Space

Emily Sue Harvey

T0306983

THE
STORY PLANT

This is a work of fiction. Names, characters, places, and incidents either are the product of the author's imagination or are used fictitiously. Any resemblance to actual events, locales, organizations, or persons living or dead, is entirely coincidental and beyond the intent of either the author or the publisher.

The Story Plant
The Aronica-Miller Publishing Project, LLC
P.O. Box 4331
Stamford, CT 06907

Cover design by Barbara Aronica-Buck

Print ISBN-13: 978-1-61188-019-9
E-book ISBN-13: 978-1-61188-020-5

Visit our website at www.thestoryplant.com

First Story Plant Printing: September 2011

Printed in The United States of America

Dedication

I dedicate this book to all the families who have, like the Stowes, faced seemingly insurmountable odds in the substance addiction recovery of a loved one. Who have, inside their own home and beyond, for the sake of family or friend, sacrificed their own space for the rescue of a loved one.

To the ones who, through either tough love or the gentler kind, never gave up on the addict. Whose love helped the "beaten down" one to experience the soul nurturing and hope that only family and unconditional love can give.

To Karen Aho, a precious, courageous friend. And to Angel Callahan, my faithful assistant.

To Leland, my husband and greatest supporter, whose unreserved love ever buoys me to greater heights than I ever thought possible.

To Father God, the one who "don't make no junk" and is always there to finish lifting the willing, healing one to full redemption and helps them see that, like with the American eagle, after the excruciating pain of renewal, life is more beautiful than ever.

Acknowledgments

Space is work of fiction, one that was not easy to pen. I have the passion for it, but the subject matter many times veers readers into dark, desperate places where one is reluctant to enter. In this setting the characters feel real emotions and cry out in pain and confusion and anguish, often grasping at the will to even live. Not a cheerful scenario by anyone's standards. Yet the story is provocative because all around us, behind closed doors, many seemingly normal, happy families live this drama. It has become all too familiar. The tribulation inside those walls is staggering.

I took the liberty of using fictional South Carolina settings, such as Brattsville and other locales. The characters are composites of many folks I've known and some I haven't personally known. Most are purely figments of my zealous imagination.

My insight into dealing with this timely challenge came from both personal and second hand experiences. Those who allowed me to use their own occurrences to weave into this tale are many, some of whom I will not name for obvious reasons. You know who you are, and I am eternally grateful for your transparency and unfailing generosity.

Bright family moments weave together the Stowes' story. A special thank you to Michael and Susan Cooper and their beautiful "miracle" children: Caleb Michael ("Faithful"), Rachel Gabrielle ("Little Lamb"), Moriah Jordan ("God is my teacher"), and Danielle Isaac ("Laughter"). This wonderful family was divinely put together and inspired the groundwork for the Stowes' odyssey.

Thanks to both Susan Cooper and Jean Scroggs for their invaluable adoption status input. And heartfelt gratitude to Dr. David Barnes, counselor and friend, a genuine, present-day Good Samaritan. And to the Rev. Bob Roach and wife, Pat, whose medical expertise helped flesh out the story's coronary crisis.

Thank you, Rita Allison and Doug Brannon, SC State House Representatives and friends, for your wise counsel and input during the creation of this book. Two other Good Samaritans!

And finally, much gratitude to those former addicts who generously shared experiences of stolen lives, utter despair, and finally the climb from the pit and back up to the mountaintop of redemption. Who want to encourage others on the same path from destruction to learn to fly with the Eagles.

Above the storm.

Be blessed, dear reader and enjoy triumph in its purest form.

Prologue

"Don't be afraid of the space between your dreams and reality. If you can dream it, you can make it so."

– Belva Davis

"Now, let's go through this area. I think the space we're interested in leasing for a restaurant is right through here," my sister Lexie said, uncharacteristically business-like for her, the family joker. She and her husband Adam continued to guide Dan and me through a maze of back rooms in this business plaza section.

"This is a short cut," she explained. "Quicker."

Dan and I cut our eyes at each other, wary yet curious. Lexie had, all week, enthused about her new interest in opening a restaurant on the outskirts of Greenville. In suburban Taylors, actually, a perfect, according to Lexie, South Carolina setting for the Ma and Pa establishment she'd "always dreamed of."

Strange. I'd never heard of this particular dream.

Short and athletic, freckle-nosed, spiked red-haired Lexie was known for her sense of adventure. Her wiriness and strength could have made her a star gymnast. Her balance and physical prowess always left her older sisters, Priss and me, behind in a blinding dust storm. Yet, she'd migrated toward marriage and motherhood and it fit her like tight leather pants.

So today, when she asked Dan and me to come along and give our opinion on her choice of a future business site, we agreed. Mainly because we enjoyed Lexie and Adam's company. Never a dull moment. I also liked that she trusted our opinion on such an important matter. Besides, she threw in a bonus.

"We're gonna treat you to a scrumptious meal," she gushed.

"Where?" I ventured.

She grinned, her nose tilting becomingly. "It's a surprise."

So, as we made our way past the stockroom paraphernalia to yet another door, she knocked.

Then Lexie said, rather loudly, "This must be it."

I scowled at her volume and halted as she opened the door and stepped back for Dan and me to enter. The room was pitch dark.

"Where's the light switch?" I asked, slightly irritated at all the drama, fumbling inside alongside the door frame. My fingers contacted it and ...

Click.

"SURPRISE!!" screamed a room full of lively, raucous humanity.

"Aaii!" I nearly jumped into Dan's arms.

"What the heck?" I shrieked, glaring at them, shaking from the trauma, certain we'd wandered into the wrong room.

Dan stood there beside me, slack-jawed and rather pale from the jolt.

"Happy anniversary!" yelled a familiar voice. My sister Priss' beaming face honed in, and her husband Earl's. My knees, by now, warbled like Jello.

I spun in a wobbly circle to face Lexie. "*Liar*! I should have known." Lexie's face- splitting grin was pure Cheshire. "There is no restaurant deal, is there?" I accused.

"If I ever talk seriously about opening a restaurant, please take me out and shoot me," she said, laughing uproariously.

Adam, a bit more sensitive to my frustration, stepped forward and murmured, "Sorry, Deede. That's the only way we could get you here without you suspecting something."

"Am I forgiven?" Lexie implored, still grinning and holding out her arms to me.

"Of course," I snapped good-naturedly and hugged her hugely, swaying to and fro. And when she released me, Priss grabbed me for her bear hug.

Then my little white-haired mother Jean Eagle ooched in for her hug. "Congratulations, honey," she said. "I'm so proud that your and Dan's marriage made it when so many others didn't." She kissed both my cheeks and released me back to Priss, who, in the throes of celebration, took me by the shoulders and then, impulsively, embraced me again.

"We wanted to celebrate your and Dan's thirty-fifth with you. We knew you two romantics would rather do something alone so we had to resort to treachery," she gushed, breathless with excitement.

I turned to the gathering of family and friends and laughingly scolded them. "So this is why nobody remembered, huh? Not a soul has even *mentioned* our anniversary." Our family, the Eagle clan, made a big to-do over everything, so to ignore such a significant event was totally uncommon.

After a big round of applause, as one, the throng morphed into team-mode, escorting Dan and me across a portable dance floor to a platform where two white easy chairs — which I recognized as from Lexie's house awaited us. Red roses and vibrant English ivy, from both Priss and Mom's gardens, bedecked the entire setting. I felt like Queen for a Day. I was grateful that Lexie had suggested Dan and I dress sharp-casual "for the fancy restaurant we're gonna take you to."

The little sneak.

As Dan and I were ceremoniously seated by nephew and niece, hunky Jensen and pretty Betty, I realized the chairs were arranged so Dan and I could hold hands, comfortably maintain eye contact and chat throughout the evening. Their thoughtfulness impressed me to no end. A local disc jockey did the honors of keeping music streaming.

Kool and the Gang shot things off to a boisterous start with *Celebration.*

I gazed at the youthful mass pulsing to the music and smiled. My other nieces Chloe and Ginger gyrated uninhibitedly alongside Jensen and Betty, and I thought how dancing had changed since my younger days. Among the dancers, I recognized high school friends of theirs, as well as our daughter Faith's.

But where is Faith?

Faith, our twenty-four year old, recently divorced daughter was not the greatest social mixer in the world, but she would certainly be here for this event. Yet, since her divorce, we never knew exactly what to expect.

I motioned Priss over and whispered. "Does Faith know about this?"

Priss nodded. "I called her personally and invited her. Said she was coming but would probably be late. She asked me to pick up Maddie at her Daddy's and bring her, and there she is." She pointed out our little five-year-old granddaughter, now bug eyed at the teens' exuberant twisting and pivoting and posturing.

"Faith will probably be along any minute." Priss squeezed my shoulder and returned to sit with Maddie.

Be here any minute? I seriously doubted that.

Faith was becoming an island unto herself.

I had, I felt, made peace with that. I turned off negative thoughts.

Tonight was our night. Dan's and mine.

Thirty-five years together. Our gazes connected then and that magical flash of excitement shot through me and I thought how it had never diminished. Not one smidgen. Those green eyes held mine with as much magnetism as the day we met in USC College English class. He'd asked me to help him study for an upcoming exam.

Hah.

"Was that not a brilliant maneuver?" he asked me later, preening. I had to agree it was indeed brilliant, as was everything else about Dan Stowe. He was working his way through college by doing weekend construction work, a thing that prepared him for his future asphalt business. The business degree he earned enhanced his economics savvy.

It also molded his slender frame into something I called streamlined strapping.

Dan never said 'I can't.'

Me? I was head-in-clouds Deede, a classic writer, with all the melancholy and artistic temperament attached.

Dan was everything I was not. And vice versa.

While in an exceptionally poetic mood one day, I told Dan, "I've figured it out. True love is knowing a person's faults and loving them even more for them."

"That's the sweetest thing I've ever heard," he said, totally impressed, and kissed me soundly. "But then, look who's saying it."

Oh, ours was a mutual admiration alliance all right.

I delighted in the fact of Dan's masculine strength, his rough yet tender hands. He loved my softness and femininity, my gentle, maternal side. His nature was tough, from a rough childhood, but he'd learned to govern and control his sometimes dysfunctional reactions to everyday life happenings.

We shouldn't, according to the astrology chart, have married. But since we put no stock in astrology reading, we ignored the naysayers.

With us, it worked.

Oh, how it worked.

Tonight, all stops were on go as family and friends shared Deede/Dan vignettes from way back when.

"Dan, I hope you don't mind me telling this," our brother-in-law Earl stood and said. "But when Faith was born, Dan was the proudest man alive. He's a man's man, but," soft-hearted Earl paused, swallowed soundly and cleared away the lump in his throat, "at the hospital, when he heard Deede and the baby were doing fine, he broke down and cried like a baby."

Sniffles and soft coughs rustled all over the big room because the story of our Faith's birth had, by now, become family lore.

Where is Faith?

Earl grinned then, swiped away tears and continued. "Then there was that man who Deede accidentally bumped into one day in Wal-Mart — who loudly and rudely told her where to go. Before you could say 'scat' Dan had him by the collar. 'Tell my wife you're sorry,' Dan said under his breath, 'or you'll wish you'd never been born.'"

Earl shook his head, grinning proudly. "That man apologized to Deede and then ran out of the store so fast you could hear the wind whistling around him."

Lexie piped up, "Remember when Gene proposed to Priss? Dan said, 'just think about it, Priss, he'll be changing your name from Priss Eagle to Priss Eagle Byrd.'"

Everybody burst into laughter as the memories continued to flow. Some funny, some somber, others simply tender.

A wonderful buffet was spread to one side of the large room, where folks quietly filled their plates and feasted at white-clothed tables centered with red rose and ivy arrangements. During this time, the lights were lowered. A screen appeared to display videos featuring the Stowes.

I was touched that Priss and Lexie had spent hours selecting and organizing the video presentation. Now I knew why Priss had plundered my old pictures while recently visiting me. She'd somehow sneaked them past me and out of the house. Tonight, photos of days gone by tugged at heartstrings and drew more tears and laughter.

My sweet mom sat near us with grandchildren, like dibbies, surrounding her table, and she would catch my eye all along to smile her eloquent message to me. *You are special, Deede,* it said. Dad had only recently passed away. I could not yet let myself think about him without dissolving into tears. Tonight, I pushed back thoughts of him.

The photographs of Dan and me with our little Faith were especially poignant.

I looked around again, growing uneasy. *Where is Faith?*

The music struck up again.

You're the Best Thing That's Ever Happened to Me drew Dan to his feet and he reached for my hand. It was one of our Gladys Knight favorites. He led me down the steps to the dance floor and pulled me into his strong arms. We danced as we loved, as one. We'd always had that inexplicable soul connection. Everywhere. Doing anything. It was simply *there.*

As we moved to the music, Dan whispered in my ear, scattering goosebumps all over me. "Just when I think it's impossible to love you any more, you prove me wrong."

"Mmm. I know what you mean," I murmured.

A few moments later, he whispered, "How did I do it?"

"What?" I rubbed my cheek against his.

"How did I get you? The prettiest girl to come out of Brattsville, South Carolina?"

I looked into his eyes. "It was meant to be."

"Destiny, huh?"

"Divine destiny."

"You bet."

He reached down and kissed me then. And a round of applause and whoops of delight rent the air.

That was when Dan's cell phone vibrated against me as it jangled into Latin strains of *Girl from Ipanema*. "Yes?" Dan held it to his ear, straining to hear.

I watched him turn pale, then ashen.

"What?" I leaned close, fear gripping me. "What is it?"

"We'll be right there." He snapped his phone shut. "It's Faith."

I felt the blood leave my head. "W-what? Has something happened to her?" *Oh God, no! Please.*

He saw my panic, took my hand and squeezed reassurance. His eyes conveyed, *everything will be all right.* But I'd glimpsed the flash of fear a second before he covered it.

"She's in the Greenville ICU. Let's go."

Priss was there in a heartbeat. "It's Faith," I told her as we moved through the crowd, her trailing anxiously along. "I don't know the details yet."

"Keep me informed, sis," Priss called after us as we rushed out the door, leaving behind more stunned faces.

I asked Dan, "What's wrong with Faith?"

"I didn't want to say anything with the whole world listening. She's unconscious." He looked at me then, his eyes tortured as he swept me along with his long strides. "She's ODed on drugs, honey. Our Faith is on drugs."

"No," I cried out, feeling my legs beneath me turn numb. I nearly stumbled.

Dan's strong arm went around me and he propelled me to the car.

We didn't know it in that moment. We glimpsed only through a cracked door into the immediate. But our perfect world, as we knew it, our togetherness-dream, was beginning to shatter into a million tiny pieces.

Chapter One

"...things that are never satisfied...the grave and the barren womb."

– Proverbs 30:16

My craving for a baby started in adolescence. My own adopted baby sister Alexis, Lexie, joined our family four years after my own adoption. My older sister Priss' adoption preceded mine by four years. She and I both were gaga over little Lexie. Mom and Dad freed us to lavish her with affection. That arrival triggered my maternal leanings and later, Priss' two little girls Ginger and Betty fanned them into fervency.

After Dan and I married, we wanted to begin our family. At first, we were both working our way through college and didn't mind when we didn't quickly conceive. After all, we had plenty of time. Later, after we both graduated and Dan launched an asphalt paving company and I was hired on at the local newspaper as a features writer, we began in earnest to try to conceive.

My craving for a genetic link was understandable. Priss and I both talked about it. "We've got the best parents on the face of this earth," I told her one day. "But it's not — normal. I feel guilty even saying it. Aww, Priss, you know what I mean."

"'Fraid so, honey. I've felt it, too. That —" She rolled her eyes upward, searching for the right word.

"Connection," I supplied.

"Exactly. That's why —" She suddenly choked up and tears filled her eyes. "That's why my little Ginger and Betty are so precious to me. Do you realize they're the first blood relation I've ever personally known?"

My mouth dropped open. "You just put into words the – the *uniqueness* of my existence here on earth. It's isolated from any real *genetic roots."*

Priss and I lounged side by side on my sofa, bare feet tucked beneath us, turned facing each other. We nibbled on her famous homemade walnut fudge, enjoying bursts of flavonoids and serotonin ecstasy. Priss washed down a bite with milk, took a deep breath and moaned, "Much more of this fudge, you just call 911 for a comatose female."

I laughed with her, lightheaded myself from the sugar surge.

Then my sister sobered and reached out to touch me, her gray eyes gentle.

"Don't get me wrong, Sis. I love my family. I couldn't love you more than if we'd occupied the same womb. It's just that —"

"You don't have to explain to me, Priss. I know what you're saying. Exactly. That's why I want my own *little connections,* running all over the place. Then they'll have me as their roots, and I won't be hanging out in the hemisphere without my own space."

"Couldn't have said it better myself." Priss wiggled her brows and we burst into laughter, watching Johnny Depp on Oprah and finishing off the fudge in time for her to pick the girls up at nearby Brattsville Elementary School.

From that time, Dan and I switched into overdrive efforts to impregnate me. My parents were supportive and couldn't wait for me to produce more grandchildren for them to pamper and spoil. Louis and Jean Crowe were very involved in their grandchildren's lives. Mom was a school teacher and Dad worked with the State Income Tax Department.

Month after month passed, and still, I did not conceive.

Miraculously, Priss and I had always been soul-mates. I say miraculously because it was not genetics that wired us so. So we figured fate, parental nurturing and some Divine tuning had figured in. We adored Lexie, who'd always followed a different drum cadence than ours but always, during important times, marched our way and lingered.

Whatever, we were truly sisters.

Yet — with all my heart, I craved my very own *connection.*

~ ~

"When are you going to stop putting my daughter through this torture?"

I overheard Dad's impassioned plea to Dan. They stood apart on the far side of the room. From my hospital bed, I called out, "Don't you dare blame Dan, Dad. I want a baby and with each procedure I've gone through, it was of my own volition." I was livid and my father was properly chastised, an unusual confrontation because he was so wonderful. But I couldn't have Dan being the object of anyone's frustration.

And I was already shredded from the procedure so my emotions ran rampant.

"I'm sorry, Dad," I murmured, seeing his stricken features.

"It's okay," he said. "I understand."

I could tell Dan was proud of my response, though he ended up putting an arm around Dad's slumped shoulders and giving him a sympathetic squeeze and mumbling encouraging words.

The previous year, Dan and I had run the gamut of charts, fertility pills and HGC shots.

This last procedure, a uterine biopsy for which I had no local anesthesia, had been the most painful of all. Again, the path led to defeat.

"It's all my fault," I sobbed after the last test showed negative. Dan had enough sperm to populate the world.

"Don't say that, honey." Dan gathered me in his arms, and I felt the tension in his body. I knew he wanted to splinter the wall with his fist.

Our obsession — it had become an obsession by now — began to close us into a dark, bubble-like vacuum together, shutting out everyone except God. And though I came from a close family, I withheld details of our ordeal from them. Not even Priss — initially - knew the real depth of our fixation. Mine and Dan's passion seemed out of sync somehow when exposed beyond our invisible bubble, so we clutched it protectively to our bosoms.

~ ~

"You have polycystic ovaries, Deede," Dr. Wingo said gravely.

"What's that?" I asked as the old familiar dread snaked through me.

"That's a disease where the ovaries produce an egg, although it's not a mature egg usually, but the hormones are imbalanced. So the egg never releases. The egg then becomes a cyst." His concerned, aged eyes peered through his bifocals, assessing my reaction. He'd been my ob-gyn physician for several years now and knew every nuance of my maternity fixation.

"W-what happens then?"

"Well, eventually the ovaries become thick with cysts, enlarged and lumpy. I want to do a procedure on you called a laser wedge resection of the ovaries."

"What does it involve?" I asked in a whispery voice, not wanting to hear more but knowing I had to know. I could not give up at this point.

"It's a surgery that will drain the cysts." He made it sound so simple that I relaxed.

Everything was going to turn out right, after all.

~ ~

As it turned out, the surgery "drained" more than sixty cysts. Because the operation left the entire surface of my ovaries without a *covering,* they *healed* by sticking to other parts of my insides. These were called adhesions, causing extreme scarring. I ended up with ovaries stuck or adhered to my urethra and abdominal wall. My fallopian tubes did not escape either, becoming scarred in the process. One even folded into itself like a crimped hose.

After I healed and still did not conceive, Dr. Wingo said, "I'm going to do a dye test on you, Deede, and see what's happening inside."

By now, I'd become somewhat shell-shocked by all the battery of tests and procedures. Still — that maternal longing stirred strongly and deeply. So I managed to jerk myself up and buck up for whatever it would take.

Early in the a.m., blue dye was injected into me, showing both fallopian tubes completely blocked. "This prevents pregnancy even if you ovulate, Deede," Dr. Wingo said kindly as I lay there in the hospital bed. "The egg has no way of getting through the tube and become fertilized to implant in the womb."

I felt disappointment settle in me like cold cement. "So …?" I said through numb lips.

"So," Dr. Wingo took my icy hand in his, his eyes pools of sympathy, "In summary … with the scars and blocked fallopian tubes, Deede, there is absolutely no way you can become pregnant."

All hope. Gone.

I closed my eyes. It can't be, God. *Please don't let it be final.*

Please help my faith.

~ ~

One day, my phone rang. It was Lexie, my baby sister. "I'm pregnant, Deede," she gushed. I could hear her excitement. "Can you believe it? Me and Adam, parents?"

The world seemed to tilt.

The words pierced my heart in an odd way. Oh, how I wanted to rejoice with her, but the deadness inside me refused to give way to life. "Hey, that's great," I said, hearing the flatness in my voice and knowing that she, too, detected it.

An awkward silence ensued. Stretched out. Still no celebratory words bubbled up and separated from my dark funk

"Well," she sounded deflated, bewildered. "I'll let you go. Just wanted you to be one of the first to know." I heard the hurt in her words. Oh, how I hated that I'd shot her down. I felt despicable.

"I love you, Lexie," I murmured, the knot in my throat growing bigger.

"Yeah," the reply was weak. "Me, too. Bye."

I shared the news with Dan. Huddled on our bed, we cried together and tried to sift our feelings. "It's not that I don't want *them to* know the joy of a child," I sobbed against his shoulder. "It's just — just that I can't help but wonder, why can't it be us?"

"I know," Dan held me close. "I know, honey." His ragged words sounded as confused and desolate as mine did. It had nothing to do with Lexie and Adam. It had everything do with us. We were so raw and bleeding at the time that their glowing celebration of a new life made our own barrenness ring more dissonant and hollow than ever.

We burrowed even deeper into isolation. At Hope Memorial Church, where all our family clan attended, we avoided Lexie and Adam. We knew they were hurt, but in our vulnerability, we felt we had no choice.

Soon, Lexie and Adam left and joined another church. The disapproval of my parents smote me. They didn't understand, and I knew, in their zeal for family solidarity, they were deeply troubled over this schism.

"Say, you two haven't yet found out how it works, huh?" Priss' husband, Earl, teased us one Sunday as we were hugging their two girls after church. Earl's slightly Rockwell-ish features were pleasant beneath thinning, premature graying hair. His good humor matched Priss', a thing that first attracted her to him like bees to pollen.

"Shh," Priss sternly shushed him, leaving poor Earl looking more than mildly befuddled and I realized — true to character — Priss had not involved him in the current family dissonance.

"It's okay," Dan said weakly, trying to look nonchalant.

"Yeh. We know." He left it at that and we promptly departed as Priss, who'd by now lent me her shoulder to cry on more than once, informed Earl of his blunder. She was my only family confidante and only recently so. I'd asked her not to tell anybody of my pain, feeling somehow that if no one knew, things would eventually turn out right.

The teasing from well-meaners was coming more frequently lately, and it stung.

"Y'know," I told Dan as we drove home that day. "If it were anyone else acting as we are, I'd call them incredibly self-absorbed."

"Yeh." Dan huffed a sad laugh. "Me, too."

All we knew at that time was that our emotions were grief-charged, like those of bereaved parents, and we had no idea how to resolve them. "Did Shakespeare write 'it's better to have loved and lost than not to have loved at all?'" I asked Dan at one point.

"That's us, Dan. We've never even had a child to love."

~ ~

Months later, one last ditch effort wavered before us: In vitro fertilization: a test tube baby. As we awaited the results of this last procedure, mom called and told us Lexie's baby, a nephew named Jensen, had been born.

I could hear the appeal in Mom's sweet voice, but Dan and I were so immersed in our own battle that we had nothing left over to give.

Lexie and Adam's time of joy became the day of our worst defeat: we learned none of the test-tube embryos survived. We were devastated. We retreated further, hoping for a Divine mercy visit inside our desolate lair.

All hope — gone. We would never have a child.

I could not bring myself to call or see my sister and her baby. I told myself it wasn't jealousy that caused my reticence. I don't truly believe it was that simple. It was so soul-deep, the grief and hunger, that just the sight of a baby could set off the old familiar anguish.

One night mom called. We'd always had an incredible relationship. I adored her.

"Deede," she said gently, "you need to reach out to Lexie more. She's hurting, honey. She feels you're rejecting not only her but little Jensen, as well."

The world crashed in upon me. I quickly hung up and burst into tears.

When it rang again, I let it ring, sobbing for the pain I felt and also for the hurt I was unintentionally inflicting upon my loved ones. Mine and Dan's was a perpetual, consuming sorrow. An emptiness no one, save our Creator, seemed to understand. So we prayed much to Him.

And then ... somewhere in the darkness, a tiny spark ignited.

~ ~

A few weeks later, Dan said, "How would you feel about adopting?"

I tensed up. Then I realized how futile worry had been in the past. It had become a blasted habit. I was a wreck, reacting to anything to do with procreation and parenthood.

Did I believe in adoption?

I sighed. "I don't know." Then my palm slapped my forehead. "*Of course,* I believe in adoption. *Duh*. Look at me!" He didn't laugh and neither did I. I shrugged limply and sighed. "I don't know, Dan."

"Let's pray about it. Think on it, y'know?"

I nodded. And in coming weeks, we prayed together. I began to relax about the whole thing.

Slowly, I began to realize I could now accept adoption as an option. After all, look at Priss and myself. And what joy little Lexie had brought into our family when she was adopted. I still loved her as my own.

With adoption possibilities, I could chill out. Bide my time. I was still young so there was no rush.

"Let's wait for just a while," I suggested to Dan. "Maybe for a few months. Let's enjoy each other, just the two of us, for a while longer." I didn't know why — it just seemed the right thing to do at that moment.

Dan grabbed me, and we fell onto the bed in a tangle of limbs and fierce embracing. I pulled his face to mine and beneath my hands, felt the solid beat of his heart and it touched me profoundly, that declaration of his life. It spoke of his being. It spoke of his energy and drive. It spoke of how precious he was to me.

"Let's just, for a time, think of us," I murmured against his lips. "We have each other, Dan."

"And in the end, that's what counts," he whispered and kissed me soundly. Which led to more kisses that made me feel warm and languid, dulling some of the sad, awful memories of recent days. We were *alive and together, Dan and I.*

Then for the first time in years, we made love simply for the pleasure of it. And I thought of how much we had missed. Our coupling was as passionately rampant as in our early days of marriage. And in the aftermath, with Dan holding me closely in his arms, bliss stole over me, contentment unlike any I'd ever known. The warm sensations still trickled through me, now gentle and soothing. It was the last thing I felt as I drifted off to sleep.

~ ~

"Hey, big boy," I cooed, holding little Jensen, a chocolate-eyed version of Lexie, his mother. "Those eyes are definitely your dad's." I blinked back tears and looked at my profoundly proud sister, whose turned-up nose still sported light freckles. Her red hair still spiked becomingly, but recently, she'd experimented with some different color, adding brown to the hair, making it auburn and then highlighting the ends blonde.

It was actually cute on her.

Since birthing Jensen, our little athletic smart-aleck of the family flowed gracefully and displayed a splash of maternal mellowness that sat well upon her.

"I'm so happy for you," I said. And it was true. All my angst of the past was gone.

"What a prize you are," I said to my handsome nephew, grasping his strong little hands and letting him pull his weight into upright standing position on my lap. I laughed at his strength and determination. "My little football jock," I called him, gurgling with pleasure.

Having caught a fresh perception of life, I now resigned myself to the fact that I would never naturally birth a child of my own, I'd begun to adapt to the idea of adoption. Actually began to get excited.

In March, everybody in the family got a virus. Mom, Dad, Dan, even Priss' family had the stomach monster. I rarely got the bugs and felt pretty smug as I typed my news for the paper column. Then suddenly, it hit me.

The virus lasted three to four days and left everybody as suddenly as it came.

Except me. The queasiness lingered. It irritated me that I couldn't bounce back. So I suggested we go out to dinner on the second week. "It's all in my head," I insisted to Dan, who remained dubious, concerned.

"Sure you don't want to see the doc?" he asked.

"Nah. I just need a good square meal to turn me around. I'll call Priss and Earl to join us at the Red Lobster."

Although the smell of food still tied my stomach in knots, I ordered my favorite seafood plate.

The meal turned me around all right. Right to the Ladies' Room to vomit every last vestige I'd ingested.

I returned to the table pale and shaking. Priss looked at me strangely, Then she grinned.

"Deede Stowe. You are pregnant."

"Oh, yeah. Right!" I rolled my eyes and swallowed against the knot of queasiness.

Priss's grey eyes sparkled with glee. "You. Are. Pregnant."

"It's not possible," I muttered, dismissing her teasing, feeling a bit irritated with it to tell the truth. Priss knew how much I'd wanted a baby. She knew all the medical facts and that I could not get pregnant. Yet — she was insistent. A little seed of something sprouted inside me and when, on the way home, I asked Dan to stop at the drugstore to buy a pregnancy kit, he chuckled and shook his head.

"I just need to prove Priss wrong," I insisted. "She won't shut up till I do."

When the test turned out positive, I shook my head in bewilderment. The next morning, I bought another kit and drove over to Priss' house.

"I just did it wrong, is all," I told her, determined to prove it to her and yet — a cluster of butterflies flapped in my stomach.

Again, the test showed positive. Puzzled, both Priss and I decided I should call Dr. Wingo. Knowing my history, he scheduled me for an ultrasound. During the screening, he began to mumble. "Well," he said, "it seems to be in the right place."

He peered at me through thick lens, scratching his balding head.

"What is?" I asked, alarmed.

"The baby," he said. My heart nearly leaped from my chest as he pointed to the monitor of shadows and light. "See?"

Numbly, I nodded, suddenly weak-kneed and filled with wonder.

Dr. Wingo looked at me, shaking his head. "There's no medical way this baby should be in your uterus." He continued shaking his head. "You must have gone to church right." Then he laughed and patted my arm. "You need to see an ob-gyn man."

"You mean —" I pressed my fingers to my mouth as tears rushed to my eyes.

"You're pregnant, Deede."

Chapter Two

"Parents can only give good advice or put them on the right paths, but the final forming of a person's character lies in their own hands."

– Anne Frank

On December 10, Faith Jean Stowe was born. Faith was the only name that fit and the middle name, Jean, was in honor of my mother. "She's our child of faith," Dan insisted.

I agreed. Our little tan-haired, blue-eyed daughter was named for the time we believed God for a child. It was only after we relinquished our ungodly passion to Him that He gave her to us.

The first time I held her in my arms was the highlight of my entire life. The tiny, perfectly round blue eyes latched onto mine and I would have sworn there was an electrical surge of love that flashed between us and encompassed me until I felt I would burst with it. What I felt, holding her to my heart, was so intense that it could have burned a hole clean through me. Dan was equally beguiled.

I had expected a solid, forceful link to form, but nothing of this magnitude. This maternal love was a force of nature, not at all what I'd expected. It was fierce and all consuming.

I was looking at a part of *me.* Never before had I had the opportunity to see a part of my genetic self. This was my *connection.*

Wonder and joy gripped me as I watched one tiny fist flail about and brush rosebud lips that immediately began to suckle it.

"Ahhh," I breathed and felt a sudden burn of tears. They trickled over.

I looked up and saw that Dan, too, was moved to tears. He sat on the bed beside me, arm around my shoulders as we adored our creation. Our miracle.

She was flesh of our flesh and bone of our bone.

I was finally someone's roots.

Faith's.

Since that moment, I've never been the same

~ ~

Faith was an adorable baby. That wasn't just my opinion. Everywhere we took her, folks were drawn to her like hummingbirds to nectar. Her cornflower blue eyes seemed always alight with some undisclosed joke.

"Hi, Faith," Priss pealed at our first family Christmas dinner when Faith was six weeks old. Faith's spontaneous eruption of belly laughter had a domino effect and soon the entire clan of twelve was laughing with her until teary-eyed. They pressed into a circle to engage her with goofy greetings and she never failed to respond with glee.

"How'd you luck up so?" Lexie pouted in jest. "Jensen took three months to find his tickle-box."

"Hey, he's just as delightful." I gooched him in his chunky tummy to demonstrate and his mouth spread wide, spilling laughter, rewarding me with a deep-seated pleasure, that sense of belonging that only family provides. Jensen, already in his second year, was evolving even more into the little jock. He loved balls, any kind or size and already watched football games with Adam, his dad. Yet, his spirit was gentle and generous. He watched over Faith like a nanny.

Amazingly, when Faith would begin to cry, Jensen's lips would begin to wobble, and he, too, would cry.

Later, from toddler-hood up, those two were soulmates. When Jensen was four, Lexie gave birth to a daughter, Chloe, a beautiful raisin-eyed minx who would later rival her cousin Faith in manipulation.

But in those young years, Faith looked up to Jensen as her Alpha. I won't say he was exactly a role model because, from early age, Faith always did her own thing. But Jensen came as close to being her iconic hero as anybody in her life. Looking back, I think this was one of the cornerstones of a vicious rivalry between cousins, Faith and Chloe: their mutual vying for Jensen's affection and alliance.

~ ~

Oh, how I tried to not hover and smother Faith. So did Dan. And I think we did pretty well considering how long we had waited for her. We did discipline her when necessary, but that didn't happen often.

She was a happy little girl. Faith never met a stranger and was a real social creature. When she was six, I allowed her to visit nearby friends in the neighborhood and vice versa. One day, she was gone longer than usual.

"Tanya," I called to her next door playmate who was swinging on her jungle-gym, "isn't Faith over there?"

"She was," Tanya yelled. "But I haven't seen her for a while now."

My alarm grew as I searched up and down the street. No one knew where Faith was. I called Dan at work and he rushed home. By now, neighbors were involved in the search, knowing how frantic Dan and I were.

Two hours passed, a suspenseful time that shredded my nerves to confetti. We had, by now, combed the neighborhood and night was swiftly encroaching. At a neighbor's house several blocks from ours, we were able to trace Faith's whereabouts until she got on the bicycle with a little girl named Bobbi. That's all we knew. The neighbor lady was on the phone, still trying to help locate her.

Pacing, I watched the scene through a haze. A sense of impending doom seized me.

"Call the police," I told Dan. He nodded.

"I'm going home to wait for her," I said weakly. My knees felt rubbery and my breath shallow. "She may come home and I want to be there."

Dave called the police and dropped me off at the house. He left again to meet the police at the place Faith was last seen. I sat down in the den and waited, praying, begging God to please bring my baby home.

I know you didn't give her to us for something like this to happen. I cried and prayed some more.

I waited for a long time until I could sit no longer. I began to dust and shuffle things around. Anything to keep me moving ...

A car door slammed outside and I froze.

I turned to face the door. Fear gripped me.

Please, God. Please don't let it be bad news.

The door slowly opened. In walked Faith, wearing a little blue housecoat and slippers. Her damp hair was freshly shampooed and neatly combed back.

"Faith," I held out my arms and burst into tears.

She ran into them, and I sat down and pulled her on my lap. "Honey," I sobbed. "I was so scared."

She burst into tears and wailed. "I'm sorry, Mama. I was at Bobbi's house. They asked me to eat supper with 'em and — and then Bobbi's Mama gave me a bath — this is Bobbi's housecoat and slippers. I didn't mean to scare you."

We hugged for long moments and I thought how sweet she smelled, like shampoo and soap and talcum powder, and then I called Dan and told him Faith was safe.

Faith and I were still sitting there in each other's arms when he got home.

~ ~

I realized Faith marched to her own drum beat by the time she was seven, when she allowed some adolescent neighborhood kids to go into our cellar and haul out barrels of discount liquid soap from an abandoned networking venture. They proceeded to use an empty barrel into which they poured the contents from others. By the time they finished filling them with the water hose, suds covered half of our back lawn.

Dan and I had left Faith that afternoon with Sandra, a teen baby sitter, to do some early Santa Claus shopping and when we returned, our mouths dropped open at the sight of the monstrous white foam wall rolling around the side of our house and encroaching upon our front lawn.

When we sprang from the car and squished around to the back yard, ankle-deep in suds, we saw the five-gallon buckets and a larger barrel, hose still hooked over the side spewing water into the ocean of liquid detergent.

The culprits had just moments ago fled. Probably heard our car coming. Dan rushed to turn off the water. I marched into the house where the baby sitter watched television soap operas and sipped coke. "Sandra, where's Faith?" I cried, startling her.

Blinking, she looked around as though it was the first time she'd thought about it. "Uh, she was through here a minute ago. I think she went into her room." I renewed my vow to be more selective when hiring baby sitters.

There, I flung open the door. She lay on her bed, feet bare, arms crossed, head propped on pink pillows, watching a Disney Channel. "Who made that mess outside, Faith?" I asked, barely controlling my anger.

"Tracy and Doyle Harrigan," she said calmly of our adolescent neighbors. "I told them you wouldn't like it."

She was so laid-back about the whole thing that we never suspected she was involved. Only years later did it occur to me that Faith must have been the ring leader because the two boys were nice kids and would not have done such an in-your-face thing without Faith instigating such "entertainment." After all, she alone knew where the unmarked soap was stored. And her feet were bare when I checked on her that day. Her socks were probably soaked and tossed in the laundry basket with wet towels.

At the time, however, Faith was a quiet child. She'd never given me a moment's concern. No back talk. Total respect. She listened and simply observed. For several of her middle childhood years, I knew little of what she was actually thinking. I thought I did. And I felt peace about her development. She spent much of her time reading and doing crossword puzzles while I did my newspaper writing.

We did lots of family things together in those early years. Faith would, I think, have loved to have had siblings. We were never again able to conceive.

~ ~

"Mama, let's help with the church's Thanksgiving free meals for the poor," eleven-year-old Faith ventured. "Pastor Hanover said we could serve if we want to. They need two or three more helpers."

"Sure," I said, hugging her snuggly and thinking again what a big ol' heart beat inside her.

"Hey!" She pulled away, her eyes wide with inspiration "I'll call Jensen. He can help, too." She rushed to the phone to call her favorite cousin and within moments it was all set. "Chloe is coming to help, too," she added magnanimously.

Glory be. Even at nine, Chloe could out-wisecrack Jensen and hold her own with Faith any day of the week. That Faith had included her astounded me. In a very good way.

And when we served the needy that Thanksgiving, her social gene went into overdrive. She and Jensen made those folks feel like royalty. She truly loved everybody in those days. Hers was the unreserved brand of love that spurred her to unabashedly pamper each diner as though he or she were the most important being on planet earth.

She and Chloe even called a truce in their shameless competition — raging by now — to out-do each other. Their focus was any given moment's reigning accomplishment. Whatever achievement shimmered on the horizon automatically drew disdain from the lagging cousin. But today, they worked beautifully, side by side with nary a snarky-jibe at each other.

It was a rare time of peace.

I couldn't have been more proud.

Another day, Faith came in from school teeming with injustice at the death penalty. "Mama, it's just not right! Killing people like our country does is wrong, wrong, *wrong*."

"It's just in murder cases," I explained to her. "When —"

"Mama," she looked at me incredulously, those blue eyes so clear and persuaded they seemed steeped with translucent tears. "It is *never right* to kill. Life is too — too precious. Don't you see?"

I nodded because I did, indeed, see.

Her propensity to *see* was vast, her IQ extremely high according to her school placement tests. To tackle any subject was effortless to Faith. We never pushed her because we didn't have to. She always seemed on top of whatever challenge engaged her. I learned early that she operated on her own steam and did not require supervision.

Was that where it went wrong, I've asked myself all these years later?

At such times, I remind myself that Faith's strong will was already fully operative. Untested.

It was untested because there was no provocation for a battle of wills. The most serious skirmish was one of laughter.

"Mama," Faith squared off in front of the freezer door in her jeans and white Reeboks. "Buying fat-free ice cream is *child abuse.*"

At that time, Faith was everything we'd ever dreamed our child would be. And more. We wanted to allow her to make her own destiny-choices. With her great mind, we were confident she would make good ones.

We attended church together faithfully, where Faith immersed herself in any youth program or drive in progress, displaying incredible versatility in many areas, including music, dance, drama, as well as advanced people skills.

She was, we were convinced, headed for a beautiful, successful adult life.

~ ~

One Christmas Eve, I lay on Faith's bed with her for a mother-daughter time of reminiscing. "What was your life like, Mama?" she asked quietly. "Being adopted and all."

I sighed deeply and smiled at her. "It was marvelous," I said, truly meaning it. "I was always aware that I was with my mom and dad because they chose me. I didn't just — happen." I grinned at her then. "And you, too, can feel that same sense of pride that you were chosen, Faith. One great miracle did God give us. And that was you."

She smiled sleepily and reached over to hug me. "I love you sooo much, Mama. You're the best. Thanks for hanging in there, okay?"

"Okay," I said, laughing at how, when she'd popped up in my life, it was such a surprise. Such a miracle.

This was all Dan and I had ever prayed for. To have a child to love.

And one who loved us back.

~ ~

"No, Faith," Dan said. "You cannot go to the mall and hang out. It's too dangerous."

"But all the kids are doing it, Daddy." She sported a black outfit and matching fingernail polish. Amid her pale features, onyx lipstick and mascara stood out in stark relief. I'd cocked my brow a few times but resisted critiquing this Goth phase too harshly. I felt that, in time, *this, too, shall pass.* And eventually, it did.

"Honey," I inserted. "Daddy's right. It's too dangerous. There was a girl named Tammy who was kidnapped last week and they found her body in a lake just today. I heard it on the news. She was grabbed from a launderette."

The grim news failed to daunt her fervor. "Ya'll don't ever let me have fun," she grouched, her lips and cheeks puffing in a pout. "I hate being an only child. You always think of the worst thing that can happen." She stomped out of the den and slammed her bedroom door.

Faith, twelve, now a middle school student, was entering peer-kingdom, where she sought to do things with friends. *Everybody's doing it* became her mantra.

I understood.

Many of her school friends were from broken homes and while I sympathized with their unique problems, I saw Faith begin to adopt their mode of operation in her dealings with Dan and myself. And their extreme MOs did not fit into our family dynamics.

Anger began to take seed when Faith compared her life to her friends' lives and felt that since two divorced parents — many times competing and vying for their child's affection — bent the rules and overcompensated with her friend, that we should do the same with her. Of course, we did not.

Faith came to hate the word "no."

Because she'd flowed pleasantly in earlier years, we'd not had to often refuse her what she wanted and needed.

Now, the variables — her wants — began to drastically change.

But Dan and I tried to be patient through those times.

At thirteen and fourteen, things got worse.

"No, you will not go to that concert in Atlanta," Dan all but shouted, unusual for him. He'd always been the more patient one. "I won't have my daughter sleeping in the park all night. God only knows what could happen."

"But Daddy, Geena, Patty and Laura are going. We'll be chaperoned by one of the mothers."

"No. I don't care who'll chaperone. Females are vulnerable in that kind of setting, especially in a big city like Atlanta."

Faith was fuming. I could tell, even though she didn't say anything more. Dan sensed it, too. "Faith, do not — I repeat — do not buck me on this because if you do, I'll — I'll whip you. I don't want to do that, but I forbid you to go to that concert. Do you understand?"

I held my breath, struck by how things had spun from negotiation to drastic ultimatums so quickly.

Faith, eyes set straight ahead, face unreadable, nodded slightly.

"Good. Then we understand each other."

I knew Dan used the threat as a last, desperate resort. He was terrified that something bad would happen to her. We'd just that week read about a woman and her two daughters being abducted and murdered while vacationing in a remote area of a South Carolina state park.

But when Dan relayed this information to Faith, she was not impressed.

The next day, the day of the planned exodus to Atlanta, Dan and I drove to the school to pick up Faith. She was not there waiting as usual. Dan and I began to grow uneasy and asked some students standing nearby if they'd seen Faith.

"She left in a blue Ford Lexus," one girl told Dan.

"That's Laura's car," I said, a knot of dread tightening my chest. We drove to Laura's house where the car was already being packed. I could see luggage in the open trunk. Dan strode to the porch and banged on the door. When Laura answered, Dan demanded, "I want to talk to Faith."

"She's not here."

"I know she is," Dan insisted. "And if she doesn't come with me, I'll report you to the police for harboring a minor." His threat was, again, out of desperation and at the same time, I think he would have followed through.

Laura disappeared into the house. Presently, Faith came out and without a word climbed into the car. Her face was closed. Resigned.

The ride home was silent. When we got home, Dan sat Faith down in the den. "Faith, I told you that if you disobeyed me on this, that I'd whip you, didn't I?" he said softly. She nodded, eyes straight ahead. "I have to follow through. Come on upstairs, Faith."

I knew Dan would rather cut off his right arm than do this. "Deede," he'd said to me as we'd driven to Laura's to pick up our daughter, "I'm losing control of the situation. I have to get her attention. Make her see that this is the wrong way."

Faith followed him up the stairs, her back straight, chin high. My emotions swirled and agitated in a blur.

I knew that Dan felt a need to teach her a lesson. I'd had whippings, too. Not bad ones, just enough to get my attention. Some folks, I knew, didn't believe in corporal punishment. In the South, at least in my slice of the

South, it was tolerated as a means to justify the end. And it had never hurt me, Priss or Lexie. To me, it said my folks cared enough to confront.

Today, I heard Dan's and Faith's voices begin to rise from the upstairs and then Faith began to scream and wail. I didn't know exactly what transpired, but I knew Dan loved his daughter and wanted only what was best for her.

One thing I did know: a battle of like-spirits raged.

Faith's passion, in the face of what she considered unjust acts, was legendary.

Faith hated pain.

I put my hands over my ears until the ruckus stopped and Dan came downstairs, pale and shaken. He walked past me and out the door. I heard the car leave and went upstairs to check on Faith.

She lay face down on her yellow bedspread in her yellow butterfly wall-papered room, head cupped in arms, silent.

"Faith?"

She turned over and looked at me with red-swollen eyes that immediately filled with tears again. "He hurt me, Mama," she whimpered disbelievingly, her grief spilling over that this man who'd been her stalwart protector had "hurt" her.

I took her in my arms. "I'm sorry, honey," I whispered, torn between the complex variables of the father-daughter conflict.

Later, Dan told me Faith began to fight and grab the belt. It became a battle of wills — the first real one between those two. Definitely not the last. Dan's temper flared, and the licks were harsher than he'd intended. He wept about it later.

"God, I hate to hurt her," he told me, tears in his big, generous eyes. "I don't want to ever do that again." And he did not.

The next day, at school, while Faith changed clothes for dance class, a friend saw red welts on her back and legs. "What happened?"

"My Dad gave me a whipping," Faith replied, by now, she told me years later, resigned that all kids got whippings when they truly deserved them.

The friend went to the school counselor. The counselor called the Department of Social Services.

The next day, at work, Dan received a visit from a DSS officer. Dan was chastised and humiliated. I don't think he was ever the same after that day. He felt betrayed that Faith had told on him, knowing she had willfully disobeyed a direct order, knowing the consequences.

I tried to smooth it over. Truthfully, I told Dan, "She didn't intentionally get you in trouble. Someone saw the welts, Dan, and reported them. Not Faith." And indeed, Faith denied she'd known her friend had reported the incident until the DSS guy showed up at school to question her.

How did I feel about it all? I hated that Dan had lost his cool during the discipline. He shouldn't have struck her so harshly and I told him so. He apologized and vowed he would never again allow himself to be trapped in that same situation.

Of course, I grasped that DSS intervention could cause Faith to revoke her forgiveness toward Dan. With such authoritative weight behind her father's chastening, at the very least challenging his administering of the "rod," regardless of the critical nature of Faith's transgression, she would automatically feel abused.

I explained to Dan that Faith had not been aware of all the repercussions of the disclosure.

Still, Dan felt a rip in that close, snuggly relationship. From both the disobedience and then what he perceived as betrayal. He'd always adored — no, *worshipped* - his little girl. Now, when he'd said "no," to protect her from danger, she'd changed from our quiet, almost docile daughter to one who would go to awful lengths to get her way.

At least, that's the way he saw it.

Me? I saw the collision course falling into place. I would try and try in years to come to ward off the crashes. The DSS cleared Dan of abuse charges. When Dan asked the officer what he would have done under identical circumstances, the man had smiled tightly and said. "I'd have done the same thing. Only I wouldn't have left any evidence on her."

Personally, I don't think physical punishment, beyond token spankings, accomplishes much. Add to that troubled temperaments, and it can tally up to big trouble as the child enters the adult world. But then, who has all the right answers?

How can a parent harness the stampeding, raging force of a mutinous child?

How must a parent save an offspring from their own self?

What works for some can be disaster for others.

So from that day, I put much effort into keeping peace in our home. It would become my great mission in life.

~ ~

That Christmas, our clan met at Lexie's house. I held my breath because of Lexie's daughter Chloe's territorial stance when Faith dared enter her domain. Faith and Jensen, now teenagers, were tighter than ever. Jensen was a high school senior and Faith a junior. Freshman Chloe struggled desperately to outshine Faith at every opportunity, resorting to dirty tactics when the occasion arose. I knew on some gut level that jealousy of her big brother's soul-mate status with Faith had a bearing on Chloe's desperation.

Perhaps Faith's aura of self-assurance and confidence rattled Chloe's rickety cage. Whatever it was, when Faith drew near, Chloe was wary as a cat in a room full of pit bulls.

"Now Faith," I took her by the arm before entering my sister's elaborately decked out house. "Please behave. This is family time."

She gave me an innocuous look. "Who, me? Mama, I'm always sweet to Chloe."

I scowled at her blatant lie. "I've heard how you tease her mercilessly, Faith."

Faith stifled a laugh. "Jensen teases her, too."

"Which is even worse, Faith. He's her brother. You two need to be kinder to her. She's younger and looks to you two for leadership."

"Hey," Faith muttered under her breath. "She asks for it. She is so stupid at times."

"Faith!" Her callous attitude shocked me.

"Just kidding, for cryin' out loud!" She laughed then. "But it is kinda true, y'know, Mama? She puts herself right out there, asking for it."

I had to concede that Chloe had become a real drama queen, adept at conjuring up calamity at the drop of a paper clip. I shook my head, appalled that Faith was drawing me into her distorted logic.

"You should never disparage someone because they're skinny or have a big nose or ears that stick out. They can't help what they're born with —"

Lexie appeared at the door then, resplendent in green sequined sweater and black velvet slacks, "Come on in out of the cold, you guys. Merry Christmas!" We all hugged and I turned loose of Faith with an uneasy feeling in my gut. I was not particularly warmed by what I was learning of my daughter's relationship philosophy.

"Look at you two." Lexie planted her hands on her hips and slanted us a bright-eyed approval. "I love that satin crimson blouse with those black velvet lounging slacks, Deede. Sexy. Faith, you're gonna have to loan me that holiday vest and turtle neck. I love it!"

"Yeh, right." Faith cackled, then snorted. "Hey! You'd get lost in this outfit and wouldn't show up again before New Year's."

Lexie's hugely blinking crimson necklace and matching earrings, her customary touch of the ridiculous cracked me up. "You look cute," I said truthfully, kissing her on the cheek. "Everything smells delicious."

"Sam helps me," she winked at me. "Discount, y'know? Their food fares fool everybody." Then she whispered in my ear. "Promise not to tell?"

I laughed, delighted at her candor, and whispered. "Promise."

I added my own food contributions to the turkey and trimmings, my own special recipe of dressing and gravy, homemade cranberry sauce and chicken bog, a scrumptious rice, chicken, smoked sausage, onion dish that had become a tradition in our family. Last, I lifted the dome on my pedestaled three-layer Italian cream cheese cake.

Priss arrived bearing ham, pasta salad, yams, veggies, assorted pies and her lip-smacking orange slice cake. She looked festive in Santa hat and red sweatshirt emblazoned with sequined "Santa's Helper." Jeans, sneakers and red socks completed her comfy attire. Her two girls, Ginger and Betty, college gals, wore green elves hats and matching "Helpers" sweats. They contributed an array of goodies, from walnut fudge to peanut butter balls to sandy fingers. All spawned from Priss were excellent cooks.

Our men all adjourned to the den to watch any sports event available, each wearing Christmas-y sweaters over turtlenecks.

"Mom," we told our aging mother, "don't you dare cook anything but your macaroni and cheese pie." Under threat of serious disapproval, she complied. Jensen went to pick her up because we wouldn't let her drive after dark. She was resplendent in Mrs. Santa Claus garb, complete with frilly apron and cap. In years past, she'd always done the lion's share of food preparation, deliriously happy to do so.

"Now, it's our turn," we corporately insisted at each approaching yuletide season.

Dad had, those last holidays of his life, gone against the tide to insist, "I'm doing my coconut-egg custard pies. It's no trouble a'tall." We did not resist because his custards – that would rival Paula Deen's – were ones we'd eaten at every holiday during childhood days.

A tradition.

Oh, how we missed them now that he was gone.

Family, to us, was everything. Its solidarity was something neither of us siblings took for granted. Neither did our precious mom and dad.

So, with the Faith-Chloe rumblings, I went into high gear protecting it.

After dinner, we voted for the most imaginative holiday attire. Mom moderated, calling each family member forward and asking for applause.

Tonight, Chloe won hands down when she did a dainty spin around the room in her days gone by ballet costume from the Nutcracker. Thin as gossamer, she was remarkably engaging with her flushed cheeks and sparkling, victorious dark eyes. The prize was a beautiful ceramic American eagle, wings spread for flight, compliments of Nonie Eagle.

A chorus of "Woo hoos" and applause deepened Chloe's blush of pleasure.

The gifts were dispersed and Jensen took Faith out for a drive in his first car, a used, but well maintained, silver 280Z.

Chloe immediately appeared, fiercely offended. Her colorful Sugar Plum Fairy role would have been extraordinarily charming had she stayed in character.

"They didn't even ask me to go." She plopped into a vacant easy chair and crossed her arms, finely tuned features ablaze with umbrage.

"It only has two seats," Lexie reminded her in a tone of voice that matched my own hackles-risen response.

Chloe crossed her matchstick thin legs and swung one defiantly back and forth, insuring that all gazes would be tethered to her. "Faith has my new tennis bracelet on. I haven't even worn it yet."

My heart lurched. Why, *why, why*? Faith knew better. She knew Chloe's proclivity for scenes. I dialed Faith's cell phone number.

"Get back here," I ordered quietly.

"Why?" she shrieked. "We've just left."

"You have on Chloe's bracelet."

I heard her muttering.

"Do not use that language," I ordered. "Get back here and straighten it out."

Within moments, Jensen and Faith entered the front door. Faith was livid. She marched straight to Chloe and tossed the bracelet into her lap. "There. Satisfied?" Then she stalked from the room.

"Wait," I called after her. "Come back here. You owe Chloe an apology."

She zoomed up to me. "For what?" She gazed at me as if I'd grown horns.

"Because you left wearing Chloe's bracelet. Without permission."

"I asked her if I could try it on," Faith said, tossing her cousin a look of disgust. "Did I not?"

Chloe's chin shot up. "But you didn't give it back to me. You walked off with it on."

Jensen spoke up then, in his laid back way. "Chloe, just chill out. Okay? It's Christmas."

"You always take her side," Chloe wailed, visibly shaken.

Oh, Lord. A perfectly good occasion. Ruined.

Again.

I gathered my family and leftovers together minutes later and left.

On the drive home, Faith snorted. "Little drama queen did it again. She is so disgusting."

Dan huffed disapproval and shook his head, yet refusing to be drawn in as he drove to our home. He maintained a distanced stance nowadays, leaving me feeling abandoned during Faith's misconduct episodes.

"Stop it, Faith," I said. "You weren't totally innocent. You knew you had that bracelet on when you left with Jensen. It's never right to simply take over someone else's belongings. I think you enjoy prodding Chloe."

I looked at her over my shoulder. She was gazing out into the night, her lips curved into a sly smile.

And I hoped — prayed — that the two of them would outgrow it all.

~ ~

Unfortunately, Faith's and Chloe's obsession with outdoing one another did not go away. For a while after Faith married and gave birth to Maddie, an uneasy truce did develop between the two of them. Chloe could not resist little Maddie, and to get to her, she had to go through Faith so she began, at that particular time, to pick her battles more carefully.

The faux-peace prevailed until Faith's decline into drugs. In the past, Faith had shown discretion in how far she would push Chloe and vice versa. I think that, to Faith, taunting Chloe had, somewhere along the way, become a sport.

Chloe, still unmarried and attending a local college, had some of the same recklessness Faith possessed, and when the peaceful tide began to turn turbulent, Chloe's anger regained momentum.

After drugs clogged Faith's already warped sense of right, all stops were pulled out.

It drove the family crazy. Lexie and I tried to remain neutral, let the girls duke it out, but sometimes, maternal reactions would pop up.

"Chloe said Faith took one of her favorite sweaters the last time she stayed at Faith's to baby sit Maddie,"

Lexie said one day, looking a bit tense when she dropped by the house for a cup of coffee together. "Chloe looked all over for it and Faith pretended she didn't know where it was."

"I'll talk to her," I replied, uneasy with Lexie's accusatory leaning in the use of "pretended." Faith had already told me about Chloe's "hissy fit" over a "tacky old sweater I wouldn't be caught dead in." Faith swore she'd not seen the item and had to practically push Chloe out the front door to get rid of her. "I don't want her baby sitting for me anymore," she decreed.

Lexie and I agreed it was difficult to know who was telling the truth. Both girls were pretty even-Steven in meanness and retaliation and stretching the truth to fit their purposes.

Today, as she prepared to leave, Lexie added, "Chloe said Faith shoved her out the door. She felt Faith was high on something."

"I'm sorry, sis," I muttered, confused and disappointed. Also a bit defensive.

What was to become of our family?

And more critically, what was to become of Faith?

~ ~

Dan's hands-off stance with Faith's discipline continued. Oh, he showed her affection, but the old Daddy-Princess connection had slackened until the knot had slithered loose.

To understand Dan would be to know his background. His childhood was riddled by alcoholism and abuse and abject poverty.

"We never knew if we'd have food," he told me.

From a family of seven kids, Dan knew what it was like to not have enough heat in the house during winter and to run out of food before being filled. He knew deprivation and what it was like to work odd jobs from the age of eleven and buying his own clothes.

"Nobody ever did anything for me from that time. I saved and bought my own cars. Dad even borrowed mine when he would wreck his during drunken rampages."

Dan's was a heart-wrenching story of betrayal.

"The anger was the worst thing I had to deal with. Dad, when he was sober, was a fine man. But put alcohol into the mix and he was a nasty drunk. Mad at the world. Mama? She was his enabler."

Dan's was a different perspective of life than mine.

"I had a peaceful childhood in which I was validated every day of my life," I told him one day during our porch rocking, intimate sharing time. "How lucky I was to know I was loved. I had a place where life itself was sacred. Revered. Peace reigned."

His next divulgence touched me profoundly.

"It was different in my family," Dan said. "Kids ran wild everywhere I turned. I never had a space of my own," he said. "So I found this little cubicle in the rafter of a new room being built on our house — one that remained unfinished for years — and I put all my little treasured things there so no one would bother them. It was mine, that space."

"We just *happened*," Dan said. "Sex was for procreation. Period. Our walls were thin. When we heard the night noises, we knew. Soon another baby would arrive. And the food wouldn't go as far. And the drunkenness would get worse. And the anger would be like a wildfire."

He looked at me then and smiled tenderly. "It took you to show me the difference between animal coupling and real love. Romance was just a word until I met you."

And that he had wanted a baby as much as I had still amazed me because I knew Dan's early life deficits. He'd come so far during our marriage. That man of the past had disappeared behind our pitch perfect family harmony in the first years of our marriage.

"I want to make life beautiful for Faith. To give her the happiness that I never had," he declared over and over through her early years.

More recently, however, after that disastrous Christmas day at Lexie's, I saw the struggle as Faith pushed her father more and more to the limits. Dan bought her a white 280Z and she was ecstatic. She and Jensen were proud of their near identical cars.

Dave and I felt that, despite her lapses, our daughter was equipped for a life of happiness and success.

~ ~

Success to Faith, we soon found out, did not include college.

Though we'd hoped for her a degree and her choice of career, she'd long ago grown bored with book learning. With her fancy car for mobility, she'd secretly dropped out of school in her senior year, using her daily food and gas allowance to hang out with friends.

By the time we discovered her truancy, she'd been expelled for her absences.

Broken-hearted, we tried to look at the bright side of things. During those hooky days, Faith met twenty-four-year-old Jack Kenyon, who, we discovered, was a nice man who loved her and wanted to marry her.

Not exactly our dream for her but, at least, it offered a solution to her finding safe haven. Maybe our prayers were being answered after all.

Now a beautiful nineteen-year-old, Faith seemed ready to settle down.

Her wedding was grand. Much grander than we could afford, actually. But Faith loved beautiful things and wanted to have a memorable event. And she was our only child. The funny highlight was when Jensen stood in as Faith's attendant. But she didn't care a fig about what people thought.

At the time, I laughed. Later, that same trait would come back to haunt me.

Chapter Three

"There is no pain equal to that which two lovers inflict on each other."

– Cyril Connelly

In the beginning, Faith easily slid into her housewife-y role. She and Jack purchased an attractive three-bed-room house in our middle-class neighborhood. She never wanted to be far from us, which never ceased to intrigue me, given her assertive, don't-tell-me-what-to-do spirit.

Yet, at that time, there was a redeeming balance to her.

"You and Dad come over for dinner tonight," Faith would suggest at least once a week. "I'm barbecuing a roast. It's already so tender it falls off the bone."

Jack quickly flowed with our extended family. Every-one loved Faith's spouse. Especially Ginger and Betty, Priss' girls, both in college and, according to them, defi-nitely *not* blind to his beauty. I noticed Chloe's eyes co-vertly following him, too.

"Jack's a hottie," was a common, shared sentiment among our females. And he was with his smooth, blond good looks. His work ethics were exemplary. He was am-bitious, yet not obsessed with work.

The men loved Jack just as heartily as the females. While too lean and handsome to be considered an iconic tough "man's man," Jack fit into the family's masculine order of things. We knew he'd come from a broken home and that he felt that set-adrift thing at times, the flashbacks peculiar to kids shuttled back and forth between mother and father's residences, never quite tethering securely to either home.

But for a long time, he seemed well-adjusted and, while not overly attentive to Faith, seemed content and provided well for her.

"He's not romantic," Faith told me one day in her detached, up-front way, like describing the milk man.

"Maybe you should tell him what you need," I suggested.

"I have," she replied and rolled her eyes. "It's like talking to a chair."

"Keep trying. Sometimes, it takes a while for men to catch on."

I admitted to myself that from the beginning, Faith and Jack's relationship lacked the intimacy, the passion that earmarked my own marriage. Little things, like holding hands or hugs or soft words ... long warm looks ... were rarely there.

Faith's pregnancy soon pushed aside the romance subject because she was totally in awe of the emerging tiny new life inside her. It was during those magical months of change that we spent the most quality mother-daughter time ever together. I was so proud of my daughter's brand new maternal leanings. Definitely a new facet of her.

"I'm not smoking," she understatedly announced one day.

"Great." I wished fervently that the vow become permanent.

"It's not good for the baby. Besides, it makes me sick." And she stuck to that decision until Maddie was nearly a year old. Then she took up the habit again but indulged outdoors, not exposing her daughter to second-hand smoke.

I was happy. Dan, too, was elated that our daughter was settled in to a good life with a great man.

And our Maddie was the crowning touch. I smiled at the notion that I now had a second generation little *connection* toddling about.

We had our space in life, Dan and I. It was right and perfect. One we'd worked and planned for all through the years.

Life was good.

~ ~

"Mama, I need another refill of Lortabs." Faith had undergone an emergency appendectomy and now recuperated at her home. Jack's work took him out of town so I spent time there watching three-year-old Maddie and doing general cooking and cleaning, pushing my column writing up to the late night hours.

"Are you sure it has a refill?" I asked. It had been a week and a half since surgery and from my own experience with my hysterectomy, I knew that, as a rule, severe pain subsided within one and a half weeks.

"Yeh. I'm still cramping in here." She indicated her lower abdomen. I shrugged. Maybe hers was different from mine. Dan drove to the pharmacy for the refill. I thought how I'd always avoided continued use of pain killers. But this was Faith's first experience. She'd never done pain well. On some level, I sensed Faith enjoyed the "la-la" euphoria but didn't feel overly concerned. She was a big girl now. A mother, in fact.

Old enough to make good choices.

I had not a clue of what awaited our family in the wings.

~ ~

I don't remember exactly when the deeper rumblings began in Faith's marriage. After all, Faith and Jack never displayed that magic that marked Dan's and my union. Too, I'd slowly lost touch with my daughter. At first, I attributed it to her having her own life, apart from mine.

A good thing. Right?

She'd also started working part-time, from home. Soon she had both her realtor's and appraiser's licenses. When Faith set her course, there was no stopping her.

The new freedom sat well upon Dan and me. The time we spent with Faith and her family was quality time. But slowly, without my even noticing it at first, the dinner invitations grew fewer and the intimate chats ceased.

Seemed one day, Faith was a young mother and wife who cooked delicious meals and did laundry and the next, she was a stranger whose blank eyes stared at me unseeingly. It was as though Faith, the Faith I knew, disappeared, leaving someone hollow and alien in her place.

When had it happened?

Was it when Dan and I had been enjoying cruises and weekend excursions to the mountains or seashore, romancing it up like we hadn't for years? So enthralled that we hadn't noticed the slow decline of Faith and Jack's marriage.

Later, I would wonder if I could have helped more.

~ ~

"I don't want a divorce," Jack tearfully revealed one day. He sat in my den, needing reassurance and encouragement.

My heart went out to him. I wanted with everything in me to tell him it would all blow over. But I knew in my heart of hearts that it would not. Because Faith would do what she wanted to do.

Period.

He'd come to me, devastated that Faith wanted a separation. I was stunned. Seemed the smooth river of my life had changed overnight into rampant, savage rapids. The bends no longer ran smoothly but in jerks and stops with jack-in-the-box images popping up in dissonant chaos.

Faith's dialogue involving Jack had evolved into total negatives. She never gave him a kind reference. She spoke of a side to Jack I'd never even glimpsed. I had witnessed her out-maneuvering him with her sharp wit and tongue, a thing that visibly shook him.

"Faith," I told her after one such display in front of the family, "Jack simply needs you to be nice to him. He's evidently not had too much positive feedback in his life."

"He's not really smart, Mama. Haven't you noticed?"

"He's not stupid, Faith. His intelligence is just different from yours. He's got so many great attributes. He's a wonderful provider. A great dad and, my Lord, honey, he's as handsome as a movie star."

"I'd rather have a craggy brain who knows how to romance a woman."

"But you can take him *as is* and with your intellect, with kindness and wisdom, you could have him eating out of your hand. You could have everything you want,

Faith. There is no Mr. Perfect out there. You've got some of the most beautiful raw material to work with that I've ever seen."

My counsel fell on deaf ears.

Faith had made up her mind.

Dan and I tried to convince Faith to give her marriage another chance.

"*What?*" She glared at us. "He's a jerk. He treats me like crap. You don't hear how he talks to me sometimes. He hit me, Mama! I can't believe you take up for him."

As always, Faith's passionate convictions smote me, gave me pause. Was I really blind to Jack's faults? Was their "behind closed doors" a place of horrors? Were there really two sides to him?

Of course, there were. Everybody is multi-faceted, depending upon a current situation. He wasn't perfect, but neither was Faith. I knew she'd learned his buttons as he had hers. And she, too, carried a potentially aggressive streak just beneath the surface.

Something about the change in Faith deeply disturbed me.

This wasn't in my dreams for her.

~ ~

Jack and Faith had grown violent. One two a.m. call from the police had propelled Dan to their house to collect a sleep-fuzzy Maddie as Faith and Jack were hauled off to jail for domestic violence.

"They both were guilty of hitting each other. Faith's fingernails left bloody trails on Jack's arms and she had bruises where he'd gripped her arms tightly," Dan later explained, his features weary and stunned. "Jack had called the police to come and subdue Faith and was surprised that they arrested him, too."

Poor Jack, I couldn't help but think.

And poor Faith.

During that time, the world of justice began to open up to me. I did not always like what I saw.

Dan and I finally bailed them out of jail a couple of days later. Rage emanated from both of them. Against all my hopes that they would forgive and begin anew, that was only the beginning. I didn't then, nor do I now, understand such vehemence.

Dan grew silent. He watched. And one day, he looked at me as one on death row.

"Deede, if Faith and Jack divorce, we'll never know another moment's peace."

In that heartbeat in time, I did not believe it, thought he was over-dramatizing.

Now, years later, with twenty-twenty hindsight, I realize the veracity of his prophecy.

~ ~

In horrific resignation, I watched the death of Faith's and Jack's marriage. In the divorce, Faith gained primary custody of five-year-old Maddie. I felt no sense of triumph. Rather, I felt a deep grief when Faith excised from our lives, as succinctly as a surgeon, the man Dan and I had come to recognize as a son.

Initially, to their credit, Faith and Jack remained outwardly friendly, for Maddie's sake.

I tried, oh, how I tried, to be happy for Faith. She commanded it.

"I don't see why you can't just walk away from this, Mama," she would say. "I was never happy. Can't you see that?"

"I just — feel that Jack's heart is broken over losing us, honey. We were the family he'd never had. He told me so. It's going to take time for us all to heal."

"Well, he's not family any longer. I can't see why you can't be on my side."

I rolled my eyes and tried to scrub out the *taking sides.*

How I detested that term.

"Anyway," she switched mid-stream on me, "we're friendly now. I want to keep things as pleasant as possible because of Maddie."

That placated me somewhat. At the same time, something inside me held complete peace at bay.

Something about Faith — something elusive and offbeat telepathic — hinted that she was just beginning to search for that something she was missing in her life. That, in itself, gave me serious pause. Because since her miraculous birth, she'd had the greatest opportunities available to a beautiful, positive life.

She had so far rejected them all.

Dan's wariness and concern were contagious. Darkness seemed to hover over us.

I wondered, where would she go from here?

Where was my daughter gone off to for all those years? Where and what had been her space? Now, years later, I realize that I don't know her. Haven't for a long time.

I want to. With all my heart, I yearn for that reconnection.

Faith is at once my miracle embryo, my sweet-smelling infant, my toddler and my little girl … my adolescent who adored me and emulated even my mannerisms at times ... the teen who wanted to be her own person, yet still lingered, at times – if not clutching – fingering the apron strings ... the young married woman held spell-bound by motherhood.

The deadlock that is ours is agonizing. I detest it. The three of us seem wrapped — no, *chained* — together in a nether region of no return. Together, yet apart. Dan, Faith and I are in a horrific limbo with no idea how to escape. We — Dan and I — have prayed, but the *how-to* and the what are not yet revealed.

Something must happen to break the hex that ensnares us.

I pray with all the faith that is mine that it *will* happen.

Soon.

Chapter Four

"Recovery is a journey between two stations. One station represents total chaos, and the other represents total serenity. What is important is not where you are but what direction you are facing."

– A recovering drug addict

Five years later

"I'll pick her up in about thirty minutes," Priss said over the phone. "You two definitely need a break from each other."

I rocked vigorously in the white rocking chair on our shaded front porch, one of four Dan and I had purchased years ago from a local Cracker Barrel. "Understatement if I ever heard one." I snorted, venting frustration. "Thanks, Sis." I clicked off my phone, feeling my insides slowly begin to unfurl, to un-knot and allow my chest to take in deeper drags of air.

Then I arose, marched inside to my downstairs study and planted myself solidly at my computer to resume working toward my newspaper column deadline.

My current homeland stress-register had, in recent weeks, shot right out the top of my head. My older sibling,

Priscilla, "Priss," was, like the ever-lovin' Cavalry, rushing to our rescue during another hard time. Those times were growing more and more difficult for me to handle.

"Mom?" from upstairs yelled my divorced, live-in twenty-nine-year-old daughter Faith, who had in the past year completed a round of drug rehab. "Can you help me get my things together?"

I closed my eyes tightly, gritted my teeth and yelled back, "Why can't you get your own things together?" I was *not*, by any stretch of ambition, her maid. Nor was I doing her any favors by allowing her to dump her responsibilities on me. Despite my suspicions that she was classic ADD, I knew she was functional enough to get it all together on her own. If she chose to.

That big *IF*.

The daily battle raged.

She breezed past me on her way to my bathroom to collect some of her infinite hair paraphernalia strewn helter-skelter, cluttering my space. The over-the-shoulder glimpse I caught of her reminded me of the downward physical transformation of my formerly model-beautiful offspring.

Her five-feet-nine inch frame carried an extra thirty pounds and her auburn hair, once lush and groomed, sprouted haphazardly from atop her head, tethered by a pony-tail holder. Her former vibrant olive-complected face now sported blotches and uneven skin tone, while the finely chiseled features remained set in a morphing shift of expressions ranging from apathy to disdain to umbrage to rage.

Faith's choice of clothing was any garment nearby, whether on the floor or stuffed in a drawer or sometimes, when desperate, perhaps snatched from the used laundry basket.

Even the smell of her was different. Rather than *Ralph Lauren* or *Armani,* she now reeked of stale nicotine. My request, that she wash up after smoking, fell on deaf ears.

I noticed because first on my daily agenda was a hot soapy bath, deodorant and a dusting of bath powder. I dressed in clean, appropriate clothing. Next, I applied a minimum of makeup to look nice. A light spritz of *Bill Blass* completed my toilette. All this occurred in less than an hour. Then, putting aside further obsessing on appearance, I was ready for anything that presented itself during the long day.

Our differences here loomed as deep and wide as the Grand Canyon. This had not always been so. At one time, Faith's stunning beauty caused passing male drivers to veer off the road at times. Faith's fastidiousness in her grooming habits prevailed until her slide into drugs.

The mother in me had difficulty holding my tongue at times. Yet, I'd learned, by now, to choose my battles carefully. And as ridiculous as it sounds, this one ranked rather low on the scale compared to others.

The goal now was to save Faith from this alien she had become.

Her worst enemy.

Drug rehab, I now realized, was only the beginning. Chances of relapse loomed as thick in the air as cluster bombs' poisonous smoke.

Besides, any mention of better sanitation merely drew more defiance.

"Mom? Help me? Please?" she repeated, a nudge that set my teeth even more on edge because it was, even in its polite wording, a command. Something about it re-curled my insides into a pulsing ball of protest.

"Hey," I swiveled in my desk chair to peer at her, "I don't ask you to help me with things I can do for myself, do I? Why can't you carry your own load, Faith?"

Now, this battle was pretty high on the scale. So I dug in.

"I don't need a lecture right now. Okay? I'm in a hurry." She grabbed her things, clearly agitated, yet speaking in that lofty tone exclusively hers. Then, in a blink, it changed to petulance. "Why are you so mean to me?" The inner-child's bratty head popped up.

That hit me like a cannon blast. "*Mean?*" I stared at her incredulously. "Faith, I've chauffeured you all over the county this week, taking time away from my work. I don't think that adds up to *mean!*"

"Mom," she squared off and peered at me with a disbelieving light in her blue, blue eyes, "what's more important, work or family? Huh?"

"Hah." I swiveled back to the computer. "Depends on who's asking that question and in what context."

"I know your writing is important, Mom," she threw over her shoulder as she sauntered away, "but does it have to —"

"Look," I stopped typing, took a deep breath and closed my eyes. "This is my life. *I need* a life, for crying out loud!" I heard the shrillness creep into my voice. "I have a deadline here, and I'd like some respect and some danged *space!*"

"Stop shouting at me," she said so calmly I wanted to hit her.

I call it Faith's rebound tactic, when she veers a situation from herself to use against her antagonist. "I thought we were going to be more polite to each other and now you're shouting at me again. So much for niceness." Now that she'd gotten in the last word, a virtue in her book, she self-righteously spun on her heel and stomped up the stairs muttering.

Repeatedly, *meanness* filtered clearly through the jumbo-mumbling.

Shaking with frustration, I took deep breaths to level out my staccato pulse. Don't know why she could get to me so — so *fiercely.* Over and over, I would dissect and analyze.

It always added up to a whopping *honor* issue.

I'd always honored and esteemed my own parents beyond measure and didn't quite get it with the current generational irreverence. At least, I blamed it on a generational curse. Made it easier to shake off.

Outside, on the porch, I found her planted like an ancient oak in her rocker. The picture she made, a forlorn, beaten down one, caused the anger in me to fizzle.

How vulnerable she looked.

Yet, a peculiar energy oozed from her.

It sucked up the oxygen and sunshine, leaving only something dark and heavy.

The air grew suddenly thick with portent. I took the chair near her and waited, dreading.

"I can't go on, Mama," she said quietly, staring into middle space. "I don't want to live. Really, really, don't want to. I need to check out."

"Don't talk like that, honey," I murmured, my heart plunging to new depths.

"Besides Maddie, name one thing I have to live for." Her voice was as dead as her eyes. "Huh? Name one." She didn't look at me, only gazed unseeing at a mocking blue sky with whimsical white clouds.

I felt helplessness snake its way through me.

Hurry, Priss. The thought flew through my mind like startled bats. I knew that her Aunt Priss always had the right words to soothe Faith.

So, today, after yet another crisis and SOS to Auntie Priss, I looked at Faith sitting morosely there in that rocking chair, crying out for help. Thinking *suicide.* My weary heart floundered, struggling to respond. Trying to form the right words to comfort and not stir the terrible anger.

The despair. Because, in the end, Faith would do what she darn well pleased. That realization always caused my heart to freeze with dismay. Faith's will was self-propelled with her own unique brand of force, one that overrode anything and everyone who attempted to shape or alter her persuasion

I was exhausted from the previous night's sleeplessness, when Dan and I had words and he'd slept upstairs in the guest room. Again. Over Faith.

Always over Faith.

Priss' car pulled up, scattering my thoughts, and she climbed out, her soft fine wedgy cut, silver-streaked dark hair glistening in the sun, a cheerful smile on her pretty face. My sis is pleasingly fluffy and happy with herself that way.

Oh, she occasionally gives it a shot — weight loss — but ultimately, life and food flaunt their festivity and she gives dieting a sabbatical. She chooses clothes for comfort rather than to make a fashion statement. Her flip-flops free her feet to breathe in cool air and move unencumbered.

Lord knows, I try to be casual about such things but just can't divorce myself from the bathroom scales and full-length mirror and fashion detail. My chestnut, wheat-streaked hair remains fashionably cut and styled, one of my rare indulgences. I constantly monitor and adjust my appetite and weight while Priss sails contentedly through life experiencing all the epicurean delights her heart desires and chooses loose, comfy garb.

Her favorite quote is "I keep trying to lose weight, but it still finds me."

Thing is, she's not an unhealthy size. "Big-boned genes," she quips. "From God only knows *who*." She pulls humor from every source, even her adoption status.

Priss knows how to enjoy life. And she helps me, by taking Faith home with her, to regroup and to once more see the good and the salvageable in my daughter. In life.

"Hi, Priss." I stood and hugged her as she joined us.

Our tiny, fluffy rust-brown Pomeranian, Poopsie, did her little celebratory spin round and round and proceeded to bark with excitement as Priss reached to ruffle her fur then lift her into her arms for a smooch.

Yeah, Poopsie was named after her less than desirable leanings when we were trying to housebreak her. But the name stuck.

My little caricature Poopsie doesn't smooch me because I wear lipstick. At least, I tell myself that's the reason. Secretly, I fear she detects something about me that I don't. You know how dogs can sometimes sniff and sense health issues and I find myself fearing —

Nah.

Probably, she just doesn't feel that way about me, you know?

Poopsie loves Faith. Faith is Poopsie's Alfa.

Poopsie *adores* Dan, who is Poopsie's Ultra-Alfa.

Poopie is *wild* about Priss and yelps so fiercely in celebration of my sister's arrival that I'm almost moved to tears.

Me? I'm at the bottom of the heap, but Poopsie is fond of me. I feed her.

Priss and Faith began to load Faith's overnight gear into the Honda. Faith called over her shoulder, "Mom, would you mind running upstairs and getting my cell phone? I'm sweating like crazy." She wiped her face with her hand to demonstrate.

I paused, counted to ten and reminded myself that she'd just recently been hospitalized with a malady as yet undiagnosed. One that had sporadically caused high fever and sweating. Actually, the thermometer registered 104.3 degrees when EMS had arrived at our house and hauled her off to the hospital as she convulsed with fever and pain. In the ER, they managed to bring down her fever by putting her on antibiotic IV for several hours before releasing her with medication.

The blood test results had not yet been tracked down.

The symptoms hinted at meningitis. But tests were negative.

The ER doctor on duty suggested it was maybe a rare, tick-bite related fever-ailment. Exotic and long-lasting. Like Faith.

Too, I revisited my resentment of her long love affair with street drugs, one that had played havoc with her health. Her once beautiful, perfect white teeth were quickly deteriorating. I had, just last week, paid eight hundred dollars for a root canal and crown for her. Her thick, naturally wavy auburn sun-streaked hair, so like Dan's, had long ago lost its luster.

However, even on her good days, Faith's sense of entitlement waxed boldly.

Grinding my teeth again, I trudged up the stairs, found the plug-in phone charger and delivered it to Faith, not even looking at her.

"Thanks, Mom," she muttered and watched Poopsie rush to the open car door and jump into the front seat. Faith yelled, "She's wanting her ride around the block, Aunt Priss."

Aunt Priss' once-around-the-block with Poopsie was a tradition so she climbed in and cheerfully cranked up, allowing Poopsie to stand in her lap, prop paws on ledge and peer out the window, black button eyes aglow and tiny tongue lolling out of her mouth, anticipating the cruise.

"I'll wait here and smoke a cigarette," Faith decided and returned to a rocker and lit up again. Feeling again that bothersome concern-jolt, I stood and went into the house, just now being air-conditioning cooled in early spring's fluctuating heat.

And I knew in my heart of hearts that my concern for Faith's health wasn't a controlling thing with me.

It was overload. I simply wanted the best in life for my daughter.

I wanted her to heal.

I wanted her *to live.*

Plain and simple, I loved her.

~ ~

"What do you think, honey?" Dave asked me, as uncertain as I'd ever seen him.

I poured milk and Stevia sweetener into my decaf coffee and stirred, watching black turn creamy brown and thinking on his suggestion. "Buying Faith a car *will* get her out of the house and into civilization again. It will also solve another problem. I won't have to chauffer her all over creation. I'll get more work done."

Last night, I'd shared with Dan about Faith's suicidal thoughts. He, too, was apprehensive about her mental stability.

"But do you think she'll be responsible?" he asked. "She hasn't done too well in the past. We've already had to junk three cars after she drove them. And how will we know she won't go straight to druggies ... I don't know."

He drained his cup of black coffee and then looked across the kitchen table at me, his generous green eyes appealing. "Help me out here."

I sighed deeply, feeling the weight of stress. "She's going to have to start making her own decisions some time." I sipped my coffee, letting its warmth soothe me. "I think Faith will appreciate wheels because she's been without for quite a spell. As for taking care of it — there's only one way to find out, don't you think?"

I shrugged. Beyond that, no solution presented itself.

"Well, my insurance settlement from my collision a while back will enable me to find her a fairly nice car. I could certainly use this money for us, but I won't have another opportunity to do this for Faith. As you know, our reservoir of free cash is empty."

"I know." I smiled at him and his generosity. Just when I thought it had run out, here he upped and surprised me. He certainly had a right to his misgivings about this pursuit.

Both of us kept hoping that each of these hand-out episodes would be the magic bullet to get Faith on her feet and sailing in the right direction.

"She needs a life," I said. "Something to keep her occupied. And being stranded won't cut it. She can't even get a job without transportation."

"Yeh," Dan agreed, rising to depart for work. I envied him because he was usually out of the war zone Faith and I shared. At the same time, I was glad he was spared because of the complexities of his and Faith's relationship.

He leaned to kiss me soundly. "See you later. Love you, darlin'."

"Love you, too."

His gaze slid slowly over my face, his big hand cupping the back of my head.

"Love you more." Another kiss and he was quickly out the door, having had the last word.

I grinned, warmed, feeling extremely lucky.

Blessed.

Then I heard the upstairs door open and close and Faith's footsteps descending the stairs. Instinctively, I braced myself. I never knew which Faith I would get on any given day.

Actually, this was early for her.

Faith was rarely out of her bed in recent days and neither Dan nor I dared to wake the sleeping dragon. When she did finally roll herself out, headaches or equally debilitating ailments assailed her and had her grunting monosyllabic replies to my attempts at conversation.

Most of the time I left her alone. Like now.

I needn't have worried. Faith sailed past me without a word, dumped dirty dishes she'd carried upstairs in the sink of hot soapy water I'd prepared. Without pausing, she snatched her cigarettes and lighter from the counter where she kept her stash and headed for the front porch, her preferred roost.

I sucked in a deep breath and blew it out, looking at the sink full of dishes crusted with dried food. I walked over, counting to ten, scraped them and ran a little more hot water to cover and soak them. It always made me angry.

The entitlement issue.

Before I knew what was happening, I found myself headed for the porch to confront her. But — on the way — reason took over. I could attack her and guarantee an explosion. Or I could wisely strike up a neutral conversation to prelude the duties discussion.

Maybe I would tell her the good news about the car.

I took the white rocker near Faith. "Daddy and I were talking this morning—" I began and Faith interrupted.

"Talking about what a mess I am, I imagine," she snapped, then took a long drag on her cigarette. "I know how you feel about me."

The words whiplashed me. For long seconds, every nerve and sense in my body burned and spun. I squeezed my eyes shut and gulped deeply of fresh air. How could she jump to such rash conclusions? Then, I swallowed back an angry diatribe.

"Faith, your father is one of the most generous men I know. He's constantly doing for you."

"Huh." She snorted. "And he never lets me forget it. Tells me almost daily what a waste I am. So don't bother to defend him."

I felt sick over the love/hate thing with them. The antagonism.

Then the ashes mess caught my eye. Something about the litter and stain, heaped atop my pulsing edginess, stung me more than usual.

"You need to sweep the cigarette ashes off the porch," I said, trying to sound civil. "And pick up the butts that have fallen on the floor."

"I know, I know," as in *nag, nag, nag.* "All you ever do is tell me what I'm *not* doing." Another flippant pull on the cigarette. "I'll sweep them off in a minute. Don't know why we can't just have a normal conversation without lectures." Her flat reply, as always, left me feeling even more desiccated.

I marveled again that she was such a master at playing with one's mind. Her ability to skirt the actual subject was legendary. Faith knew her father and I both hated that the entrance to our home resembled a ghetto movie set. Neither did I like seeing her dirty dishes dumped in the sink, forgotten, for hours at a time.

"When are you going to wash up your dishes?" I then asked. "I leave the kitchen clean each night."

"In a minute."

Irritation sizzled. "You never wash them quickly —"

"There you go again." This, trailed by expletives. "I'll wash them in a minute. After I smoke."

Smoking preceded everything. Always. And I knew she would not wash the dishes right away. They would sit for hours.

That was invariably the direction of our "duties" exchanges. I don't think Faith planned it that way, but somewhere along life's way, she developed this extraordinary sense of control.

"Faith missed her calling by not becoming a prosecuting attorney," I told Dan repeatedly. He agreed. "She's a genius at turning words to her advantage."

Even worse, somewhere along the way, she decided she didn't care what others think of her. She didn't give a hot dang about orderliness. Trying to teach her to have a place for everything and to put everything in its place was like daily banging my head against a chipped, bloodied cement wall.

Intermittent bouts of neatness did seize her following the drug-riddled years. But they soon stifled and fizzled beneath an impatiently discarded outfit followed by a ton of others.

There is, to Faith, a flame-like aura, one fired by an eagerness that, when prodded, instantly evolves into snapping impatience. Her rash disregard of decorum, I think, comes from gestational hard-wiring.

I do not excuse it. I simply observe her struggle to conform, when over and over, the impetuosity wins out.

Dan and I *do* care what others think of us, but in a wholesome way. A messy, cluttered house is *not us.* Cleanliness. Little things like self-respect and character and ethics of behavior remain important to us.

We're into relationships.

Faith is a near-recluse. She avoids extended family get-togethers except on rare occasions. And she hasn't been interested in the opposite sex for a long, long time.

Today, I pushed these thoughts aside. Weary beyond words. Thought about how unnatural this was, to have an adult child under my roof.

Needy. Demanding. Controlling.

I stood and started into the house.

Then stopped.

I turned. "By the way, Faith. Your inconsiderate, stingy, unloving dad is planning on buying you a car."

Her mouth dropped open on that one. She looked at me, truly looked at me.

"You serious?"

"Has a cat got a tail?"

I slammed the door behind me.

~ ~

"Thanks, Dad!" Faith gushed and threw her arms around Dan. He patted her back as she squeezed exuberantly, allowing the luminous warm side of her to emerge. Nobody does affection quite like an overjoyed, abandoned Faith. He handed her keys to the mint-condition, white Mercedes Benz he'd found.

One owner. For whatever reason, the owner was letting it go at a price Dan could afford.

Parked in our driveway, it glistened beneath the afternoon sun.

Moments earlier, Dan had sat Faith down and laid out the rules.

"Faith, nobody, but *nobody* else is to drive this car. The insurance will not cover anyone else should an accident happen, in which case, your mother and I could be sued for everything we own."

"I promise, Dad." Faith rushed to reassure. "I understand perfectly. Believe me, I'll take care of this car — protect it with my life."

Oh, how I hope this will happen. Hope floundered up in me like an injured butterfly.

Her past track record was not encouraging. She'd trashed the last three vehicles we'd helped her acquire. They'd not even limped home. They'd died and been towed to the car graveyard.

Now, with wheels, Faith's demeanor did an abrupt turnaround. Her voice even changed. Gone were the snippiness and the biting retorts. Her social life cranked up. At first, Dan and I were pleased to see her engaging with other peers. Though we collectively held our breath, praying the peers would not be of the drug culture.

The day she first sat behind the Mercedes wheel, she said, "I'm going to visit a friend. I'll be back in a couple of hours."

Dan didn't let her off that easy.

Thereafter, he would push for accountability. "Give me a time"

"By nine." She would mean it. I knew she did.

And for several weeks, she kept her word. Then, she began slowly to take liberties, adjusting rules to her own time clock and agenda. Pushing closer and closer to the edge she lived on.

I worried. Dan obsessed.

"She's getting into something she's not supposed to," he insisted, frantic with misgiving.

Faith's explanations were given so convincingly that we had to give her the benefit of the doubt. Her weight loss was the most profound change. Seemed overnight, she ceased to care about food.

Eventually, Faith moved closer and closer to the dark precipice, driving Dan crazy.

More and more, she would leave "for a few hours" and not be back for two or three days, calling regularly, however, to check in.

"I'm over at Betsy's. She's sick and needs me to help her out. I didn't want you to worry about me."

The reasons were sound. Still —

Our calls to Faith's cell phone would go unanswered. Suddenly, she was completely inaccessible.

That really unglued us. Especially Dan, whose vigilance increased in those coming weeks.

Her explanations were simple. I couldn't get a phone signal there or I dropped my cell in a puddle of water and it wouldn't work for a while or I forgot and left my phone in Betsy's car overnight."

Faith's excuses were instant and conceivable.

"I hope she's wise enough to not screw up this chance," Dan said repeatedly, looking as though an elephant sat upon his weary shoulders.

"The pull of drugs is powerful," he added, almost to himself.

"She'll be okay," I reassured him. "She's had enough crap happen that she won't let it happen again."

And I tried to believe that experience is, sometimes, the best teacher.

With all my heart, I wanted to believe it.

~ ~

Faith's times with Maddie were her most treasured slices of life.

So when she began to disappear when Maddie was at our house for entire weekends, I truly began to worry. Her absence was so unnerving that, perversely, Dan and I ceased talking about it.

It was as though the air grew thick and black with possibilities too horrific to speak of. So we grew more and more taciturn and tried to enjoy the time with our little third grader. We avoided mentioning Faith's rapid weight loss. She was beginning to look frail.

"Why isn't Mama here?" Maddie asked me one evening as we lay piled up on my bed watching her favorite Disney cartoons. Her blue eyes, so like Faith's, implored me to make it okay.

"She — has a sick friend she's helping." I hobbled through the half-truth. Faith's host of "sick," faceless, nameless friends had grown in past months.

The mystery surrounding Faith suffocated me.

"Does she love me?" Maddie asked, not meeting my eyes, plucking at her pajama button.

"Of course, she does," I insisted, my finger tugging her face up until our gazes met. Hers was moist and inordinately sad.

"Yes," I repeated fiercely, knowing it to be true. Then I hauled her into my arms, tightly to my heart, fighting back tears. "She loves you very much, precious. No matter what happens, always remember that."

No matter what happens.

Now *what*, I wondered, made me say that?

~ ~

Dan answered the phone as I peered, bleary-eyed at the bedside clock.

Three-fifty a.m.

"Yes, this is he."

I sensed Dan's tensing as he listened to the male voice on the line.

"Was anyone hurt?" he asked in a flat voice.

The voice seemed to go on forever, with Dan replying monosyllabically. When he finally clicked off the connection, he looked at me over his shoulder. "Faith's car has been totaled."

My heart lurched. "Is Faith —"

"No, Faith wasn't in it," he said quickly as he lay back on his pillow, arms thrown back, hands beneath his head. His eyes glimmered in the dim of night. "It was just as I feared would happen," he said quietly.

Resigned.

"What?" I did not want to know.

"Faith let this guy drive her car. He was drinking. He and his buddy went for a joy drive and completely totaled the Mercedes."

"Oh God." I closed my eyes, instantly sick. *Why, Faith, why?*

Then another fear hit me. "Was anybody hurt?"

"Nothing life-threatening." Dan slid his arm around my shoulders and pulled me closer. "But only because they were drunk as skunks. Ahh, honey — this is what I dreaded. We could be sued over this. We could lose everything we have."

His angst reached out and enveloped me.

"Why were they driving the car?"

"Apparently, Faith gave them the key."

"When did it happen?"

"Two days ago. That was a state trooper, clarifying some things about the title."

"So this is why she hasn't come home," I said. "She's afraid."

"She's got reason to be." Dan's voice rang silkily, ominously in the darkness.

And I knew.

This was the beginning of more sorrows.

~ ~

Will Tollison brought Faith home. She introduced us to the handsome, winsome guy. Tall, blond, tanned and fashionably buffed, he wore designer clothes and had a killer smile revealing perfect teeth that rivaled a celebrity's. Dan held his peace until Faith's new interest departed in his flashy car.

Dan met it head on. "What were those guys doing in your car, Faith?"

"I asked them to take it to Will's apartment and park it," she calmly replied.

"They told the officer you gave them permission to drive it. Where were you at the time?"

"At a party. At the Sheraton. I only told them to drive it straight to Will's, a few blocks away, and park it," Faith insisted.

"Why, Faith?" Dan shook his head disbelievingly. "You knew the rules. Nobody else was to drive the car."

"Dad — I did not tell them they could take it for a drive."

"When you handed them the keys, you gave them permission to drive it. That's all that's relevant if one of them decides to sue me."

I wasn't sure of the legal ramifications, but Dan felt certain he was vulnerable and culpable should such a suit materialize. I didn't know if what he said was one hundred percent accurate or if some of it was a little paranoia. Whatever, it had him — *us* — over a barrel at that precise time.

"Faith, you promised me that you would be responsible with this car. As far as I'm concerned, it's over. My helping you get wheels. In the future, you're on your own."

When he walked from the room, he never revisited his decision.

"Why am I not surprised?" Faith snapped as soon as he was out of earshot. "I had a mixed drink that night and it made me sick. You know I'm not a drinker, Mom. That's why I asked them to drive my car back to Will's. I couldn't tell Dad that. He'd have really busted a gasket."

True.

"I wish I'd been in the car when it crashed," she said flatly and tromped up the stairs. "I'd be better off dead."

I closed my eyes.

Full cycle. Back to suicidal.

Wham. Her door slammed so hard a wall picture crashed to the floor.

No, more than full cycle. This time, I felt something more menacing in the air.

~ ~

When Faith learned Dan forbade her use of our other vehicles, she went into an emotional tailspin. I suspect partly it was because she realized all that she'd forfeited by breaking the rules. Too, "no" still did not sit well upon Faith. Dealing with accountability was excruciating to her.

She began to disappear in strange cars with strange people, staying gone for days before slipping back in during wee hours and staying in bed for days on end. Her weight continued to plummet.

When Dan or I protested, she declared, "I'm of age. I can go and do what I want to."

"You're still living in our house, Faith," Dan would remind her. "Where are you going? And with whom? We have a right to know."

"I have a right to my own life, too," Faith insisted, chin out, defiant. It was like she'd already lost everything. Dan and I had no leverage except to threaten to turn her out.

This became a pulsing, beckoning option in the worst of times.

By now, I'd discovered a hypodermic needle in Faith's room one day.

"They belong to my friend George," she immediately explained. "He takes B12 shots with them."

By now, Faith was a seasoned liar.

~ ~

The explosion came a few weeks later.

Faith had been gone for over two weeks. We had no idea where to look.

Mystery shrouded our daughter. When she wanted to disappear, she simply vanished in strange vehicles. A dark underworld out there swallowed her, leaving not a trace.

"She's my daughter, but I don't know the first thing about her," Dan said one day.

"Me, either." And it truly alarmed me that Faith and I had wandered so far from each other.

Dan was like a silent pressure cooker just before the steam begins to hiss. Dark and brooding. "Where is she getting money to survive this long?" he asked.

"I have no idea." She'd not even bothered to pretend to look for a job.

Dan's cell phone rang.

I stood at the sink, washing dishes and gazing out at the birds doing their springtime nesting in one of our hanging ferns out back. I sighed and thought how relaxed this time was.

Faith was gone for the time being.

"What?" I heard Dan's voice turn wispy, a sure sign of bad news.

"We'll be right there." He clicked off his phone and looked at me, a stunned look on his face. "It's your mother." His declaration held both shock and weariness.

"Oh, no," I moaned. "What —?"

"She's in the ER. Chest pains."

At the hospital, we met Priss and Lexie. Mom was ashen but responsive. "Don't worry, honey," she reached out to take my hand. The oxygen mask fogged with her laborious breathing.

"Don't talk, Mom," I said gently, fighting back tears. "Just rest. Everything's going to be okay. We're all here."

Mom's eyes closed as the sedative kicked in.

My sisters and I looked at one another, mirroring each other's fear. How would the Eagle clan fare without Mom, our sunshine? Hand in hand, we walked to the hospital chapel and prayed.

The ER doctor on call, Dr. Lahti, was optimistic. "The heartbeat is irregular, but I don't think it is anything life-threatening at this time. I suggest she be scheduled soon for a battery of tests, however, to make sure her heart is in tip-top shape. At her age, one can never tell."

Overnight, Mom stabilized and was free to go home.

We followed a hospital staffer pushing Noni in a wheelchair. Hospital policy. But when we got to the car, she stood to her feet and grinned at us all.

"Can't keep a good Eagle down," she quipped to her offspring lined up like royal subjects, her eyes alight with the sheer joy of living

I smiled and waved until Priss' car was out of sight. She was taking Mom home. And, oh, how I missed my Dad since his sudden death three years ago. I realized then that tears blurred my vision and that I trembled. The trauma of Mom's crisis mingled bitterly with the one we found ourselves embroiled in with Faith.

Another shock wave hit me.

Where is Faith?

~ ~

Dan must have felt it, too, because he hardly said a word on the way home beyond expressing thanks that Mom was okay. I felt the tension thicken when we reached home and Faith still had not returned.

I tried to turn it off. Let it go. But denial never quite worked for me.

Dan disappeared for a while and as I prepared lunch, I heard him bumping around upstairs in the attic, where he locked valuables in a safe.

"Lunch is ready," I called up to him for the second time. "Your food is cooling. You don't like cold chicken and dumplings."

Moments later, he appeared, pale and shaken. "Look," he held out a check book, "she's taken checks from my business account — several checks are missing."

Within hours, Dan discovered that several thousand dollars were missing.

"The bank president asked if I wanted to prosecute." He looked at me with haunted eyes. "I couldn't do it, Deede. I know she deserves it but — she's my daughter."

"Our miracle child," I whispered, stunned. "What happened, God?" I gazed upward, truly mystified, shaking my head. "Where did we go wrong?"

"Maybe we didn't go wrong, Deede. A person chooses their own path. Looking back, I don't see anywhere we didn't always have Faith's best interests at heart. We tried to do the wise thing every time we faced a crisis with her. And what has she done? She's thrown it all back in our faces."

I saw Dan's anger gathering into a violent storm. I, too, felt betrayed but handled my anger differently. But for once, in that moment in time, Dan and I were on the same page.

Our daughter had dishonored us to the nth degree.

Faith needed to go. She'd crossed a point of no return.

How could we ever trust her again?

First, we had to confront her. But how?

We didn't even know where she was.

~ ~

Three days later, she showed up.

During those three days, along with Dan, I'd alternated between rage and utter despondency. Had I seen her during those seething moments, I envisioned myself slapping her up side the head. A visceral itch. During the down times, I simply moved zombie-like or curled into a fetal knot of despair. Dan threw himself into work.

When Faith did appear, my reaction was one of mingled relief and confrontation.

"Faith," I met her at the door. "We know about you taking the checks and spending our retirement."

She dropped her head as she brushed past me to head to the kitchen for a glass of water. I saw her hands tremble as she drank thirstily.

She looked at me with gaunt eyes. "I know. I knew you would —"

Dan walked in from the back door and stopped dead in his tracks. If looks could kill, Faith would have hit the floor before the next heartbeat. "So. The prodigal daughter has decided to come home, huh?" His voice could have cut cedar.

"I came to apologize," Faith said.

"Apologize?" Dan stalked to her, eyeball to eyeball. "*Apologize*? You steal from me, knowing how hard times are for us and go out and blow it on drugs and God only knows *what* and that's all you can say?"

Faith's eyes filled with tears. "Daddy, can you consider for just a moment that it was a cry for help?"

Dan stared at her for long moments, barely holding his rage. "Help? You could have *asked*. You didn't have to steal from us money we worked hard for. Money we cannot replace."

Faith nodded, snuffling and wiping tears from her cheeks, unable to speak. She trembled with fear and, I strongly suspected, remorse. But I knew Dan was less inclined to believe her vulnerable.

"I want you out of here," Dan said quietly, lethally. And I knew he meant it.

"I don't have anywhere to go," Faith rasped, virtually wringing her hands.

"That's your problem. You've dishonored us for the last time."

"Please, Daddy ..." Faith swallowed the lump in her throat and pleaded. "Please don't make me leave. I'll do whatever you want to make things right. Anything."

Dan paused at the door, hand on knob, not looking at her. "Let me think about things, Faith. I don't know that I can get past this last thing you did. Let me think on it." He closed the door firmly behind him.

Faith gazed at me, remorse pouring from her red, teary eyes. "I'm so sorry, Mama. I've got myself in such a mess I don't know what to do."

"I'm sorry, too. This last thing threw us for a loop. Daddy's so distraught." So was I. But I had to buttress up to keep Dan encouraged. Sane. After all, he was the 'golden goose' who financially kept the lot of us afloat.

"I don't know how he can take any more of this." I shook my head slowly, beaten to a pulp inside. I felt like curling into a fried crisp fetal shape as life seemed to ooze from me.

Faith burst into tears. "Mama, I don't know what I'd do if something happened to either of you because of me —"

I sighed heavily. I had no answers. I didn't know if Dan would even permit Faith to remain under our roof. And I knew he — *we* — had every right to make her leave.

Faith began to collapse, catching herself before staggering the sofa and folding herself onto it, looking like something a feral cat dragged to the door.

"I do love you both, Mama," Faith sobbed.

And I believed that she did. As much as she was capable of loving.

But — to quote Faith - she'd made a royal mess of things.

~ ~

Dan and I talked and prayed during the next twenty four hours, trying to make a wise decision. The final verdict was Dan's. I trusted his wisdom. In the case of Faith, I did not always trust my own prudence. I was aware that my maternal leanings tended to color my judgment in this crucial matter.

At the same time, I prayed fervently that mercy would flavor Dan's choice of action.

He sat the three of us down around the kitchen table the next evening, which was encouraging since that's where our more intimate times passed.

Today, however, Dan looked anything but cozy — his implacable demeanor a witness to his tough upbringing. "Faith, I will allow you to continue to live here under the following conditions. You will get a drug test today to enlighten us as to your addiction status. Then you will check in at a methadone rehab center until you're drug-free. You will not drive our vehicles. Under any condition. Period. No discussion."

Faith nodded, desperate for clemency.

For survival.

"You will honor your parents henceforth or you will leave."

"I will, Daddy," Faith vowed passionately.

Please God. Make it so.

Chapter Five

"A brother (or father) offended is harder to be won than a strong city..."

– Proverbs 18:19

The following year was hell.

Dan arose each dawn to chauffer Faith to and from drug rehab, a twenty-minute jaunt one way. Methadone had a terrible effect on Faith. So much so that we felt guilty that we had instigated the "cure."

Had we known, I'm sure we wouldn't have gone that route.

Within weeks, her slender frame began to bloat and swell. The weight began to balloon. "I'm so hot," she complained incessantly. Regardless of the season or temperature, sweat beaded her face like a second skin.

"You're freezing my fanny off, Faith!" I wailed daily when she plunged the air conditioner to record lows.

Dan reacted. "Faith! Do not mess with the air! I'm already paying a king's ransom to keep our utilities running. You're driving us to the poor house."

In winter, she turned heat down to 50 degrees. "I live with a bloomin' Eskimo," I moaned, rubbing together and blowing on my icy hands. And that was just the tip of the — pardon the pun — iceberg.

Still, Faith sweltered and wiped her brow amid arctic temperatures.

Methadone wracked Faith's body, causing her to eat everything that didn't move and stopped her menstrual periods. Her teeth began to show signs of the effect.

Faith was born hard-wired to be temperamental. Methadone therapy escalated her moods, swinging the index , with little provocation, from catatonic to whirlwind, to thunderstorm, to hurricane, to tornado. We experienced them all, sometimes in one day.

To his credit, Dan tried to be understanding when things blew up in his face.

Much of it, I blocked out. I could only stomach the memories in increments. These were bridges I tried to burn behind me. Ones I wish Dan could release.

Her favorite cousin Jensen faithfully visited Faith often during her most difficult times.

"Come on, Faith. You don't have but four months left," he said during those last weeks. "I'm really proud of you."

That was a day when her teeth were clattering with mild withdrawals. She was trying to cut down more than the recommended dosage. "I-I'm g-glad somebody's p-proud of me," she stammered, wrapped in a blanket.

This was the only time she experienced the freezing sensation, during withdrawals. Interspersed were muscle spasms, all over, causing her to cry out in agony.

"Why don't you switch to suboxone?" Jensen asked her the next week. "I've been on the Internet studying treatments and suboxone seems to have the least side effects."

"Show me where to go," I said to the family computer whiz. Jensen's college degree was in computer science.

After thoroughly studying the pros and cons, we decided to switch Faith off methadone and onto suboxone. Her side effects seemed to diminish somewhat. The most dramatic shift was in her emotional state. Suboxone leveled out, to a degree, Faith's high-strung temperament.

Her angry outbursts and irrationality took a downward swing.

Even so, as she slowly tapered off the drug, she battled more, but less dramatic, withdrawal.

Somehow, miraculously, we muddled through it.

We celebrated Faith's "graduation" with a weekend trip to Myrtle Beach. Jensen and Maddie went along, exploring sand and surf with Faith, gallivanting all over and in general, making spectacles of themselves.

Dan and I? We enjoyed air-conditioned comfort and stolen moments of intimacy while the younger crowd romped and played outside during daylight hours. After wonderful restaurant seafood dinners, we would all meander to the Myrtle Beach Pavilion for rides and entertainment.

Dan and I managed to soak up a little sun. But I'd already discovered that at our age, sun did really weird things to skin, which in my case no longer simply freckled. No. Blotches and fuzzy brown protrusions appeared, things I always thought were reserved for witches and wizards and relics of humanity.

Besides, the heat was atrocious. So Dan and I munched away at junk food, watched movies and basked in the cool suite, gazing out at the rolling, blue Atlantic and enjoying the lulling sound of surf and wave.

I look back on those four days and sigh contentedly. How idyllic they were.

How peaceful.

And I'd let myself think — during that sweet interlude — that the dark times were all behind us.

How wrong I was.

~ ~

Those next months, till this day, stand out like a three-dimensional horror saga.

That Faith had ceased to do drugs did not bring back my daughter.

And now, my husband, the man I'd known all through the years — Faith's father — was but a shell of himself. Seemed that since that day Dan discovered the theft of his checks and subsequent funds stolen, he'd not been the same.

The proverbial camel's straw had crashed down on him.

Faith? After the initial triumph of getting clean, she slowly morphed into this new version of herself. The silence surrounding her was deafening at times. She remained an enigma. I could not, for the life of me, solve the riddle of who she was.

"I don't really know her," I shared with Dan in those early post-rehab days. "Will she ever come back, the Faith we knew?"

"I don't know her, either. Haven't for a long time." That was pretty much the extent of Dan's allusion to Faith. He simply turned her off.

Click.

The disconnection blasted like a cannon. Reminded me of the time the DSS officer had investigated Dan for child abuse. He'd felt betrayed by Faith. Now, he succinctly abdicated the Daddy-stance. It whammied my gut every time he excised her out of our discussions. "I don't want to talk about it," was his pat reply.

"Can you not forgive her?" I pushed him for clarity.

"It has nothing to do with forgiveness. It has to do with trust."

Anything I said beyond that resulted in his walking out.

But I knew.

Yes, trust was an issue.

At the same time, his growing aversion to Faith had *everything* to do with forgiveness.

~ ~

"Hi, Jensen!" I greeted my nephew, Faith's soul mate, at the door on a rainy summer day.

He stooped to hug me, scooped me up and swung me round and round until I was drunk as a skunk, then set me down, steadying me, laughing like a hyena.

I blinked away the loopy stars and took his beautiful face in my hands. "I love you, sweet boy!" I gave him a big kiss on his bristly cheek. "When did you start growing a beard? Huh, I ask you?"

"About fifteen, twenty years ago, Auntie. Where's ol' motor mouth?"

"Shut up, Tank," Faith yelled from the kitchen and came out toting a bag of cheese Doritos, stuffing her mouth. She walked up and hugged him and held out the Dorito bag for him to pilfer.

"Wha's happening?" he asked her as they plopped on opposite sofas, feet planted on the glass topped coffee table.

"Well, I took my period two days ago and it's already dried up. I'm like an old woman with raisins for ovaries."

Jensen threw back his head, arms spread wide, fingers orange with cheesy powder. "Lord. Do I have to listen to stuff in 'this is more than I want to know' category?"

"Oh heck, Jensen. You're just one of the girls."

From the kitchen, which opened up into the den, I laughed out loud at that one. Jensen, at six three, two hundred pounds of solid Stallone brawn and exotic male beauty that rivaled the composite features of Keanu Reeves and Johnny Depp, propelled by the wit of Ryan Reynolds, was the farthest thing from anything resembling a girl.

"Aunt Deede," he called. "Do I have to sit here and be insulted like this?"

"Absolutely not."

"You just come by here to pick a fight with me," Faith sniped, crunching into another Dorito.

And something inside me fluttered upward, happily acknowledging that this side to Faith rarely emerged lately. The one that engaged and entertained. Celebrated.

"Nope," he got up, yanked away her chips bag and dug out a fist full. "I came to see what's going on with you." He dropped the bag back in her lap. "You've not been answering your phone. I've left you at least a dozen messages — very seriously *concerned* voice mails, mind you — and you haven't had the common courtesy to respond. I take extreme umbrage." For emphasis, he popped several Doritos in his mouth and crunched his way back to the sofa.

"If you two will excuse me," I said, "I'll go work on my column." Actually, I felt they needed some privacy to hash out what was ailing Faith. She was notorious for ignoring calls and text messages.

But ignoring Jensen's messages?

This was not an encouraging development.

"Sure, Aunt Deede," Jensen rose and gave me a solid peck on the cheek.

As I silently typed in my office, their voices drifted in and out. And as Faith gained momentum, her voice grew characteristically strident. I didn't eavesdrop. The sound rode to me.

"I thought when I got off drugs, everything would magically turn out right. That everybody would be happy with me." She snorted with disgust. "Wrong. I'm so unhappy, Jense. I'm really screwed."

"Faith, you've got lots of life ahead of you," Jensen implored.

"*Hah.* Tell Dad that. He says I've already blown it. That I'll never amount to anything. And —"

"Faith, I know Uncle Dan and he wouldn't say —"

"Maybe not in those exact words, Jensen. But they add up to the same thing. Dad hates me. Plain and simple."

"He does not hate you!" Jensen insisted. "You've got to realize that you've ticked him off with all your crap. Know what? If I'd stolen from my parents, ended up in the slammer over and over, costing them caboodles of cash, and dishonored them like you, they'd have already kicked me out. You can betcha bottom on that."

"Huh."

A long silence.

"Faith," Jensen's voice gentled. "I've got something to tell you. That's why I tried to call you so often this past week. "

"What? Are you getting married or something?" Faith's relief at subject change was apparent in the lilt of her voice.

"Something." A long throat clearing. "I'm being deployed next week."

"What?" Faith shrieked. "Jense — where?"

"Afghanistan. For a year."

Jensen had served in the Air Force Reserves for the past four years and so far, their unit had been exempt from war duty. Now, seemed the luck of the draw had run out. Tears rushed to my eyes — our little Jensen going to war.

I heard Faith burst into tears, an unusual thing, and I half rose, then thought better and resettled into my desk chair. Reeling with shock that Jensen was being deployed, I had to remind myself that this was not a time for me to intrude.

"Why *you*?" she wailed. "What am I going to do without you here, Jense? I have *nobody.*" More sobs. "I just wanna die."

"Don't talk stupid." I heard the worry in his voice.

My heart felt strangely squeezed that she felt I was not there for her. And that the loss of Jensen was more than she could bear. I snuffled and swiped a Kleenex off my desk.

"Listen," Jensen said gently, "you'll do just fine with me gone. You're stronger than you think, Faith. Trust me on this. We'll stay in touch online. Daily. I'm going because I can be of use in communications. My quote 'computer skills' unquote will come in handy. So they say."

I knew Jensen, like no other, could divert Faith from dark solutions.

A snuffle. "Online? Really?"

"Yeh." A soft chuckle. "Ol' computer nerd here done already checked it all out. See, they have these two Internet lines. One is civilian and unclassified and open to everybody — which you and I will daily use to stay in touch. The other is, of course, the classified network. So, no probe-lem, chick-a-dee ..."

The conversation continued to more upbeat data. Light teasing.

A few minutes later, Jensen approached my chair, swooped and kissed my cheek.

He whispered, "Bye, Aunt Deede. Hang in there, y'hear? We'll get through this mess soon."

If anybody in the world knew Faith, it was Jensen. He loved her unconditionally.

Still.

I reached up and hugged his muscular neck. "I overheard about your deployment," I confessed.

He grinned, showing Mario Lopez dimples and teeth. "I figured you did."

"You be safe, now, and do stay in touch with Faith. And with me."

"You got it."

"But I'll see you Sunday at church. Right? We'll connect there."

"You betcha."

On his way out, I heard him call to Faith. "See you in church Sunday."

A joke. Usually. Because Faith had, by now, become the clan "heathen."

Did she care? *Hah.*

But this time, Faith surprised me and called back, "Yeah, see you there."

~ ~

Faith ping-ponged between going and not going to church on Sunday morning. I left her alone. I'd learned many years back to not push Faith. That perverse streak in her was entirely too quirky and unpredictable.

In the end, she appeared downstairs fully dressed, makeup and hair in place. "Ready?" she called impatiently, grabbing her Marlboro 100s from the kitchen counter. "I'm gonna take a minute and smoke."

"Hurry up and wait," Dan mumbled in mimicry. His handsome brow furrowed as he pulled on his suit coat and straightened his tie. "She is such a control freak," he muttered. He opened his mouth again, then clamped it shut.

I knew he was about to complain about her bad nicotine habit again but opted to let it go in the name of harmony. Sundays, he said, were a time of peace.

True.

The drive to the church was silent and tranquil. It was a time to gather our thoughts and sift them until the junk fell away. Until the focus moved from worldly cares to spiritual serenity.

At church, I was pleased to see a burst of wall banners in the vestibule with gigantic Kinko's enlarged, grinning photos of Jensen in various poses, surrounded by messages from everyone wishing him *Bon Voyage, Be Safe, Take Care, Stay in Touch* and touching patriotic thanks for laying his life on the line for his country.

I was weeping by the time I finished reading them.

So was Faith.

In fact, she wiped her eyes and blew her nose all throughout the preliminaries and music, flanked by Dan and me on one side and Jensen on the other. Chloe, was planted at her brother's other side. Jensen kept teasing and poking Faith gently. His cajoling helped slake the sadness during the preaching hour. Chloe kept peering around Jensen, her eyes flatly surveying Faith.

Following services, a luncheon in Jensen's honor was held in the fellowship hall. Ladies of the church brought dishes from home and joined the family in bidding farewell to one of their own.

Chloe rushed to quickly plop down in the vacant seat beside her brother before Faith could get there. I sized up the situation. Lexie already occupied the space on the other side of her son.

I motioned for Lexie to come over as I filled my plate and whispered. "How about giving Faith your seat, Sis, and you joining Dan and me at Priss' table? That way both our girls can get their way."

"Sure," Lexie said, rolling her eyes. "I'm only the *mommie,* for goodness sake."

"If you'd rather not —"

"Just kiddin', Sis." She grabbed my shoulders, laughing. "Lighten up, for goodness sake."

"I just don't want this occasion to be ruined —"

"By our obnoxious offspring."

"Exactly."

We hugged and finished filling our plates and joined our other clan members. Afterward, the family lingered at Jensen's table, each storing up these moments for the months ahead without him.

Faith, now seated at Jensen's side, grew more and more quiet. She looked unusually pale and distant. Later, when we said our goodbyes, she hugged her soul-mate for a long time, crying quietly as he gently and jokingly reassured her that he would return safe and sound.

Chloe tolerated it, I suspected, because she'd have Jensen all to herself for the final goodbyes the next morning.

For the moment, she sat at the table, arms folded, gaze averted, her crossed whip-thin leg swinging impatiently.

Jensen patted Faith's heaving shoulders and said, "Remember the old Eagle slogan, huh? We fly above any and all danger. Don't forget that."

Back at our house, Faith rushed into the house ahead of us, ran upstairs and soundly locked her door. Somehow, I knew she would not come out for a long, long time.

And I wondered, who will she confide in now?

~ ~

Dan's and Faith's relationship spiraled downhill from the day Jensen left.

It was as though a part of her went with her cousin. From babyhood, they'd cried together, laughed together, finished each other's sentences and, in the worst of times, been there for each other. Many a time I'd called on Jensen to help Faith through difficult times when my counsel did not set well.

Now, I had no backup except Priss, at least not anyone who seamlessly bonded with Faith.

Faith was and is one of the most complex people I've ever known.

Her relationship with her father had deteriorated so badly that I dreaded the times when Faith truly needed money for necessary things.

"Dad, could you loan me five dollars?" she asked one day.

"Loan?" he said flatly. "What for?"

"Just — some personal things I need," she snapped, irritated at the inquisition.

"I don't have any cash on me," he said and started out of the house. He stopped at the front door and turned. "When are you going to get a job, Faith? Huh?"

"I'm going to put in my application at some places this week." Her voice turned frosty at the turn of discussion.

"Yeh," Dan shook his head, agitation rising. "You've been 'going to' for months now. You never follow through."

"I will," she visibly reigned in her temper. "I just need five dollars, Dad."

Dan stared at her. "I can't keep handing out money like this. I'm already paying child support payments to keep you out of jail. And cigarettes, you know? And you know how I hate buying them for you. Makes me mad as blazes, knowing they're slowly killing you. You could stop, you know?"

Faith rolled her eyes, fighting to hold her tongue. "I know," she grudgingly conceded.

"But you won't," Dan said disgustedly. "I don't have five dollars."

He slammed out the front door.

Faith did not take kindly to "no."

Dan met these flaws head-on. Brutally frank.

"With Faith, you build up no favor. Each new crisis negates the former crisis resolution," Dan would say in frustration. "Enough is never enough."

"True," I agreed.

Her sense of entitlement, in the worst of times, knew no bounds.

Inevitably, a crisis would detonate and the fangs-bared Faith emerged.

Like today.

"All I need is *freakin'* five dollars for some chocolate," she unleashed on me as soon as her dad was out of earshot. "My hormones are messed up and I've been craving chocolate. I'm going out of my skull sitting in the house all the time." Another choice profane-phrase followed, turning the air blue.

"Would you please respect me enough not to use that kind of language?"

She didn't address my request. The language was a regular point of conflict. To Dan and me, it was the quintessence of contempt.

It dishonored us.

"Anyway, I don't have five dollars, either. Remember, I paid two hundred fifty dollars to circuit court yesterday?" My ire began to rise. Why didn't she ever say "no" to herself? I did it all the time.

"You always throw in my face all that you do." There was that absolute "always" again, her favorite gibe.

"That's because I do all that I do. Where's gratitude, Faith? Huh?"

An expletive erupted from her. "I don't want your money! Just wait till you want something from me." And after the famous last word, up the stairs she stomped and slammed her door.

"Good ol' Retribution-Faith," I muttered and returned to my writing.

The dissing was so bizarre I had to delete it as soon as it appeared. Yes, I could have responded with ultimatums and chastisements — and I had in the past. But most of those times, we ended up screaming at each other, saying things I'd rather not have said and hearing more dissing I'd rather not have heard.

So I decided one day that I wouldn't lower myself to shouting matches again. It was too much wear and tear on me because though Faith, characteristically, was over the upset within minutes, the emotional upheaval would usually decimate me for hours, sometimes days.

Today, I poured my heart into writing a column about a local Good Samaritan act. Next to the Man upstairs, it was my salvation.

I closed my eyes for a long moment, regrouping.

Please, God, make more good things happen around here.

You know, I really, really need them right now.

~ ~

Dan was a church deacon and daily read his Bible and prayed.

So I wondered at times, how he could go at the situation with Faith so differently from me. Oh, I understood why he lost his cool at times.

So did I. Often.

"Why can't you compartmentalize your feelings for Faith?" I asked him one day.

He looked at me, his eyes going flat. "What do you mean?"

"Can't you deal with her aggravating ways, do your spiel — once — and let it go, rather than going on and on about how hopeless she is? She is, after all, our daughter —"

Dan's gaze narrowed and sparked. "Yes, she is my daughter. If it weren't for that fact, she'd have been out of here long ago. But, Deede, by my making things so easy for her, I've become her enabler. She doesn't need that."

Enabler.

That word set off something inside me — a desperation — that swelled until I felt I would burst and then collapse into a flat, smouldering, desolate heap. I didn't, but I sure came close at times. Rather, I held my tongue for ten counts, then appealed to Dan's understanding.

"Honey, what I mean is that Faith has genuine needs. Can't we — you — deal with them without being so angry —"

"I'm not *angry,*" he growled. "I'm getting older, Deede. I stay so tired I can hardly breathe deeply at times. I can't keep up this pace I'm going at. And what, pray tell, will happen when I can no longer provide financially for Faith's needs? You can't meet them. We should be on easy street by now, traveling and enjoying life together, honey."

He swiped fingers through his thick salt and pepper hair. The waves fell right back into place. How I loved his hair. How I loved him.

"I know, darling. I feel the same. It's just — I can't survive large doses of anger. It does something terrible to me."

He pulled me to my feet and into his arms. "I'm sorry. I don't mean to dump on you."

"Who else can you dump on?" I melted against him, embracing his comforting warmth.

"I don't want to put stress on you," he murmured against my cheek. "I see how mine and Faith's skirmishes leave you."

It was true. Depression ate me alive lately.

"Dan," I approached the subject gently, "let's get counseling. The entire family."

He looked down into my eyes. I saw sorrow swimming in his. "That can be costly, honey. I'm stretched to the limit."

"I'll find someone with a reasonable fee. I'll work it out. You okay with it?"

"Sure," he said. Then he held me close. "Anything for my girl." He nuzzled my neck and whispered. " Thank you."

"For what?"

"For being you."

In moments like that, I felt everything would work out.

~ ~

"Mom!" Faith called from the office where she checked her e-mail on her laptop. "C'mere."

She shared Jensen's latest joke with me, one that had us both laughing till tears puddled. "Don't put both feet into mouth at the same time," one proverb stated, "or you'll not have a leg to stand on."

More laughter. "Now, that's funny," I gasped.

The only time Faith seemed to come alive was when she got emails from Jensen. And then, once she disengaged herself, back to the porch she went, planting herself in a rocker and smoking as though her very life depended on it.

I worried that her sequestered existence was so unhealthy. But no matter how hard I tried, I could not draw her out of her numinous shell.

"Priss, do you know any good family counselors?" I asked her that very week during our sisterly coffee summit in my kitchen. "Someone cheap but good."

Priss's laughter pealed. "You know those don't go together, don't you? Cheap and good?"

"Aw, you know what I mean," I laughed, too, at the absurdity of expectation. "I know you get what you pay for. Only thing — we can't afford to pay much, what with all the load we're already carrying."

"I'll check with Lexie and see what we can come up with."

The next day, she called. "Dr. David Shedd. He's a certified counselor."

"I can't afford —"

"He's a Christian who helps folks like you guys even if you can't pay. He feels it's a ministry."

"I wouldn't expect him to work for free," I said.

"You can pay him what you can. In his own words. He emphasized 'don't worry about money. The main thing is getting help'."

I closed my eyes and breathed a prayer of thanks for those merciful ones willing to help.

"Grab a pen and take down his number."

Dr. Shedd worked in Social Services and came by our house on his way home from work to counsel our family. We each, in turn, took our medicine. Yes, foul-tasting medicine it was because neither of us wanted to be turned inside out.

Lordy. It was rough taking off the rose-colored glasses and really taking a gander at ourselves.

Dr. Shedd tried to convince Dan not to be so dogmatic and controlling with Faith. Dan countered with how Faith insisted on controlling him. Dr. Shedd asked Dan to think on it.

He advised me to not react to Faith so much. I agreed that I overreacted at times and was willing to meet halfway. But that I felt I was already doing that. He asked me to think on it seriously in the next week, every time a conflict arose. He suggested to Faith that she consider herself a guest in our home and to behave as a guest would. She agreed but gave him reasons why she felt abused. He asked her to think on being a guest versus being an entitled family member.

The next week, we all admitted that we could improve our attitudes. For a time after the next sessions, we all three moved in a semblance of harmony, each acknowledging the other's space.

Then, months later, Jensen failed to e-mail for several days in a row. Faith called me up to her bedroom, a messy chamber that didn't embrace me. That had not changed dramatically. But I tried not to take in the clutter and focus on Faith.

"He's not responding to my messages, Mama," Faith moaned, on the verge of panic. "Do you think something's happened to him? I see every few days where car bombs and stuff happen and kill troops. You don't think it's happened to Jensen, do you?"

My heart lurched at the distinct possibility. But I forced myself to remain calm. "No. I'm sure these lapses happen for legitimate reasons. They're not just sitting there twiddling their thumbs, waiting for e-mails."

She huffed impatiently. "That's not funny."

"I know it's not. But try not to worry." I would call Lexie as soon as Faith was out of hearing range to check it out.

"Mama," she slumped back against her pillows and I noticed the paleness of her puffy features. Dark shadows beneath her desolate eyes lay vivid against skin's whiteness.

"What, honey?"

"Pray." She reached out and took my hand and closed her eyes, rolling over and curling into a fetal knot.

My heart constricted. Faith was not prone to ask that. She wasn't an atheist. Neither was she agnostic. She believed. But most of the time, at least in recent years, she'd neglected her spiritual self. Even, at her worst times, scoffed a bit.

Today, I held her icy hand and prayed. For Faith. For Jensen's safety. And for our home. When I finished, I kissed her cheek and tasted the salt of her tears.

"Thanks, Mama," she whispered.

~ ~

"We've not heard anything from Jensen, Deede," Lexie's tense voice relayed her own concerns when I phoned her a few minutes later. "He's not e-mailing me, either. I'm trying not to worry. I figure there will be times like this, when he's busy doing his thing there."

"I didn't call to alarm you, Lex," I reassured her. "I don't think there's anything to worry about. Faith has a tendency to obsess lately, is all."

"Poor thing. She and Jensen have always been tight. This separation has to be hard for her. And her trying to get leveled out after rehab and all."

"Yeah." I sighed. "Take care and let me know if you hear from Jensen, okay?"

"Sure thing, honey. Love you."

"Me, too."

As soon as I rang off, I turned and nearly bumped into Faith.

"She's not heard from him either, has she?" Her words were almost slurred, her eyes dead.

"Faith, are you taking something?" Alarms buzzed through me.

"There you go," she turned away, cursing. "Always suspecting the worst."

"Are you?" I followed her to the stairs and watched her climb them, mumbling under her breath, sloughing heavily, weaving.

Her door slammed and I heard the loud *click* of her lock.

"Faith!" I called, banging on her door. "I wasn't trying to start a fight. I'm concerned, honey. Can I please come in?"

No response. The moments slid into minutes as I stood there, forehead pressed against door. Would this never cease?

I turned and retraced my steps downstairs. I tried to watch television until Dan came home. I couldn't harness my mind to focus. I found myself going over the past weeks. The counseling had fizzled when Dan and Faith continued barreling down a collision course.

I tried to be a mediator and keep my cool. But with a misspoken word here or a misguided look there, things between Faith and me began to slowly unravel. With Dan, Faith usually soft-pedaled and learned to dance around outright implosions. With me, in private, she left a trail of antagonism as solid as the Great Walls of China.

Did I stand up to her?

Strongly. At times, fiercely.

For the record, there is not one shred of martyr's complex in my psyche. I've been told that I have a healthy self-image. And I'm known as an expert negotiator. Dan always sends me ahead to the business-bargaining table. I've never in my entire life had difficulty in that arena. Relationship-wise, through calm discussion, I usually accomplish a meeting of minds, even in disagreement, and everyone walks away with mutual respect and a modicum of dignity intact.

But somehow, Faith's repertoire of how-to-go-at-life deleted *negotiation*. She was, from birth, equipped with a keen mind and even sharper tongue. She's adept at maneuvering and turning one's own words against one.

As Dan is fond of saying, "She's way ahead of us." Yet — I think she has more of Dan's emotional make-up than he is aware of. The driven part.

Only thing is, Dan's drive is focused and disciplined.

Faith's is rampant, unruly and disruptive.

I heard the front door open and shut. Dan was home. He came into the den where I sat, TV remote dangling in one hand with me staring unseeing at the screen.

"Faith's not swept her cigarette ashes off the porch," he muttered with disgust. "It looks terrible."

I looked at him and sighed. "I know. It does. But she's having a terrible day."

"Huh. She's always having a terrible day. It doesn't take two minutes to clean up her roost out there. But will she do it? No. I think she leaves messes on purpose, to tick us off. Pull our chains. To prove a point." He marched to the kitchen and put on a pot of coffee.

He came to sit opposite me as the coffee made. "If she would just — be nice, you know? Honor us? Show a little appreciation? It wouldn't be so bad having her here. Heck, I wouldn't mind helping her. Not at all."

I nodded. I felt the same.

He continued, getting more irate by the moment. "But she's not grateful. She feels that whatever is ours is hers. She's not willing to work flipping burgers. It's beneath her." He scowled and shook his head. "I don't get it. And she stays angry all the time, upsetting you and wearing me down. She's not teachable."

His anger was building and so was the tension inside me. "Dan, Faith has been doing better … until this thing with Jensen came up. It seems to have spun her out."

"I'm sorry, Deede, but I don't see a big change. I see that she still yanks our chains and demands and uses and shows no courtesy or kindness. The least she can do for us is to hold her dirty tongue and be kind." He shrugged. "I don't see that happening."

Dan went outside to water the flower garden, his niche. He loved to watch things grow and kept our landscape meticulously groomed. He also used the activity to sift and sweat away frustrations, to neutralize stress.

"Mama!" Faith called from the top of the stairs. "Help me!"

I ran just as she crumpled on the stairs, catching her before she began to tumble. I held her in my arms, listening to her gasping and turning white. "I'm dying," she muttered. Then the spasms set in.

"Dan!" I screamed to the top of my lungs. "Help!"

~ ~

"She's running a fever of 104.5 degrees," the ER doctor told us. "We're doing an IV to bring it down."

"Are you testing her for drugs?" Dan asked.

I glared at him for a moment, but he ignored me and plowed ahead.

"She's been through drug rehab but — does she seem to be on anything?"

"We can't know until we get the blood work done. I'm going to admit her because she seems to be in some kind of trauma. She will need overnight monitoring at the least. After that, we'll see."

Lexie and Priss arrived at the hospital a few minutes later. I'd called them after dialing 911 and waiting for an ambulance. They rushed to embrace me in the waiting room. "How is she?" they asked in unison.

I filled them in and then asked, "Have you heard anything from Jensen?"

"Yes, thank the Lord!" Lexie took a deep breath as tears brightened her eyes. "He called today and said he hoped we hadn't been concerned about him. His unit had been working round the clock and he couldn't contact us."

I caved in with relief. "*Thank God*. Faith has been so worried about him. We all have, in fact."

I took them into Faith's cubicle, where they both kissed her pale cheek, but her eyes remained shut and her breathing shallow as the IV pumped life-saving, med-laced fluids into her.

We returned to the waiting area and Dan went back to spend a few private moments minutes with Faith. "Dan looks like last week's leftovers," Priss muttered, though her eyes were incredibly affectionate.

"Yeh," Lexie agreed. "Poor man. These kids are gonna be the death of us yet." They stayed for a while, reassuring themselves that Faith was in good hands before departing to feed their families supper. I promised to keep them updated.

Dan came out of the ER looking pale and his eyes suspiciously red. "I thought she was waking up at one point," he croaked hoarsely. I realized that the time with Faith had been emotional for him. Somehow, I knew that to talk about it would shatter something very delicate.

Both Priss and Lexie called, inquiring about Faith, promising to come back in the event she didn't quickly recover consciousness.

I prayed that wouldn't happen.

An hour later, the ER physician on call, Dr. Temp, came out. "Your daughter is coming around. Her fever is down. The culprit is a strain of strep."

"She's had this before," I said. "It's chronic. She's had these episodes — to a much lesser degree – since childhood. But they've just recently gotten worse."

The physician shook his head. "Probably because she's run down from her drug experiences. Takes time to recover. Lots of it."

"She's under a lot of stress right now," I said.

Dan stepped closer and asked. "Did any drugs show up?"

I looked away, my insides tightening. *Why did he look for trouble*? Why couldn't he put aside his skepticism when she was truly ill?

Dr. Temp hesitated, then looked at him. "I can't give you that information without her permission. I'm sorry."

Dan had expected this, but it still didn't prevent him from being royally ticked off. But then, we'd refused to sign the admittance form, owning any debt incurrence. Those would fall under Faith's responsibilities. Thus, Dan would not get any information about controversial drugs in the lab work.

I sensed by the stony set of his features that this merely reinforced his suspicions that Faith had secretly dipped into verboten substances.

Personally, I did not think so. I had not seen the telltale signs so evident during her addiction experiences.

But my opinion, already shared with him, fell on deaf ears.

"You folks may as well go home and rest up," Dr. Temp suggested. "She's going to be sedated throughout the night. You won't be allowed back in ER, anyway. She's leveled out. So you can relax."

We left for home.

"I feel in my gut she's been doing drugs again," Dan insisted quietly, his hands gripping the wheel on the drive home. His eyes got that hypnotic look, intense, dark, set straight ahead.

"I don't think so," I reiterated, struggling to keep it together when I felt my insides would burst and I would begin to scream and wail and howl.

"You're too trusting, Deede. She's a master at manipulation. You're too innocent for her. She's smart — way ahead of both of us. And I can't understand why her parents can't be let in on the test results."

I rolled my fingers into fists and squeezed tightly, keeping my voice calm. "Because we're not paying for the tests."

He huffed. "I support her in every way imaginable. And I'm not enlightened on her drug status? Something's wrong with this picture."

"You're right," I agreed. That's all he needed. He began to settle down.

But I felt it in the deepest part of me. The unforgiveness.

And I wondered. Would it always be so?

~ ~

With oral antibiotics, Faith continued to battle the strep infection at home. She reconnected with Jensen immediately. She let me read his e-mail account of the missing gap in his communication:

> The activity I've been engaged in was confidential. Our unit was charged with hardening computer systems against a threatening cyber attack from a foreign power. The threat was heightened to the degree that we shut down — thus restricting access to all communications systems until the threat was mitigated. I was charged with analyzing the malware's code to determine what it does, how it spreads and how to stop it.
>
> So, Faith, I had to work around the clock to accomplish this, leaving almost no time nor, indeed, access to the Internet. Actually, Operations Security aka OPSEC demanded that I could not notify my family of this changed schedule, new limits on communications or the new nature of my job. Sorry it worried ya'll. But it was not my call.
>
> I'm happy you're better after your nightmare with that crappy strep germ. It's always been a burr in our behinds, hasn't it? Remember the time – I was eight and you were seven – I went with ya'll to Myrtle Beach and we'd just gotten there, spent one night and you woke up sick and crying with strep throat and we had to go home? The pits! You and I both cried all the five hour drive home.

> Faith, I know your depression is tough. I've had it myself at times. But remember what Noni always says: regardless of all the junk and crap, life is still beautiful. That's definitely paraphrasing it. But you get the picture. Stop beating up on yourself and try to accept each day as a new opportunity to be. And don't think about doing anything stupid. It will all work out in the end. Don't forget to go to church, either.
>
> Love, Jensen.

I finished reading the message with tears in my eyes.

Faith sat in the other office chair, watching for my reaction. "He's very wise," I said. "I hope you realize just how much."

"He is pretty smart, isn't he?" Faith pushed from the chair onto her feet and headed for the porch. I heard her swing by the kitchen, grab her cigarettes and slam out the front door. And I realized she'd completely pogo-ed over the subject of Jensen's wise counsel.

Faith avoided introspection like a plague.

That had not changed since drug rehab.

She continued to hibernate on our shaded front porch, languishing in a white rocker, smoking, reading or, at frequent intervals, talking on her cell phone to non-names and faces. Rarely did she stoop to clarifying openness, melding her two terrains together to give me glimpses of her total world.

Mystique wrapped her. I did glean, over time, that these invisible friends were ones who'd usually either gone through drug withdrawal or with whom she had drug-affiliated relations.

To her credit, following drug rehab, Faith managed to cut off most of her past partying friends.

Positive changes. But dregs of the alien-Faith, who'd gone off to another planet in years past, remained, alive and well.

In recent days, any attempted engagement with her drew either disdain or suspicion. My conversation topics were viewed skeptically and critiqued before Faith would proceed with civility. Despite all my efforts and contributions, which seemed at times infinite, it never seemed enough.

Today, Dan came in for lunch. I heard him reprimanding Faith — again — for flicking her ashes on the porch.

"I'll sweep them off," she insisted, though much nicer than had I reminded her.

"When?" Dan called over his shoulder as he came into the house.

"I'm so sick of her messes," he snapped and pulled out his chair. I set his plate of homemade chicken salad, greens, fruit and cheese before him and joined him. Faith might or might not eat with us. She lived on her own timetable.

My head already pounded from Dan's "ashes" litany and from the fact that it was true. But it was like hearing the same tom-tom drumbeat message over and over and over until it triggered a hysterical response at the first beat.

"How's your day going?" I asked, overly bright, hoping to veer his mind in a more pleasant direction.

"Okay." He drank thirstily of his iced tea. "I see she's not cleaning her room, either. I went up to ask her something this morning and that place looks like a dump. It's not right, Deede. This is our house and she refuses to honor that."

"I know." My insides flattened out as if waiting for the next stomp of the foot.

He lowered his voice. "I was hoping for some privacy during this hour home — but I can see it's not to be." His eyes relayed a different hunger from that for food, lifting my emotions somewhat.

I smiled in agreement and reached across to squeeze his hand. Our "private times" were a sore point with both of us. "Rain check," I murmured and winked at him.

Faith did come in and join us. "Dad, Mr. Smith, our neighbor across the street, has a flat tire. Would you go help him? He's having a hard time with it."

Dan looked at her. "Did you volunteer my services?" The words were low, yet biting.

"Not exactly. I told him you might be able to help him. Was that all right?"

"I would prefer that you ask me before volunteering my services. Mr. Smith is not physically challenged. So he can change his own tire, I suspect. That's what I do when I have a flat. Besides, I have a work agenda I have to meet every day. Work? You know?"

Faith crunched into a pickle. "So you won't help him?" Her voice was flat. Faith's usual timber.

Dan glared at her. "Faith you are such a control freak. Why don't you just leave me out of your plans in the future?" He threw down his napkin and stomped his way out the front door, banging it shut behind him.

"Sheesh." Faith rolled her eyes. "He's supposed to be such a fine Christian man, and he doesn't even want to help out his neighbor?"

"Stop it, Faith. You know that's not the point."

"Oh? Then what is the point?"

"The point is that you're not only speaking for your father by volunteering his time and energy, you're also judging his Christian character. You're dissing him, Faith, and I don't like it a bit." I threw down my napkin and marched from the kitchen.

"I hate this place," she groused. "All I ever hear is how bad I am."

Yes. I sank heavily into my desk chair, desperately seeking escape.

That's because that's how it is.

Dan's dark face flashed before me — and his hurried exit, as though he could hardly leave fast enough.

And I felt that heavy, sinking feeling in my gut.

His resentment was taking a toll on him.

On us.

~ ~

"Mom, do you have ten dollars?" Faith asked nicely. I stopped typing and looked over my shoulder. She smiled at me from the doorway.

"No, I don't Faith."

"Mama, you know you have some money somewhere, tucked away."

"No, I don't," I said truthfully. Both Dan and I had stopped carrying cash because it was for certain Faith would ask for it at some point in time.

She walked away mumbling to herself. I caught that she thought I was lying.

Dan was adamant that giving Faith money was detrimental.

That we were being her enablers. I agreed, in principle.

And, too, I agreed that Faith was a user.

Faith's fall from grace had been succinct and complete. During that plunge into hell and the climb out, she'd garnered all the stench that attaches itself to fallen, depraved creatures.

Now, trying to steer her to a fresh starting place, I paid her fines and court costs weekly, totaling hundreds and thousands of dollars. Yet the very next time she asked to borrow five dollars and I said "no," she would erupt in effrontery, spouting "I hate my life," or "I've got to get out of here."

Before my own experience, at about this phase of a story, I'd have been the first to disgustedly tell parents, "Toss her out on the street."

But since I was not an outsider blessed with the luxury of objectivity, I knew that I'd not started this odyssey only to quit after nearly a year of Faith's being drug-free. Our family history was extraordinary and Faith was not, in our eyes, dispensable.

These problems now facing me were part and parcel of Faith's entire recovery package. So I saved my strength for the important battles. Not the shouting matches.

Rather, now I would retreat to my room or computer and avoid talking to Faith until her anger and victim-mentality subsided. Oh, yes, after cooling off, I attempted reasoning sessions. Deeply imbedded in me is a desperate desire to live in peace with all mankind.

This was especially fervent when it came to co-existing with my daughter. My only child. But Faith and I pushed buttons in each other that shouldn't be pushed.

We both are wired for passion, but it spirals in opposite directions during those clashes.

Today, she stuck her head in my office door again and asked, "Would you ask Dad if he has five dollars? Pretty please? I need some ibuprofen for this sore tooth. I'm afraid I'm getting an abscess again."

It never ends. A crisis each day.

I sighed. Then looked at her. "Faith, I don't feel up to being a go-between for you with Dad. It's too, too stressful."

"Mom, the pain is terrible. I *really need* something to ease it." She came over, bent down and opened her mouth to expose the sore area. "Look." It was, indeed, red and swollen.

I looked closely at her and saw the misery in her eyes. Pain. She had a legitimate need.

I called Dan. He bristled but said, "Come to the work-site and pick up some cash. I wish she'd get a job and some insurance." He hung up.

I felt squashed by it all. Like a bug.

Would it never end?

~ ~

My health began slipping. Depression sank its teeth deeply into me.

"What's wrong? It's Faith, isn't it?" Dan asked when he saw me silently withdraw to my room.

"Nothing. I'm just tired." But he always knew. Could see it in my eyes and sense it in my tension.

Then he would march off to find her and launch into a diatribe of everything he'd done for her for the past ten years and remind her of all the problems she'd heaped upon us and our home.

Being of similar drives, they ended up yelling at each other.

"I'll get out of this God forsaken *prison* before nightfall!" Faith would scream.

"Good! I'll help you pack!" he would shout back.

Only thing, we all knew Faith had nowhere to go. And she knew that we knew it. She was utterly dependent upon her father and me.

And she hated it. She resented us for it.

Dan and I would shake our heads, wondering if the old proverb was, after all, true: *No good deed goes unpunished.*

And we hated it because she was stealing our life. Our peace.

Our golden-years' togetherness.

Our space.

But worst of all, the father-daughter alliance had been mangled beyond recognition.

Would it ever be restored?

I wondered, will Dan ever be able to forgive Faith?

Chapter Six

"We each need our own little corner of the universe."

– Deede Stowe

There were times when Faith and I did connect. And when it happened, it was wonderful and fulfilling. She loved going to visit Mom with me.

"Noni," she sat on the big, comfortable child-proof sofa next to my mother, holding her hand, "you are so beautiful." And she was.

Noni, pronounced Noh-nee, was Mom's choice of name when she first became a grandmother.

"Aw, pshaw," Mom said, blushing with pleasure and squeezing Faith's hand. "You're the one who has the family beauty, Faith."

"Thanks, Noni," Faith leaned over to kiss the smooth cheek. "But I hope I look as good as you when I'm your age."

Mom chuckled and I could tell she was pleased beyond measure. "Oh, you will, dear. Just take care of yourself. Are you still reading good books?"

"Sure am," Faith replied, picking up her iced tea from the coffee table and taking a long pull off it. "I just finished reading the Charles Dickens book you lent me."

"*A Tale of Two Cities*?"

"*Oliver Twist.* I enjoyed it. Thanks for your continued efforts, trying to shape me into a cultured lady," Faith said, laughing.

"No trying to it," Mom insisted in her school teacher voice she'd used for over forty years. "You *are* a lady, Faith."

"'Fraid not, Noni." It was Faith's time to blush. "I wish."

Faith's subjugation to Mom was to me, and will ever remain, a wonder. I can see why because, I, too, adore my mother and submit to her like a love-starved kitten. It's just that Faith does not easily select and pay homage to those worthy of admiration. Period.

"No," Mom insisted, patting her hand. "You are what you want to be, honey. Underneath all that junk you carried around for a while, beats the heart of a fine lady. And don't you forget it."

On the way home, Faith reached over to take my hand. "I love you, Mama," she said. "I'm so lucky to have Noni, too. She's so — *special,* isn't she?"

"Yes," I replied, feeling tears gather behind my eyes. "She is."

"I miss Papa Eagle," she said, gently squeezing my hand.

"Me, too," I said. "Noni's handled his death well, don't you think?" Better than me, I sometimes thought.

"Yeah." Then she chuckled, "but then, she tells us that Eagles always fly high."

"Lots of wisdom there. We do fly over the clouds when it's called for."

Then Faith did something she rarely did anymore, she laid her head over on my shoulder and asked softly, "Do you love me?"

"I sure do."

"How much?" she asked in her little girl's voice, "This much?" She held up her hands to measure width.

I chuckled, reminiscing over our little ritual from her childhood.

"Honey," I said, "more than you'll ever know."

~ ~

"No, Faith, you cannot drive the car to the store," Dan snapped, tired and irritated and just having walked in the door after a hot afternoon of outside work. I whiffed the odor of tar on him as he passed. Asphalt has its own unique aroma.

"But, Dad," Faith plodded on, "it's only a mile away. I'll be really careful and —"

"It's not going to happen," Dan said over his shoulder as he walked away. His take was *give Faith an inch and she'll take over completely*.

I could not disagree with that assessment.

"I'll take you," I quickly volunteered, going for my car keys.

Once inside the VW, as we drove to the nearby Lil' Cricket, Faith said, "Mom, it's really hard being cooped up like a twelve-year-old. And, worse, being treated like one."

"I understand, honey. I really do. But remember that you *did* ruin several of our vehicles when we let you drive them." I tried to stick to the immediate issue, which was, in this case, our refusal to allow Faith to drive our vehicles. So I avoided the twelve-year-old reference, knowing that it could, in moments, evolve in a quagmire.

"That was *then.* I'm *clean* now, Mama. Why won't Dad trust me again?"

"That comes with time. Just be patient."

Things between Faith and her father escalated so I began in earnest to hide from Dan any crisis between Faith and me so as not to add fuel to the illustrious fire. Dan's take on Faith and her current status in our home was at odds with my own. Theirs became vicious clashes with neither backing down in their heat, saying such terrible things that I would often get in my car and drive off until it was over.

I felt the love/hate thing in my bones, smelled it, tasted it and grew desperate to extinguish the bitterness.

~ ~

One day, I overheard Faith talking on her cell phone with an old friend, one from her teen years, before her drug days. About an hour later, she came into my office and asked, "Mama, can I talk to you?"

"Sure," I said, recognizing a real need for my attention and swiveling my computer chair so that I faced her. She sat down opposite me in another chair. "What's up?"

"I've been talking with Freddie Muntz, remember him from high school?"

"Sure do. Nice guy."

"Well, somehow, we got to talking about Dad. You know, Freddie always liked Dad, ever since Daddy helped him dig his car out of the muddy ditch one day. He really began to relate all the good deeds he saw Daddy do and —" She stopped and her eyes filled with tears. "Suddenly, Mama, I saw my father through his eyes. I do have a wonderful Dad." She began to cry then, great sobs of regret.

When she finally wound down and took a deep drag of air into her lungs and released it, she cut those marvelous, near translucent blue eyes at me, red and swollen now, and desperate. "Do you think he'll ever see me in a new light, Mama? Really?"

"Ah, honey, I think so."

I hope so.

Tears gathered again and her voice trembled. "I pray he will. I miss my Daddy."

And for a long time, when I had my morning devotions, Faith would join me and we would pray together for family unity. I watched her hope grow and, behind the scenes, saw Dan's stance against being her "enabler" grow more rigid.

I felt torn in two.

My heart nearly broke.

~ ~

Faith went all out trying to win back her father's affection in those coming months. I watched and waited.

And prayed. Oh, how I prayed that Dan would get a new perspective of his daughter. I watched her present him little gifts and surprises, watched him turn them away. Not hatefully. His was an apathetic attitude, stuck in the mentality of "I will not be her enabler." And in his dysfunctional view of things, any softening toward her would result in her taking advantage of him.

It was the quintessential "all or nothing" mentality of a dysfunctional.

I watched, horrified at times, not knowing what to do to defuse the one-sided standoff.

On other days, sieges of conscience and emotional need would strike Faith, rendering her so humble and contrite that I hardly recognized her. She would hug me all throughout the day with an endless stream of "I love you" and reaching out to Dan. "Daddy, can I bring you some coffee?"

"Here, Mama, taste this." She offered me bites of most dishes she tackled and actually cooked a lot. Was, in fact, a great cook. In her depressive condition, food became her entire world and pounds began packing back on her long frame. She managed to acquire food stamps, which helped tremendously during our own financial struggles and her jobless existence. We never used the food card. Only Faith used it to buy things she loved. She was generous with the goodies, always offering Dan servings.

"No, thank you," he would nicely refuse.

Because Dan feared that he was being controlled.

Manipulated.

And when he refused her peace offerings, I saw Faith's features and stance wilt. I saw her hope deflate like a busted balloon.

And I remembered something I'd once read: "Never refuse a child's gift."

Now I knew why. Yet, I understood Dan's raw nerves.

"She's not a child," he shot back when I suggested he treat her more gently. "She's twenty-nine." There was, in Dan, a touch of brutality when provoked. And I knew that it only surfaced when stress hacked away at him.

I admired Faith's resilience at such times. From one day to the next, she ricocheted from "I hate that jerk!" to "why doesn't Daddy love me anymore?"

"Just be nice," I would remind her. "Respect him. He'll have to come around sooner or later."

I saw her desperation grow. Her eyes shone more blue and intense. Her laughter and speech became more strident and intrusive.

I saw Dan's stress climb. Felt his detachment grow more impenetrable than ever.

Faith could not dig deeply enough to find "Daddy" anymore. He'd shut that door firmly. Instead, when she reached out, it was to an aloof stranger who met her material needs when what she really needed was a hug. Or a simple "I love you, honey."

"How do I look, Daddy," she would ask on the rare occasions she dressed up. "Do you like this dress?"

"Hmm. Fine," he would grunt noncommittally, hardly looking at her. I could not even imagine how badly that hurt Faith because my own father never rejected me.

But I tried to understand where both of them were coming from.

Faith's presence was forceful ... like she was limned with a misty light that brightened to blinding as she revved up. For Dan, laid-back and reserved, pragmatic Dan, she was too vivid, too booming. Too intrusive.

Too much.

At times, she was too much for me, too. But I was able to —from my maternal-reservoir — compartmentalize *me* in the midst of Faith's nuances and be conciliatory during the worst of times.

Dan's ability did not stretch that far. Perhaps his abused childhood limited him there. Whatever it was stunted him in that direction. He simply was not able to pigeonhole himself that way. I respected Dan and had to accept it.

Our family's critics are too many to name. We have engaged a spectrum of advisors from policemen to pastors to family and friends to professional counselors. The advice route starts at the police's stern "Do not be her enablers ... kick her out. Let her serve time ... wash your hands of her," and ends up at pastors' and counselors' urging that "everyone can change. Help her as long as she's trying to get her life together."

Unfortunately, Dan got stuck in the first counsel and I was trapped in the latter.

Dan had, months ago, emotionally cut himself off from our daughter.

Enabler became his chief negative word.

"Can't handle all this added responsibility at my age and with my work load."

This followed by him kicking off his work boots and socks, showering quickly and tumbling on the bed, exhausted. "Is it too early to go to bed?" He would joke, meaning it.

"Nope. I'll bring your supper to you on a tray."

And I would, with him propped in bed, so tired he could hardly keep his eyes open as he ate, sliding me affectionate smiles as I sat in the easy chair, eating with him while watching the news. Dan's asphalt company was taking hard licks with the current economy crisis and instead of retiring as he'd hoped to do by now, he was forced to lay off workers and push himself to help do manual labor he'd once designated to others.

My job as a local newspaper columnist did little to nothing to boost our lifestyle. Writers are notoriously underpaid. But the creativity gave me a sense of accomplishment.

Besides, I figured it warded off endless nervous conniption breakdown fits.

~ ~

In the early dawn hours, the sultry August heat spell broke and a clash of thunder startled me awake. I squinted at the clock. Six-twenty a.m. Dan slept like the dead beside me as I snuggled and spooned against his back, rapturously listening to the rain that came down in pelting sheets. There was something about the sound that lulled and soothed me.

I wrapped my arms around Dan and nuzzled his neck. He began to slowly stir, then rolled over and pulled me against him. "'Morning, pretty girl," he murmured and kissed me. I would remain ageless, in his eyes, his eternal *girl.* We snuggled and kissed some more. Then we made love. These private moments were precious. Rare.

Then, sated, we spooned together and dozed again, awakening only when the birds outside our window began to sing their cheerful salutation to bright sunshine that had broken through sometime during the early hours.

Dan tossed aside the covers and his feet hit the floor moving. Even with tousled hair and sleep-glazed eyes, he still looked hunky to me in only his pajama bottoms. "I've slept late."

"You deserve it, honey."

He turned and smiled at me, a lazy, flirtatious smile that went to my toes. "Don't look at me like that or you'll end up being even later."

He chuckled, shuffled back to the bed and leaned over me for one more quick smooch. Then we heard Faith's footsteps upstairs as she moved about. "See?" Dan muttered bitingly. "No danger. No privacy."

He turned and looked at me. "I can't help but resent that I've worked all my life for this time — for our time. And it's being stolen from us."

My heart, so light the moment before, plunged. I covered it with a smile. How I wished Dan's every thought of Faith was not limned in disapproval. Then I resolutely pushed it away.

I cannot change anybody except myself.

I would do well to remember that.

Later that morning, Priss came by to visit. We sat at my kitchen table sipping coffee, scarfing fresh Krispy Kreme donuts Priss had brought and catching up on family happenings. "How's Faith doing these days?" she asked quietly. Faith had gone to a movie matinee with a friend, a rare occurrence.

"Oh, fine. Same old same old. You know Faith."

Priss laughed. "Yeh. I know Faith. Do you know how much I love her, sis?"

"I do." I looked at her and sighed. "You are so — so extraordinary, Priss. What would I do without you?"

"You'd do just fine, Deede. Remember what Mom and Dad always taught our Eagle clan to say when times got tough?"

I nodded and in unison, we pealed, "Eagles always fly high!"

I laughed, as she'd intended. "Do you ever miss teaching?" I asked as I went to the stove and poured us more caffeine.

"No. Not any more. Earl makes enough money to keep up three females, don't you know?"

"You're lucky." And she was. Earl's hardware store was successful enough that after her first baby's birth, Priss had retired from the classroom forever.

"Yeh. I am. Actually, with Ginger and Betty already into their own careers, that takes a lot off of us." Her girls, always close, now co-owned and operated their own gift shop in downtown Brattsville.

"You're lucky there, too. Wish Faith would find work."

"Is she looking right now?"

"Not really seriously enough."

"She does have health problems, though, Deede. I see her struggling to get it all together. I really do."

I looked at her, truly grateful. "Thanks, Priss. I just wish —"

"What?"

"I just wish Dan could see Faith as you do. To at least try."

"He will, honey." She reached over to take my hand. "Dan has his own problems. He's like Earl. Men see things more in black and white, I think. And really? Dan takes good care of Faith, financially. He may fuss, but he won't let her down in crucial times. You can take that to the bank."

"He's trying so hard to make ends meet, Priss." I measured cream into my coffee. "But even with my pittance salary, Faith's needs gobble it all up." I added Stevia sweetener and stirred.

In drug addiction, Faith had, in the end, landed at the very bottom of the pit. It included alienating family and friends to criminal activity to support her drug habit.

"Priss, now, even after drug rehab all last year, she hasn't bounced back. You know that."

"But she will, Deede. Give it time. She will."

"Dan's finally thrown up his hands and turned his back. Emotionally. Now I feel completely alone."

"Oh, Dan's there. Just in a different way."

"But I need somebody I can talk to without setting off a Civil War each time."

"You have me, honey. And let's not forget the Man upstairs. He's always there."

"I know. That's what keeps me going. I hate this turmoil. I can't live with it. I'm so desperate for some respite, Priss." Tears burned my eyes. "I can't even put it into words."

"I understand, sis. I really do," she reached across the table to squeeze my hand reassuringly. "In time, it *will* all work out."

"Dan and I walk on eggshells much of the time in the name of peace. But now, it's not just Faith I tiptoe around. I have to soft pedal around Dan, too. Seems he has this knee-jerk reaction to any defense I put up in her name. So I have to approach him just right."

"I know, Deede," Priss said, wiping moisture from her own eyes. "But I think that's a man-thing, the tough love. That's needed here, too. But it'll get better. You'll see."

~ ~

The autumn morning started beautifully. Sun poured through the den's open blinds, and when I stepped outside, I smelled the crispness of fall in the air, tingeing the foliage and trees red, yellow and gold. I wrapped a sweater around my shoulders only to find, minutes later, that I did not need it. And somewhere deep inside me, a memory stirred of Dan's and my early courtship days and USC football games. I hugged the recall to my heart, whiffing again that unique bouquet of bonfire smoke blended with *Brut* and Prince Matchebelli's *Wind Song.*

"Good morning," I said to Faith as she came out on the porch with her cup of coffee and pack of Newport 100s.

"'Morning," she mumbled, stone-faced. Faith does not do mornings. Her lighter's *click* emitted an angry punctuation.

But something about the day brought out the youngster inside me, the one who loves everybody and wants everybody to be happy. That child is into new beginnings.

Fresh starts.

"You sure don't look happy," I gently teased Faith.

"Leave me alone," she snapped and drew heavily upon her cigarette.

Something about the succinct rudeness crushed the joy inside me. Like a deliberate pin prick bursts a balloon, so did the rejection pierce my heart. A knot immediately clogged my throat and tears burned my eyes.

"I didn't mean to —" I started an apology for being intrusive.

"Just leave me alone, will you? Please?" The cold words, echoes of Dan's to her, hit me like a tidal wave. Her rebuff was so unexpected that I had no defense.

I stood abruptly and said quietly, "I'll leave you alone, darlin' daughter. Sweetie pie. I won't bother you any more."

You see, there is not one atom of Mildred Pierce in me.

And truthfully? Faith is not Veda, the daughter born into evil. At least, this version of Faith did not appear until drugs decimated the original.

As the door slammed behind me, I heard her cut loose with a diatribe of profanity. This time, I was the one who called Priss to come and get her.

"I'll be right over," she said. "Since you two probably aren't speaking right now, I'll ring Faith — for her to get her things ready."

Today, daily newspaper column deadlines stared me in the face, and I typed on the computer furiously, trying to reign in my splintered, hurtling thoughts — to make sense of chaos. Of all the losses and disappointments.

Faith had lost custody of our little Maddie three years previously. Drugs had stolen our beautiful, intelligent daughter's life.

And ours.

It was still hard to forgive her for — through rotten choices — losing our Maddie. I still shook my head and wondered, *how did it happen*? How can something so exquisite turn so ugly?

Today, with Priss, my faithful sister, en route — again — to collect Faith and give both my daughter and me some respite from each other, I clung to my writing deadline as a drowning woman to a floating log. I breathed deeply and counted the minutes until rescue.

"Mom," Faith drawled tiredly, passing my desk as she headed back to the front porch to stroke her incessant smoking habit, "would you please, *please,* put me on some coffee? I'm so tired this morning."

And every other morning. I was still shaking from her hateful response to me earlier, and she was already over it

The mean thought poised there, quivering, then flapping like a matador's red cape. I remembered that I hadn't attended church for the past two Sundays and guilt began to gnaw at me. So I marched to the kitchen, measured out water and coffee into the two-cup pot and slammed it onto the glass-topped stove. I gave up on my column for the moment.

I wasn't fit to be creative.

I still trembled from Faith's earlier hateful response to me. She had the nerve to ask me to —

I resented that. Deeply.

Still grinding my teeth together, I went to the shaded front porch to settle into one of our rocking chairs and watch for Priss' little white Honda Civic. Even though she had two adult children of her own and knew of my daughter's indiscretions and failures, she loved Faith totally.

Through the best and worst of behavior, Priss never gave up on her niece. And when things at our house got too stormy, Faith would call her Aunt Priss to come get her. She'd only be gone for a day or two, but our respite from each other was like a warm blanket in a raging ice storm.

It gave us all a turn of thoughts. New perspective.

Faith joined me on the porch after going in to fill her Starbucks coffee cup, adding lots of cream and sweetener, leaving the kitchen counter strewn with it.

"I'm sorry, Mama," she said. "I didn't sleep but about three hours last night. Couldn't relax. But I shouldn't have taken it out on you."

Moments like this, when she truly apologized, reminded me that Faith was salvageable.

"I'm sorry, too. I know you're at your worst in the mornings. I shouldn't get in your face."

"It'll still be good for me to go over to Aunt Priss' for a couple of days. We need some time apart. Don't you agree?"

"Yes. We do."

"I love you, Mom."

"Love you, too, honey."

"Did you ask Dad about the new coffee pot? He locked it up in the closet." She rolled her eyes and took a long, gut-filling drag on her Newport 100s. She referred to our bedroom closet that Dan had combination-locked to protect our valuables from disappearing. Everything from jewelry to checkbooks to cameras now stacked the shelves and Faith didn't need an explanation as to "why."

"Not yet." I averted my gaze from her death-wish gesture. She sat there, thirty pounds overweight, bedraggled and reeking of nicotine. Limp as a noodle. But that wasn't what bothered me. That could be remedied in time. It was her passionate obsession to do herself in.

Somehow. Someday. An icy feeling of dread oozed through me.

Please, God. Help me not go there. We have, after all, come this far.

Faith had only last week stayed on the phone convincing a salesman to replace two gourmet coffee pots whose handles had malfunctioned and broken off. The company had shipped the two packages to her this week. Proudly, she'd shown Dan. Her hopes that her father would celebrate her skill and share with her had died when he locked up the spare.

"But I'll need it when I move out," she told me, nearly crying with misery, an echo of my words to Dan. *"She'll need it when she moves out."*

"Hah." His humorless huff of dismay reflected in his eyes. "She's not going to move out." He cut an agonizing look at me. "*Ever*."

This, he would say to her face if the subject arose. I knew because he had done so. Dan believed that he, as the wage earner, was entitled to say what was on his mind. He also meant the words as a challenge to Faith, to shock her into enough anger to make her try to prove him wrong.

That's what would work for him.

But Faith was not him. Nor me, for that matter. She was her own person. One of the most complex people I'd ever known. And if there was truly a magic solution for this situation, we had not found it.

I tried to help him see that his negative feedback could backfire and become a self-fulfilling prophecy for Faith. If he kept telling her that she could not pull herself up, wasn't it possible she would begin to believe it?

At least, that's how it might have worked for me in my relationship with my parents. Their words could render either life or death to me. Fortunately, I was never tested with the darker possibilities.

Now, Faith's own hopelessness reached out to me. I'd never seen her so desperate. Her father's taking the coffee pot and locking it up sent a message to her that pulled the ground from underneath her feet.

And then it hit me. She has nothing. She's totally out of control of her life. And this seemingly insignificant situation is uncommonly earth-shattering to her. She doesn't have that father's consoling gentleness that undergirds in the darkest of emotional storms.

"I'll talk to him," I'd earlier promised because Faith, by now, was beginning to realize that a discussion with her father — concerning Faith — could evolve into an open vat of pit vipers.

"I paid for the first pot and don't owe Faith a darned thing," was his tart reply when I'd mentioned it to him.

The old familiar impasse. How I despised it. How I prayed for a mercy-tsunami to flood our house and hearts. So far that had not happened.

But I hoped Dan would change his mind. This current stance was totally out of character for him, who was, as a rule, the most generous person I know. But it seemed that with Faith, he was always acting on principle.

Or anger. I could not, most of the time, tell the difference. After all, Faith's anger gene came from somewhere other than from me. I had no comprehension of that vicious arena.

Thing was, I knew Dan prayed about his decisions. He daily read his Bible and conceded that the Psalms and Proverbs spoke to him about his responsibility to hold Faith accountable for her actions. I agreed that she be held accountable, but at the same time, the New Testament spoke of mercy and forgiving "seven times seventy."

Even there, Dan and I had different perceptions. Thing was, neither of us were absolutely wrong.

I told Priss one day, "I'm convinced that somewhere in the middle a solution will arise." She agreed.

Today, Faith lit another cigarette and took two long drags and exhaled though her nose.

"It's difficult to watch you killing yourself." The words slid from me like an ocean wave's foaming emission.

"Will you please stop telling me all I'm doing wrong?" she snapped, her swollen eyes set straight ahead. "I feel like *crap.* All I have left to live for is Maddie." She sat for a few moments, eyes dully staring into middle space.

"Honestly, Mom," she murmured sluggishly, "I truly am tempted to go sign myself into some mental rehab. I don't know what to do. I've dreamed of ways to kill myself. I thought that when I got off drugs, things would change. But they haven't."

The unspoken words hung there between us. Where will funds come from for another rehab?

In the next heartbeat, guilt pummeled me. Why did it always have to be about money?

Because, reasoning took over, as vulgar as it sounds, *money makes the world go round.*

Movies and television intervention shows make it all seem so simple. They don't tell us it costs thousands of dollars to dwell and receive treatment in those hallowed rehab walls and even with outpatient treatment, drug costs eat families alive. Most cannot afford it.

Faith knew Dan and I carried no insurance on her. She'd lost hers in the divorce. I had spent all my savings, pitiful though they were, on getting her legal counsel for the misdemeanors she'd committed while on drugs. Each of my Social Security checks — gone before it settled in the bank. Dan had spent thousands on drug rehab. I had even borrowed thousands of dollars to fund the last straggling court and counsel costs.

And it wasn't over yet.

But undergirding it all was this fear in my gut. Would Faith be able to pull herself up and out of this dark place she still occupied?

Will she even want to?

Chapter Seven

"In each family a story is playing itself out, and each family's story embodies its hope and despair."

– Auguste Napier

I felt the storm brewing. Tasted it. When Faith came home from Priss', she went immediately up to her room and locked herself in.

"I'm worried about her," Priss said as she was leaving. "She's not herself. Angel has never been so — despondent, Deede. Not with me." She kissed my cheek and left.

Faith didn't come out for dinner. When I knocked at her door, she called. "Go away."

"Are you okay?"

Silence.

"Faith?"

"Please, leave me alone."

I left, aggravated with her temperamental funk. Dan had a long day at the job so I jumped in the car and visited Mom. When I came back home late in the afternoon, I noted that no ashes littered the front porch.

Unusual.

I went inside. The house was silent.

"Faith?" I called. Not a sound.

Something pulled me up the stairs and to Faith's door. I knocked.

I could hear a pin drop.

"Faith?" I called. Silence roared.

An eerie feeling seized me. The premonition brand.

"Faith?" I screamed.

With shaking fingers I tried the door. It was locked securely. I ran downstairs for a paper clip and straightened it as I climbed the steps two at a time. My fingers trembled so violently that I could hardly insert the metal tip and press the trap. It finally clicked.

I hit the door and it flew open. I didn't see her at first because she kept her room so dark, draping blankets over the windows. When I did, I gasped.

Faith lay sprawled on the floor, face down. The ceiling fan lay next to her, it's propeller across her hip. Around her neck and tied to the fan's base was a rope. Even in the moment's horror, I recognized it from Dan's workshop out back.

"Oh my God," I moaned, hysteria flailing its way through me. I dropped to my knees and felt her arm. It was cold. I pushed the fan aside and gently turned her over.

"Faith?" My voice quavered, sounded unreal to my ears.

I closed my eyes tightly, took a deep gulp of air to ward off fainting. Everything wanted to go dark on me. My hands tingled, and I flexed my fingers to do what I had to do. Everything else about me was numb.

Except my accelerating heart, galloping away like a herd of wild buffalo.

I saw a bruise on Faith's forehead and gently touched it. Her skin felt icy, clammy. Her eyes were closed. I could see a tiny white glimmer between the lids. Then I leaned in close to detect breathing. I couldn't tell so I nudged down the rope and checked her neck for a pulse, again fighting the darkness that threatened to overcome me any moment. It was suffocating. I blinked back the black spots, forced air into my lungs and pushed on.

My cold fingers probed desperately. *Please, dear God!*

Then I felt it, a faint, faint rhythm. I nearly collapsed with relief.

"Hang in there, baby. Mama's gonna get help," I groaned, now sobbing.

I dialed 911 and then Dan. "Come quick," I rasped. "Faith tried to kill herself."

~ ~

Words cannot describe the horror of those next hours. Dan, ashen with shock, drove the two of us behind the ambulance to the hospital. Priss and Lexie arrived about the time we did in the ER, along with their supporting spouses. Even Chloe came along, appearing extremely concerned. Faith looked so vulnerable and pathetic with the oxygen mask shrouding her pale face.

"What happened?" Priss asked, eyes filled with tears. I could not for the life of me, speak. It was as though I'd drained out, leaving only a hollow, numb shell.

Dan took a deep breath, blew it out. "She tried to hang herself on the ceiling fan. It held until she passed out. But it wasn't strong enough to sustain her weight long enough for her to suffocate. It fell and, fortunately, sometime during the fall, the rope slipped free of the fan's base. Faith hit the foot of the bed and bounced to the side about the time the fan crashed against her, barely missing her head. It did get in a hard lick on her forehead, giving her a nasty concussion. Also bruised her hip. They're checking her out now to see if oxygen deprivation was long enough to —" He suddenly caved and burst into tears. Violent, masculine weeping. We three females rushed to throw ourselves at him, arms binding us, tearfully sharing in this, yet another tragic family heartbreak.

It was Priss, sweet Priss, who finally dried her tears and declared, "It's a bona-fide miracle, folks, that Faith wasn't killed. Either by the rope or the impact of that heavy ceiling fan. But the Almighty simply wasn't ready for her yet."

"That's right," Lexie agreed, snuffling back more tears.

Earl joined in. "Got that right, Priss. Ol' slewfoot didn't win on this one."

"Thank God," Adam sniffled and blew his nose. "The thief comes to steal, kill and destroy. But he failed with this family. Faith comes from Eagle stock."

Dan turned and drew both men into his arms and embraced them. "Thanks," he murmured hoarsely. "I needed that." They stood like that for long moments, unashamedly weeping together in one of the most splendid displays of manhood I've ever witnessed.

I saw Chloe turned to the window, her shoulders heaving. I walked over to her and pulled her into my arms. She melted into me and cried her heart out, dampening the shoulder of my pink pullover shirt. But that was okay. Those tear were precious.

"I-I do love her, Aunt Deede," she sobbed quietly.

"I know, honey," I murmured, kissing her herbal smelling crown.

"Do you think she knows?" she asked.

"I'm sure she does."

~ ~

For the next forty-eight hours, we kept vigil there near the ER. We had no assurance that Faith was not brain-damaged from oxygen deprivation. There was no way of knowing how long she'd hung before the fan broke free of the ceiling.

"But the fact that she survived is a good indication that she didn't hang there very long," Dr. Temp said. He shrugged and gave us a tight smile. "We'll soon see."

Within two hours, Faith opened her eyes during our visit window in the ER.

Priss was with me. She grasped my hand tightly as Faith looked around blearily.

"W-where am I?" she rasped. The rope burn blazed red against her pale neck.

"The emergency room," I said hoarsely.

"Aunt Priss," she grated and gave a loopy smile. "What?"

Then she grew quiet and looked at me, questions in her bleak eyes.

"I found you," I said. "Just in time." I watched the memory return.

"Oh God," she moaned and closed her eyes. Then she grimaced. "Why is my head pounding so?"

"The ceiling fan fell and hit you on your hard head," Priss filled in, seeing me tearing up.

Faith gave the most pitiful snort I'd ever heard. "Dang it all! I didn't even get that right, did I?" she slurred, looking at me, her eyes glazed, lids drooping. "I guess Daddy's right, huh? I really *can't d*o anything right."

"That's not true, honey." I leaned and kissed her cheek.

"Yup," she whispered hoarsely, "I really screwed up this time." A smile brushed her pale lips.

"Please, don't —" I said, tears spilling over.

"Jus' kiddin'," she whispered, feebly lifting her fingers as her eyes slid shut. She was out again.

The next day, we brought Faith's laptop to her bed and let her read Jensen's e-mails to her. "How does he know?" she asked, still a bit groggy and hoarse but gaining strength by the hour.

"I told him, honey," Lexie said. "He needed to know. He was concerned because he hadn't heard from you in the past few days."

Faith smiled as she finished reading his messages.

We were all so happy to see Faith acting normally that the world fell into place once again. Dan went out and ordered pepperoni pizza from Papa John's, Faith's favorite, and we all surrounded her with love and celebration during the following stabilizing hours before her release.

Strangely, in the darkest of times, sunlight broke through, giving us respite.

Peace.

~ ~

Dan seemed different after Faith's suicide attempt. Oh, not a miraculous turnaround thing, rather he seemed not quite there. As though he was trapped in a stunned time warp. Like he'd gone through a mild tasering.

Faith slowly reverted to her former mind set, and I was a bit disappointed that she'd apparently not had a mind-shattering wake-up call with her near death experience.

She refused to talk about it. "It's over," she insisted. "I won't go there again. You'll have to trust me on that one."

So I tried to trust her, but I found myself being more vigilant than I'd ever been.

"Please," she snapped at the end of that first week at home. "Stop peering around corners at me, Mom! I know what you're doing. I told you I would never try such a stupid thing again. Chill out. Please?"

"So I forced myself to chill," I told Priss the next day when she dropped by to see Faith and have our private sister's coffee time together. I relayed Faith's words to her.

"Hmm," she sipped her hot brew. "Sounds like she means business. I suppose we'll have to believe her."

"Well, actually, Faith will do what she doggone well wants to, regardless of what anyone says or does. But I think she's serious about this, too. At least, I pray she is."

"Me, too. Come 'ere, Poopsie." She reached down for our little twirling fur ball and hugged her. She was rewarded by a thorough pooch-smooch all over her face.

"Ugh," I groaned. "I'm glad she doesn't love me that much."

"You're just jealous," Dan had come in. He reached and grabbed Poopsie, sending her into ecstasy, and received the same affectionate frenzy as Priss.

"Maybe," I joked and laughed. "But I don't think so."

He looked at me and asked quietly, "How's Faith?"

"She's doing fine," I said, overly cheerful.

He looked a little doubtful.

At least for now, I thought.

~ ~

Other things were brewing.

After Sunday church service, I huddled outside in the June sunshine with my sisters, to give them an update on Faith.

"Faith still faces a possible felony charge that could mean prison, one that spawned from the three strikes you're out Clinton Law, remember?"

"Oh God," Lexie groaned. "I hated that ruling when he made it. Each case is unique and he forced it all into one mold."

"Faith made horrendous choices back then, among them was being in the wrong place with the wrong person at the wrong time. Not saying she's not culpable, but I know this hangs over her head like the guillotine blade. I can see it in her eyes. But you know Faith. Faith does not talk about her problems. Makes them too real."

Priss nodded. "I know. Sometimes, she opens up a little to me. Just gives me a peek, actually. I know she has trouble sleeping."

"Insomnia batters her into this whimpering, hurting heap." I swallowed back the spurt of panic I still felt after having come so close to losing her. "Only then do her eyes puddle with great tears and she moans, 'God, Mama. I don't want to go to prison. It'll kill me for sure.'"

Priss and Lexie both held back tears as I talked.

And I knew it would. Somehow, I knew any tiny morsel left of the once vibrant, beautiful girl of the past would wither away in the belly of the beast.

~ ~

"Bye, darlin'." I felt Dan kiss my forehead and the door slam behind him before I could open my eyes and sit up. I pushed back the bed covers and padded barefoot to the den.

Dan would go to the post office for mail and then swing back by before going to work. It was his morning thing, chatting with the postmistress and other acquaintances who came in.

From her bed in the corner, Poopsie caught my eye, and I felt a sudden urge to coddle her. I stretched out on the leather sofa. "C'mon, Poopsie," I coaxed in my sweetest voice. She looked at me for a long moment during which I fancied that she checked my sincerity.

"C'mon," I cajoled in a more melodic way, figuring that my non-alpha status needed a bit more enticement for Madame Poopsie.

She sprang to her feet, crossed over and leaped up on the sofa, an amazing feat for such a small creature. "Good girl." I patted my chest. "Here, girl. I need a little affection. C'mon, baby." And I thought, how *pathetic* to be so needy.

Immediately, she scampered aboard and flattened out across my bosom. Only thing, her black button eyes riveted to the front door. They nearly bugged out, hypnotically staring at the doorknob. And I knew that, in her doggie mind, Dan stood just outside that door, through which he'd moments earlier disappeared.

"*Shoot fire*, Poopsie," I whined, waving my hand before her unwavering eyes. "Could you give me just a few minutes of your adoration? He gets it all the time."

Her head remained alert and her gaze glued to the door. I gently pulled her face around until she had to look at me. "Kiss, kiss?" I wheedled. That's all it took for Dan, Faith or Priss to get an affectionate snog on the mouth area. Heck, even Jensen got exuberant kisses.

She stared at me, uncertain. I could tell by the way her ears moved. Yeah, her ears talk, too. Her little black snout reached out to nearly touch my nose. She sniffed and lowered her head to lick my hand.

"Thanks a lot, Poopsie," I snarled, hugging her. "They don't know that I don't really want you to lick my face, do they? It's our little secret."

I did this often when I really, really needed Poopsie's affection. I pretended that her refusal to *kiss-kiss* didn't matter. Today, it did.

Sorta.

Dan's arrival raised her head and lifted her fuzzy little ears to full attention. In one leap, she was on the floor before he fully opened the door. She knew his footsteps, and by the time he scooped her up into his arms, she kiss-kissed his entire face.

I sighed and got over it.

"Here's a postcard for Faith," he said and deposited on the coffee table. "Looks important.

"What's important?" Faith stepped from the staircase, rubbing sleep from her eyes. She picked up the envelope, turned it over. "It's a roll call. Court."

I heard the sobering of her voice. The dread.

"This is not the one I've dreaded," she murmured. "I've still got time before the hearing."

Faith sought counsel with Otto, her attorney.

"I don't get it, Mom. But Otto said another official round of rehab would weigh heavily in my favor with the judge's decision at the official hearing later on."

I was stunned. "Where will the money come from, Faith? I cannot for the life of me follow Otto's glib reasoning. You've already done the detox and drug rehab, thousands of dollars ago."

Faith rolled her eyes and shrugged, which summed up her attitude toward Otto. "I know, Mama. Sometimes, I don't think he even listens to me. He lives off the druggie's need for his representation. His own testimony."

I had my doubts about Otto's depth, too, but kept it to myself. At the moment, he was well paid up and owed Faith his continued representation.

He owed us. Dan and me.

We certainly could not switch lawyers in mid-stream and pay another retainer fee of thousands of dollars.

"I haven't saved any money this year," Dan had only last night groaned. "We have virtually no retirement left."

Worst of all offenses, however, was that Dan and I now shouldered another burden. Faith's ex, Jack Kenyon, had, in the end, demanded retribution by filing for child support payments from Faith, whose drug habit had cost her a viable income. In a sense, his demand was justified because she'd shown him no mercy when she'd had sole custody of Maddie.

Faith's drug-fueled mean-spiritedness had, in the end, caught up with her and kicked her in the fanny. Only it turned out to our fannies, mine and Dan's.

She had been in the midst of drug rehab when she got the official notice that she was months behind in support payments. Seemed Jack had — accidentally or by design — given the wrong address to the magistrate and Faith never received the notice.

"He's such a *jerk*," she'd said, crying, frantic with fear that the police would pick her up any minute.

Bottom line with Dan was that he could not see her go to prison. Underneath that steel exterior, his father's love for Faith waxed as strong as ever.

Because Dan knew in his heart of hearts that Faith was, in our divinely ordered world, special.

But, in the end, would we have a choice in the matter? Or would Faith be swallowed up by the prison system?

~ ~

During that slice of time after Faith was unjustly declared delinquent in the child support payments, she was terrified of sudden arrest.

Jail, to Faith, equated holocaust.

"Mom!" She grabbed my arm as I drove into our neighborhood one day. "Keep driving past our street. I think there's a patrol car in the drive."

I drove past the turn off to our comfortable residence with its wraparound porch, feeling Faith's panic start to transfer to me. "No," she said, peering anxiously out the window. "It's not. I'm sorry. It looked sort of official with that luggage carrier — it's Aunt Lexie's van, I think." I glanced over my shoulder and it was, indeed, my sister Lexie waving at me from my porch, obviously dropping by for an impromptu visit.

For a time following her rehab stint, Faith had continued to wrestle with lingering drug withdrawals and panicked each time a car passed our house, thinking it might be a county patrol car coming to arrest her for nonpayment of child support.

Her fears were well founded.

One night at two a.m., a loud knock at the door startled us from sleep and on to our feet. Dan tip-toed to peer through the blinds.

Poopsie, from her bed in the den, barked and yapped ferociously.

"It's the police," he whispered and crept back to my side. "Two of them."

We remained silent as church mice for long moments as the pounding on the door and doorbell ringing continued. We quietly lowered ourselves onto the bed and heard one leave the porch. We heard his footsteps mince around the house to the back, presumably, we figured, to make sure Faith didn't escape that way. We felt Faith, being a light sleeper, would hear the commotion and hide as well as possible, in the event that they force their way in.

But we knew they weren't supposed to break in. If they didn't know for certain that we were home, we could bluff it.

So we dug in, determined not to allow them to drag our daughter off to jail over child support payments she'd not even known existed. Too, already experienced with these nighttime arrest episodes, we knew her being jailed would merely reap more court costs and fines for us. Eventually, the policemen left.

Looking back, I remembered how Dan and I looked at each other, eyes glistening sadness in the gloam of our bedroom, each knowing what the other was thinking.

So we've come to this ... hiding in the dark, and we've done no wrong.

The next day Priss, generous, giving Priss, had given Faith sanctuary at her house until we could take care of the legalities, pay the whopping fines and catch up the child support payments.

Again.

Looking back on that time, I had to be grateful for how far we'd come in recent months.

~ ~

"I think I'll lie down for awhile," Dan said as he arose from the table. "I'm more tired than usual."

We'd just finished lunch. "Sure. Why don't you?" I encouraged him.

Dan looked more vulnerable lately. Not exactly frail. Just — beyond tired.

He — *we* still wrestled with debts and obligations. With Faith's neediness. Yes, deprivation covered her like a thick cloak. But she was still Faith, with her edge and brilliance, with her air-charging impact.

In his weakened state, I suspected that for Dan, Faith proved increasingly too much.

One night, Dan and I escaped to a nice restaurant and had a thick, juicy steak with crisp salad greens smothered with Greek dressing and heavenly buttered asparagus. "You're still my hero." I shamelessly flirted with Dan.

He loved it. "And you're still *the most beautiful girl in the world*," he sang in his warbly, off key voice, which endeared him even more to me. How handsome he looked, even tired and disheveled in his constant frustration. His black slacks and shirt hugged his slender frame quite nicely. He'd not lost his youthful aura, not to me. Never would he.

"Why can you eat all you want and still stay trim?" I pouted and sipped coffee while he ate a rich chocolate dessert. I peered down at a slight padding around my middle. "Just look at me ... and I deprive myself constantly."

His green eyes glowed as they swept slowly over me. "I'm not complaining. I like what I see."

Those marvelous eyes still sparkled with passion, whether from anger or his love for me.

My view of him was, I knew, through a benevolent filter that erased lines and wrinkles from his dear Tom Selleck features. He remained fixed in my mind as that brash young man I'd loved all through the years, the man who adored me and yearned for this time alone with me.

Lately, I'd sensed a deeper strain of territorialism interlacing with that passion.

Last night, he'd grasped an eerily correct inkling that Faith and I had been locked in one of our seamless conflicts. We'd clammed up in a flash when he walked in from work.

Later, he looked at me, confused, irritated. "I don't know why I get this feeling that I'm left on the outside of the loop." He plowed his hand through his thick, salt and pepper hair, then rolled the tension from his shoulders.

"Dan, you're not left on the outside. You come first."

The dark gleam in his eyes flattened into sadness. "Sure could've fooled me. You keep things from me now. I'd call that being left out. And I wouldn't call that being first."

Only to protect you. And myself from further pandemonium.

But to express myself would only lead to more of the same. His feelings were easily hurt.

Impasse.

He'd slowly climbed the stairs to the guest room and I slept alone. So tonight's intimate dinner together was special.

It was healing.

Chapter Eight

"Families are the compass to guide us. They are the inspiration to reach great heights and our comfort when we occasionally falter."

– Brad Henry

"Mom, do you ever wonder about your biological parents?"

Faith's question struck me as surreal, referring to something I'd buried deep, deep inside me. It had remained submerged through the years, except for brief guilt-ridden moments during a movie about happy or tragic reunions, years later, between adopted children and their biological parents.

Her curiosity surfaced today during one of our *together* times on the shady front porch. They were coming more frequently in recent days. I enjoyed them. And so did Faith. Her rarely exposed sweet side struck beautiful chords in my heart.

But this taboo subject jerked something loose inside me, a clamoring, jangling alarm. I surreptitiously sucked in a deep, settling breath. I didn't want Faith to know how insecure I felt. How badly I wanted to be — normal.

Whatever that was.

"Uh, sure. At times. But not overly so. Why?"

Faith shrugged. "Why not? I've got a grandma somewhere who maybe looks like me or you. And a grandpa, too. Since Papa Eagle died, I really miss having a Papa. Y'know?"

I nodded, feeling a bit numb by it all. "I guess I always resisted thinking about it because I didn't want to hurt Mom and Dad. They've given all to raise me and my two sisters. I don't know how they would react to either of us, you know, looking for our biological parents." I shook my head slowly. "I just don't know."

"What if Noni didn't know?" Faith asked and her laid-backness about it began to transfer to me. That's what frightened me — being casual about something so significant. I would never hurt Mom.

"I don't know." I felt uncomfortable with the subject. "I need to go check on my giant white limas, simmering on the stove. They're about done."

"Mmm, I love those big white butter beans," Faith murmured.

Good. She'd dropped the subject.

I was relieved.

~ ~

"I don't like these anti-depressants," Faith had said early in her post-ER days. "They make me feel weird."

"Maybe you should call —"

"I know, I know," she said lackadaisically. "I need a brain adjustment. I might be crazy, but I'm not stupid." She looked at me then, and a loopy grin broke over her face. "Is that an oxymoron?"

I shrugged and burst into laughter, happy that she could find dark humor in the fact that she'd nearly succeeded in doing herself in. Really bizarre, I knew, but when life had been so dark in recent days, any little ray of light was almost blinding.

That Faith disliked the anti-depressants the ER doctor had prescribed after her suicide attempt convinced me that she would not take them long. I was right. Dr. Shedd, our therapist friend, had been counseling her again. But she'd soon declared that she didn't need any more counseling because "everything the shrink tells me, I already know."

"If Faith refuses to receive counsel, Deede, there's nothing else I can do for her," Dr. Shedd informed us on his last visit to our house. "She has a brilliant mind. She simply needs to harness that brilliance and channel it constructively."

I hugged him. "Thank you so much for your time, concern and wisdom."

"You're welcome. And if you ever need me, day or night, just call."

Dr. Shedd was one of those truly giving people who are like a bright falling star in the scope of time and place. He helped push back the darkness during some crucial times. But even with his expertise and judiciousness, he could not override Faith's ferocious will. One that ever migrated toward darkness.

Soon depression swallowed her up again. I tried harder than ever to avoid conflicts and confrontations.

Despite my best intentions, however, we still clashed. I simply could not resign myself to the fact that my daughter did not carry her weight as a guest in our house. Nothing big. Just the same old same old, lingering dirty dishes, ashes on the porch, clothes left strewn helter skelter and refusal to wipe down the kitchen counters after cooking.

Either talking incessantly or hibernating into near catatonia.

Clutter. Chaos. Dark despondency.

And a filthy mouth when she was agitated.

After a while of this, resentment mushroomed inside me. The eruption wasn't any more than the ones we'd had before. After the harsh words, I would shut myself in my room for a while, waiting for the smoke to settle.

One day, after an especially heated clash, I walked away and slammed my bedroom door, refusing to talk to Faith for a while. It would, I decided, be pointless to continue to exchange reasons "why" we each felt justified in taking umbrage.

Faith called Priss to come get her. When I calmed, I joined Faith on the porch. My heart softened at the sight of her in loose, nondescript garb, haphazardly bound ponytail and morose contemplation.

And I thought how lonely she must be, in her self-imposed isolation.

"Honey," I broke the ice after I settled into the rocker. "You'll feel better after you spend a little time with Aunt Priss. Everybody's uptight lately."

The late morning breeze now boasted of nearby gardenias and rampant azaleas, whose colors and bouquet began to lift my spirits. In April, South Carolina air turns warm and paints leaves and foliage vibrant, infinite shades of green. I leaned my head back and rocked a slow cadence, watching a squirrel leap from a fir limb to a power line and agilely span the distance to another tree. The tail's graceful undulating furls gave the tiny creature the illusion of flight. And I smiled at Faith's description of life on the porch, "It's like a freakin' Disney animated movie."

"Yeh," she drawled tiredly. "Aunt Priss is always so good to me."

And I'm not.

"She always talks kind to me and spends time with me."

She doesn't live with you all the time. You don't push her buttons like you do mine. She doesn't have work schedules like I do. Deadlines to juggle. But yes, she is kind and generous and I'm glad she's there for you. And for me.

She took another long pull on her cigarette. I'd never seen anyone so aggressive with lung pollution as Faith. I had to look away again. *Turn it off.* It never failed to pierce that deep maternal instinct in me. All that protection I'd given her during my pregnancy and afterward, the vitamins and good nutrition and affectionate nurturing.

Kaput.

All I'd gone through to give her life.

Life.

"She's going to give herself lung cancer," Dan insisted over and over, disgusted. Alarmed.

It was true. He'd given her ultimatums and stopped buying. She'd gone into Cruella-mode, slamming doors and slapping pans around in the kitchen and in general, causing a ruckus. Two senior citizens were no match for her tactics.

Strange thing was — Faith always knew just how far to push without driving us completely over the edge, forcing us to throw her out bodily.

Still, Dan dug in his heels about being her supplier. "It's not fair," he lamented. "I'm too old for this." Like me, Dan wrestled with guilt day by day. "Why doesn't she quit?" he'd asked just that morning at the breakfast table. "I once smoked and I decided one day that I didn't need those little sticks anymore. I put 'em down and never have picked up another one. It's all in the head." He tapped his forehead.

"Yeh," I agreed. "Only thing, Faith doesn't want to quit. Obviously." I knew it wasn't that simple for a heavy smoker like Faith. But she didn't even try.

Dan huffed dryly. "Every time I suggest that as a solution, she takes extreme umbrage."

He turned at the door and looked at me, his eyes sad. "Each time I buy Faith cigarettes, it's like buying my father liquor, all over again. Well, she'd better decide she can do without them because I'm not going to supply them anymore." With that resolution, Dan slammed out the front door, and I heard his truck roar away.

I sighed and shook my head. He would be resolute until Faith's next conniption fit. We really were stuck, wedged solidly between two merging rock canyon walls.

Yes, Faith was, at times, absolutely appalling, someone from whom even a mother yearned to flee. Yes, it was tempting to simply give up.

Yet, at what stage does a parent say, "okay, it's time to toss her to the lions?"

Because there were more mellow moments with Faith, ones that buttressed up the bad times with *what-ifs* and *when you get through all this ...*

Moments that braced it all up with *hope.*

~ ~

"I measure success by reaching out to and tackling the next barrier," I told Mom one day while visiting her alone. Faith had gone to a movie matinee with a friend, a rare treat, one she'd financed with her "tide over" money sent by faithful Lanny.

"That's the only way to do it," Mom encouraged me. "You have much wisdom, Deede. And you use it. That's the marvelous thing about you. Faith is blessed to have you. And Dan. He's doing the best he can under the circumstances. It will all work together in the end. You'll see."

"I hope so." Then I shook my head disparagingly. "Ah, Mom. I know so. You always help me level out. Thanks." I got up from her cozy maple kitchen table and went around to give her a big hug and kiss on her smooth cheek, shockingly softened by age.

"I've got to go to the hospital for a surgical procedure soon," she said as I resettled across from her.

"What?" Worry began to roil.

"Oh, just to unblock an artery. That's all. Shouldn't be too serious." She spoke so blandly of it that I blinked.

"Mom. That is serious. Why —"

"Now don't you go and get all worried about this. It'll go fine. You'll see. I called Priss and told her right before you got here. I'm going to call Lexie soon as you leave. You girls just pray, like you always do, and all will go well." She smiled, an unrestrained, generous one as love spilled from her beautiful faded whiskey golden eyes.

"Sure it will." I reached across to grasp her hands and gently squeeze my love.

"Love you, Mom," I felt tears burn my eyes.

"I love you, too, precious Deede. You are a treasure." She gave my hands one last pat.

"Now," she morphed into my strong tower again, "Tell me how things are going with Faith."

But how strong was this tower? A heart procedure loomed.

"Mom? Are you sure you're up to handling this kind of—?"

Her eyes sparked. "Don't you dare start treating me like a delicate magnolia blossom. I'm perfectly capable of engaging in my family's challenges."

How could I balk at the *school teacher* Noni?

I told her about the drive earlier that week when Dan and I had discussed Faith's needs. Her crises.

"Huh. They're endless," Dan had said while we drove through the countryside, just chilling out, enjoying simply being. "Faith's crises are never ending."

"No. Not if I take them one at a time and reach a solution."

"Good luck. Could we change the subject, honey? I want this to be our time." He reached for my hand and gave me a lopsided smile.

"Sure." But I'd already decided that when I got home, I would check on that long ago blood test that I'd never followed up on.

"As soon as I got home, I tracked down the physician's phone number who'd treated Faith in the ER months earlier."

"Good." Mom now nodded approvingly. "We never did hear from that, did we?"

"Dr. Twombley?" I'd asked, feeling a frisson of fear in my stomach. Would they show something more bizarre? "Did you ever find out what was causing Faith's high fever when she was in ER several months ago?"

"Yes. It's strep. She seems to be a carrier. It lies dormant in her until something jousts it, and it flares up and makes her very ill, like it did recently."

"Well," Mom said. "That confirms that her chronic episodes of fever, chills and inflammation were that old vicious strep bacteria." She closed her eyes and sighed. "Thank God the diagnosis was not an added ailment. At least, it's treatable." She looked at me. "We have much to be thankful for. Now we'll just get on with seeing her through to total victory, huh?"

I left Mom's feeling recharged.

~ ~

The rest of the day felt lighter. I did a mental list of to-do things that would move Faith further toward complete recovery.

I told Dan about Mom's upcoming surgery. "She says it's no big deal."

Dan looked thoughtful. "Maybe it's not. Some of these procedures are not as serious as others."

So I relaxed about Mom. She was, after all, indomitable.

I stretched out on the bed that night, my high-backed husband-pillow propping me to watch television. Dan lay beside me, dozing already at only nine o'clock. Fatigue rode him hard lately. And I knew that, as with me, stress played a huge part in it. With all the expenses of recent days, our finances continued to bottom out.

I leaned over to kiss his sharply chiseled features, one by one, lightly. He opened one eye and peered fuzzily at me before closing it again. "Love you," he whispered. "Pretty woman."

I marveled again at how our love had endured through the years. Awed that, as many of our peers threw in the towel and divorced, time had only seasoned and deepened our commitment. And I wished with everything in me that we didn't have the challenges we faced daily.

Most all of Dan's grievances with Faith were over money.

"I think she came into the world with her hand out," Dan had said that afternoon after a pleasant drive, drawing a laugh from me.

"Now, that's funny," I said, laughing again, kicking off my shoes and heading for the fridge and a fresh bottle of cold water.

Dan burst into laughter, too, following me then pulling me into his arms and kissing me soundly. Our moments of complete togetherness were hard-gotten these days. "Hey, it's better to laugh than cry. Huh, darlin'?"

"Absolutely."

"Main problem with Faith is that she doesn't believe in telling herself 'no'," he said. "She sits around thinking up ways to spend money."

In that moment, even that was funny and the laughter kept rolling.

Needy was the word.

"To be fair, though," I treaded gently, "Faith more and more only asks for money because she *does* have needs. Most of the time, they're legitimate ones."

I usually hesitated saying that to Dan because, by now, he took it as a criticism of himself. This time was no exception — his good humor vanished.

"I always end up the villain," he complained, releasing me and heading for the den.

"There is no villain," I insisted, following him. And there wasn't.

He bristled. "If she was getting in *your wallet*, you'd fuss, too." He plunked down on the sofa.

"*She is* getting in mine," I responded mildly, seating myself opposite him on the love seat, only drawing more friction. I smiled and reminded myself that, for the sake of peace, it was sometimes best to remain silent.

It was yet another aspect of my space surrendered for family solidarity.

Our house evolved into a minefield.

I simply had to learn to walk it in a way that avoided explosions.

~ ~

The evening began pleasantly. Dan stretched out on the den sofa with Poopsie napping across his stomach. I forced my voice into ultra-casual mode.

" Dan, I'm going to use your Land Rover to take Faith to the grocery store and do a couple of errands. My VW is out of gas and yours is full."

I thought some mother-daughter time together would be nice, too, but with Dan's growing territorial inclinations, I kept mum on that score. He cut me a sharp look over his shoulder as I placed him a hot cup of coffee on the glass top coffee table. "How long?"

"Probably a couple of hours at most. Shouldn't take long." I shrugged negligently.

"Hurry back," he handed me his keys and latched on to my hand, pulled me down for a kiss. "I miss you when you're gone."

"I will," I promised.

"Gosh, Mama," Faith gushed when we climbed in the Land Rover, Dan's pride and joy, "Lanny just called and said he's wired me some money for cigarettes. We'll run by Western Union while we're in Greenville. My getting some cash may settle Daddy down some."

"Faith, he doesn't fuss to be fussing. He's genuinely overloaded."

"I know," she said more gently. "I worry about him lately."

"Me, too."

We discussed the agenda for Faith's errands. She had her coupon folder, which divided into genre compartments. She'd become fairly good at rationing her food stamps with the use of coupons to stretch their value.

"Maddie's coming this weekend," she reminded me, that unique energy of hers rising, smiting the air. "I want to get some goodies she loves. That'll pretty well finish out the stamps for this month. But they kick in again in ten days. I'm not doing too badly, am I?"

"No. You're doing much better with stretching it out. You'll soon learn how to come out completely even. It just comes with practice."

Silence.

"Mom, please stop being negative. Why do you have to always tell me how much better I can do? I mean, I'm —"

"I'm sorry, honey. I didn't mean it as criticism." But Dan *was* making noises at her using up the stamps before the month ran out, after which he had to make up the difference.

"Well, it comes out that way."

We rode in silence for a short spell. Faith, always the quickest to recover, spoke as though nothing unpleasant had transpired. "Maddie loves asparagus. Can you believe that? I've only recently begun to enjoy it. So I'm gonna get a bunch to cook for her. And some linguini." Her mind was racing full throttle. Pulsing.

I relaxed and turned into the Dixie grocery store parking lot. "I'm going to sit here and chill out, Faith. I brought a novel to read. The nightlight here is bright enough for me to see, so just take your time."

I thoroughly enjoyed my down time. Faith was happily occupied. Dan was lounging at home. I was free and I felt the blessing of that simple fact.

Nora Roberts entertained me for over an hour. I lost track of time, actually.

The car trunk's opening impact stunned me back to reality. I slowly descended to earth as the Dixie employee deposited several stuffed grocery bags there and banged the lid shut.

In the next breath, Faith slammed the passenger door shut. "Let's go, Mom." She scrounged around in her coupon folder, reorganizing, muttering to herself about each transaction, heaving my senses into agitation. I fought the nervous reaction.

"I need to go next door to get the wired money." She snapped her organizer shut.

I drove to the Western Union sign and parked again. This wait was short. She was excited when she reappeared. "He sent me fifty dollars this time. Isn't that nice of him?"

"Definitely."

Lanny was an out-of-town friend, a man whom she'd known for years and who sent her a few dollars from time to time to tide her over. Faith had long ago abandoned any false pride. She had no compunctions against accepting a helping hand from a friend.

"Is Lanny — has there ever been anything—?"

"Romantic?" Faith peered incredulously at me. "*Lord, no!*"

"Just wondered." I hadn't thought so. But I'd met Lanny once, a long while back. "He wasn't unattractive."

"Just not my type."

"Hmm."

"He's just a friend," she reiterated shrugging. "He's just big-hearted. He started helping me when I was going through the divorce."

I didn't say it, but I would not have been so casual about such an arrangement. But then, I wasn't Faith.

Of its own accord, my mind veered back to the death of Faith's and Jack's marriage.

Faith's ex had felt Faith was good at simultaneously reaching out to you with one hand while pushing you away with the other.

"Jack won't romance me, Mom," was Faith's dispassionate response when I relayed Jack's sorrow. "I'm tired of being treated like an afterthought."

Dan and I loved Jack as our own son, which spun the entire thing into a nightmare. I was horrified that Faith could shuck Jack so easily, without a backward glance. How different we were, my daughter and I.

"We *are* different, Mama," she agreed testily. "Why do you always take Jack's side?"

"Faith, it's not taking sides. We've always loved Jack. Now, you expect me to suddenly see him as some kind of monster."

"He's said some terrible things to me in the past," she insisted. "And I told him what I needed, and he refused to do simple little romantic things."

I reminded her, "And you locked him out of the house again when he thought you two were back together. Didn't have a clue as to what he'd done wrong. That's cruel, Faith."

"Stay out of my business, Mama. You never see my side of things."

And it was true. Faith's callous-gene did not spawn from my pool.

Months passed, and Faith and Jack made intermittent starts and stops at reconciliation. But in the end, they both admitted they were incompatible. Each was inclined to volatile outbursts and the clashes had grown increasingly dangerous.

Soon after their divorce, Faith did the tragic slide into drugs.

How and when remained locked up in Faith's psyche vault. She'd never truly explained to me the *where* and *why* of her demise.

Tonight, I shook my head to dispel the images as Faith and I drove along I-385 to our next exit.

My mind rushed to solutions. What could fix this catch twenty-two into which we found ourselves imbedded?

A job popped immediately into my mind.

"Have you given any more thought about getting a job?" I cautiously ventured.

Faith did her strong exhale huff, a sure back-off signal. "Can't we just enjoy the evening without the lectures, please, Mama? We don't get to do this often."

"Sure."

Faith's getting a job remained a hot topic of conversation. But each time she made progress, another health crisis arose and she would be forced to quit. Her last venture had been waitressing at a local restaurant. Her tips and basic below-par pay had been pitifully little. She'd ended up in the hospital with strep infection, after which Dan told her the job wasn't worth the time.

Her health was now fragile. The long drug-siege and chronic illness had taken a toll on our once stunning, healthy daughter.

"Faith," I heard myself saying, "know what you need to do?"

She narrowed her eyes at me and cautiously ventured, "what?"

"You need to get back into the social circle and meet some nice, resourceful men to date." One of whom can marry you and take care of you.

I felt her staring at me. Felt her guard snap in. "No, thanks."

Defeat smacked me broadside. *Chill out, Deede.* And I suddenly recoiled from my desperation, envisioning some yesteryear radio and TV comics joking about a daughter named Rosa, whom they fervently sought to marry off to any male passerby.

No, my wish was for someone to come along and fall passionately in love with Faith. The romantic in me warbled a frantic operatic aria while I pictured a man who would marry, protect and nurture her. In whom she could find true love — her prince charming.

Of course, Faith was the least inclined person I've ever known to seek matrimony again. "Been there, done that. Not interested," was her blunt response.

Sometimes, honestly? I felt Faith and I were born on different planets. Seemed she moved as far as possible from who I was without plunging off the other side of the earth.

But tonight, she left her dark space to reach out. "Look!" she trilled, pulling a package from one of the grocery bags she'd kept with her. "I spent five dollars on ice cream. I could not resist it."

My stomach growled. I hadn't eaten much supper. "What kind?"

"Ice cream sandwiches with M&Ms on top."

"Lordy." Saliva poured into my mouth.

"Tell you what," she leaned in close. "If you'll help me get rid of them, I'll go on a diet with you, *Mamacita*! A deal?" She stuck out her hand.

"A deal!" I gripped it. "What the heck?"

What the heck, indeed, *Mamacita.*

And then she said gently, "Mama, I wish we could do this all the time. Just enjoy our time together.

So did I. Oh, so did I.

And for that moment in time, I let myself forget that things at the Stowe residence could turn in a heartbeat.

~ ~

Back at home, I tiptoed into the bedroom where Dan lay fast asleep, oblivious to the television movie playing, starring Tom Berensen, one of my favorite actors. Dan looked so vulnerable lying there, breathing so deeply from exhaustion that I felt a jolt of unrest.

Slam. The front door closed as Faith went to the porch to smoke.

Dan's heavy breathing halted. My hand stilled as I reached in the closet for a nightgown. His eyes opened and found me, looking slightly wild and disoriented. He raised up on his elbow. "What's the light doing on?" Anger limned his query.

"I just got in. The TV was on when I left, honey. And the light. You were awake then."

"What took you so long? What time is it?" He peered blearily at the bedside clock. When he fell asleep by eight o'clock, time to him became warped. I could feel his umbrage swell. "I thought you weren't going to be gone long."

Territory issue again. Oh, God.

"Faith had to do her grocery shopping and a couple of other errands."

"What kind of errands?"

I took a deep breath. In the darkest of times, during the greatest risks of war, I could not force myself to lie to Dan. "We had to swing by Western Union."

"What for?" he demanded.

"Lanny, Faith's friend, wired her some money to help her out."

"Huh." He sat up on the side of the bed, staring at the wall as though he'd like to take it apart, piece by piece.

"Go back to sleep, sweetheart," I said gently, hoping against hope that he would settle back down. "I'll turn out the light."

But he was already up, on his way to the bathroom. I heard a pecking on my window. I rushed over to peer out. It was Faith.

"Your lights are on," she mouthed silently and pointed to Dan's Land Rover.

I nodded and headed to get the keys in my purse. She met me at the door.

"Here," she reached for them. "I'll go turn the lights off for you."

She disappeared to the driveway.

Dan appeared in that moment. "What's Faith doing?" he asked, clearly put out for having been awakened. I didn't blame him, actually.

"She's turning off the car lights." *Please, let it go, Dan.* I felt it in my bones — disaster loomed.

He was still as death standing there. "With my car keys? You let Faith have my keys?"

"She's just turning out the lights."

He marched up to me, nearly nose to nose. "Do you realize that I work out of that vehicle? Huh? It's my office. My money pouch is locked in there, for crying out loud. We live in a prison, remember? I have to lock everything up."

"I know, Dan." And I did. God help me. I did.

After years of disappointments and betrayals, wrestling with the trust issue had become a knee jerk reaction for Dan. Tonight, awakened out of deep sleep and unsettled, Dan's entire demeanor stiffened in protest at Faith's possession of his keys.

I was able to flow with dilemmas and not overreact. Dan was not.

Dan's perception of life itself was as different from mine as rocks to pudding. But through the years, we'd managed to mesh and delight in those very differences, complementing and finishing out one another.

Until now.

This.

To me, Faith's journey to wholeness flowed like a river, each bend opening up a new view of *place*, leaving the past downstream, now cut off by a burned bridge. I did not go there anymore. Dan did; each time a calamity arose, he rushed back to peer past that burned bridge at the dark waste piles.

For reference, he said. So he remained on hold. As in *wait and see* if she's really changed.

"After all," he'd often reminded me gravely, "my father never changed. He died drunk."

Tonight, I felt I was jerked up by two hungry, contending lions and ripped asunder.

His anger palpable, Dan met Faith at the front door. "Give me those keys," he muttered in his lethally quiet way and snatched them from her. I watched her ready smile dissolve.

"Okay, Dad." Faith *knew* — she rushed to explain. "Your lights were on and I turned them off for Mama." He brushed past her and went outside to the car, to check his money pouch, no doubt. When he returned, he turned his back and climbed the stairs. I heard the guestroom door open and firmly shut behind him.

I stood there for long moments, feeling something vital sinking to my toes, then draining out. It was the sickly desperate feeling that was becoming so familiar to me these days.

Faith came into the kitchen. "Why is he so mean to me, Mama?" she asked sharply. I could hear, *feel* her hurt. "He acts like he hates me. The nicer I am to him, the meaner he talks to me."

Which was true. Lately, with fatigue and financial stress hammering at him, Dan simply wanted out of the situation. Nothing I said helped. Actually, my comments hurt because Dan felt I was aligning with Faith. That I was no longer his ally.

So now, another component clouded the state of affairs.

Territory.

Who did I belong to? Did my belonging to Dan negate any maternal responsibility to my daughter? *Heaven help me.*

Territory.

Space.

No way I turned my view satisfied Dan's need for support.

Nor could I fulfill Faith's need for validation.

"He truly hates me," Faith now repeated hoarsely. "Doesn't trust me."

Sickness stirred inside me. Nerves on edge, I turned to go to my bedroom. "I can't do anything about that, Faith."

"I know. He's a jerk!" she snapped.

I stopped in my tracks. "Please do not diss your father like that, Faith," I scolded, knowing she lashed out in pain at his rejection. She was, at once, a little girl and a nearly thirty-year-old woman.

And my mother's heart saw the ageless essence of Faith in her hurt. Still, I would not allow her disrespect of my husband, her father, to go unchallenged.

"He does for you constantly. That's the way he shows love. You must respect that."

"Huh." She took out a bowl from the cabinet and a carton of Neapolitan ice-cream from the freezer. "Respect? What about him? It goes two ways."

I could not argue that. "I guess what I'm referring to is honor. Your father deserves honor."

"Huh."

She finished scooping a dish of ice-cream to take upstairs, "I've not had my period in three months." She detoured to stand before me. "Feel my stomach. Does it feel strange to you?" My nerves stretched taut as over-tightened fiddle strings, but I poked around her abdomen and it did feel bloated. "Just swollen. I'm going to lie down, honey." That was all the compassion I could muster at that precise moment. My nerves lay in a tangled mess, shrieking *no more*.

"I know, I know," she mumbled dispassionately. "You never take me seriously."

I spun around, squinting in amazement at her. "What?" My head throbbed and my stomach knotted. *Nothing is ever enough.*

"Why do you hate me?" she asked dully.

It was like a physical blow. "What are you talking about?" Something primal and livid leaped and spiraled through me. Something beyond any calmness that nestled predominantly in my genes. I took her by the shoulders and said through clenched teeth, "I *do not hate you. But you do aggravate me out of my skull."*

She didn't react with anger as she would have done in the past. Her arms hung limply to her sides. I noted her eyes were glassy now, like deep grieving pools.

I'd had it ... but something in those grieving pools tugged at me. Disarmed me. "Look, Faith. You need a good night's sleep and —"

"That's all I do is sleep," she said in that same dead tone, as in can't-you-*fix-it?* I knew Faith's woman-to-child attitude could turn on a comma, but it always simultaneously irritated me and evoked mercy. Because I knew inside each adult is a child crying out for help.

That child may be a hellion or a spoiled brat. Or she may be genuinely in need.

It's not always easy to tell. And I wondered why I was created with so much — *feeling. Compassion.* Why did I feel others' pain?

Was it gift or curse?

I went to my room, closed the door and climbed into bed. Finally, after a long time, my eyes drooped and I dozed.

I awoke abruptly to kitchen noises. Glasses clinking, water running, cabinet doors opening and closing.

I peered at my clock. One-fifteen a.m. I climbed shakily from bed and went to the kitchen where Faith moved about as if it were eight a.m. "What are you doing?" I asked sharply.

She looked at me, clueless. "I'm cleaning up the kitchen, Mama." As in what-does it-look-like-I'm-doing?

"Could you keep the noise down?"

She wilted. "Every time I try to be nice, everybody treats me mean." She threw up her hands. "I give up."

My nerves were burning, searing, my head spinning from the abrupt transport from deep slumber to wakeful jumpiness. My mind was in a nightmare vortex. "Please stop this, Faith," I said, desperately seeking some solidness upon which to land. "Everybody's not a nocturnal creature like you."

"Stop talking mean to me." The woman reared her assertive head.

Wham. My senses slammed against a steel wall and pulsated madly. Quivering, I grabbed my skull, "*I'm not* talking mean to you."

"You hate me." The words from the child were quiet. Dead.

Again, desperately, I took her by the shoulders. "Faith," I said, my voice breaking, "please stop doing this to me." Tears welled up in my eyes. "This is going to kill me if it doesn't stop."

And in that moment, I felt mortality. Age was catching up with me. Stress layered like an onion, suffocating and squeezing the life from me.

Fast.

I left the room, sobbing quietly. "Mom?" Faith followed me to my bedroom door. "I'm sorry. I'll stop." Her woman's voice still had that lackadaisical tone, but I heard an undergirding sincerity. "Get some sleep, Mom." She gently closed the door.

I climbed into the empty bed and pulled the covers up to my chin, missing Dan's warm bulk and consoling arms. He needed me to be exclusively *his* during this golden season of our lives.

His heart-rending words from yesterday came back to haunt me.

"It's what I've worked for all these years, Deede. We should be free. Comfortable. But we've spent it all on her, just keeping her alive and out of prison."

He huffed a harsh laugh. "And it still isn't over. I don't see an end in sight. We have an adult, needy daughter who doesn't seem to have any direction or ambition to become self-sufficient."

His green eyes held anguish. "My life is being stolen. No — *our* life is being stolen."

He's having one of those anguish moments.

I have them, too, when the need for space nearly suffocates me.

Space.

Tonight, my eyes popped open and I stared through gloam at the ceiling.

Faith was fighting for a foothold to a new beginning. Me? I continued to bury myself in writing. At times, even that failed to divert me from the sick sense of failure. Yes, failure hammered me into a desolate heap. I must have done something wrong for Faith to have veered so far from her potential.

"It's not our fault," Dan insisted. "She has to decide for herself to rebuild her life. Her decisions got her in the mess she's in. Not ours."

"I agree. And she is trying, honey. She's her own worst enemy, it's true. But I watch her struggling every day to pull herself up." I carried the sadness of it all. Oh, how I wanted to understand her.

At the same time, I wanted her to simply bathe daily and have some sort of agenda to keep her functioning rather than vegetating in a messy chamber. But I'd learned long ago that counseling would roll off her like water off tarp.

Tonight, echoes of Dan's impassioned, "Why can't she just keep the porch neat?" struck me like a whip. Such a *little* thing for her to do. Her chaos was so at odds with our neat organizational leanings.

Faith would sweep the ashes on occasion, just enough to keep Dan from verbally throttling her.

And despite the continued stressfulness, Faith *had* come a long way in her recovery journey.

"Three years ago," I had reminded Dan, "we would have traded our proverbial kingdom for the progress she'd now made in getting drug free."

"She does it to irritate us," Dan swore again, ignoring my progress reference. "She knows how we feel."

Another way to dishonor, I read his thoughts because I, too, felt her perverseness to the bone. And it hurt.

Tonight, I thought on how hard Dan worked. Fatigue plunged him into deep slumber nearly as soon as his body horizontal-ed. I could close my eyes and see his beautiful calloused hands and his strong male features gentled in sleep and thought how he — even in his resentment

— loved his daughter. He gave her haven even after she'd betrayed him over and over again.

I recalled how he'd given her chance after chance to remedy the seasons of disrespect and self-serving. And I knew he tried to understand the import of my being there for her, to see her through to the finish in her final quest to find a life.

Faith wants to find her space, too. I have to believe that. I'm all she has at this moment. It's not as simple as some folks believe, to toss a child out onto the street when they're trying to pull themselves up by the bootstrings, however feeble their attempts.

And my head spins tonight as I close my eyes and seek slumber.

Why all the turmoil? What's happened *to family?*

Where is God in all this?

Nobody in our family clan wants Faith around any longer. Except Jensen, Noni, and Priss — and I sometimes wonder if that will last. I understand. Things disappeared too many times when Faith was there.

But once, long ago, she was innocent.

She can change.

Can't she? With everything in me, I pray that she can.

And will.

Am I letting Dan down somehow?

Does my belonging to Dan negate Faith's claim to her mother?

Territory.

When did I simply belong to me?

Sleep was a long time coming.

~ ~

I awoke early. After I heard Dan leave, I bathed and dressed.

I heard Faith stirring around upstairs and knew she would soon make her morning pilgrimage to the front porch.

I was right.

"Faith," I approached her as she smoked on the front porch. "Will you do something for me? For us? The family?"

I sat in the rocker next to hers. She looked at me with reservation. Yet I whiffed her curiosity. It slanted its way to me from her tilted gaze. "What?"

"Would you write a journal of your life for the past ten years? How did you get into drugs? Your epiphanies. Everything."

"Why?" She looked off into the distant sky, her complex mind sifting, sorting, weighing.

"Because I want to know who you are. Where you've been. You weren't here — with us, not for years. I want to know about that journey that took you somewhere else entirely. I want to know the whys and the hows and the wheres. I want to know what brought you back." *At least closer, if not all the way.*

She turned her head to look at me and blew out a stream of smoke. "Why?"

"Truthfully? I want to know. I think it will give me some sort of — closure. And I also think it will help you to see things more clearly, honey. I think it will help you get to know yourself again, the person you were created to be. You weren't just born, Faith. You're *a miracle."*

I watched the play of emotions skitter over her features as she considered all I'd said. She rocked softly and stared off again into space but I felt her interest gather and grow.

"Okay."

"Good," my voice didn't give away my relief and joy. I got up to go into the house and closed my bedroom door. Then, in my welling-up moment, I sat in the leather easy chair, eyes closed, and thanked God.

Chapter Nine

"I need to put things in perspective because I have a disease of perception."

–A Recovering Drug Addict

Faith

My name is Faith and I am a 29-year-old junkie. A heroin junkie. I can tell you how many months I have been clean or how many Narcotics Anonymous chips I have acquired, but none of that takes away from the fact that I am a junkie.

Always will be. The first step to recovering from drug abuse is learning that I will always be an addict. Clean or not.

The first thing non-users want to know is "Why? Why do you use? Why did you start?" Like there is some elusive, all-consuming answer to it all. Wish there were. But that's not the case. There are infinite variables involved in addictions. Some, I will try to describe.

I can take you back to the first time I smoked marijuana, but it will have nothing to do with my current junkie status. It was in no way a gateway drug. Webster's Dictionary defines "gateway drug" as any drug or addictive substance abuse — e.g., nicotine and alcohol, that may be abused, and is allegedly linked to subsequent abuse of illicit 'soft' drugs, e.g., marijuana, and/or 'hard' drugs, e.g. cocaine and heroine.

My infrequent marijuana use was merely a stupid teenage attempt to fit into some pop-culture ideal. My teen years were pretty normal. I wasn't a big alcohol drinker and was not a drug user. I enjoyed hanging out with my friends and occasionally cruising around looking for boys. That was the extent of my trouble.

My drug abuse didn't come about until years later, in my early-twenties after the birth of my daughter Maddie. Looking back, I think I might have suffered post-partum depression, but at the time, I didn't know it. My husband, Jack, traveled extensively with his job and I was regularly left alone as a new mother. Even when Jack was home, the marriage was volatile, rocky at best. Apparently, I began looking for something to numb me.

My first experience with street drugs was with my best friend Lola, but I will get to that later. Ironically, my drug dealer was not some back-alley pimp with his ladies of the night lurking about. My drug dealer was my family physician.

My enabler was my HMO.

An appendectomy and later, severe menstrual cramps justified my first narcotic prescription for Lortab (also known as Vicodin). It did ease my pain. It also provided an energetic high and excitement that I loved.

My flying phobia justified my second narcotic prescription. The Valium label said, "Take 1-2 pills every four hours for fear of flying." This prescription could be filled monthly, but with me only flying 2-3 times a year, I only filled it sporadically. It made me feel zoned out and loopy. Basically, it put me to sleep.

On one flight, while using the drug, the flight attendant had to wake me to sit upright for landing. I'd been sprawled across three seats, dead to the world. I'd told my doctor that if the plane crashed with me aboard, I wanted to be so out of it that I would be whistling Dixie. He honored my wishes.

Although it was meant for sporadic travel, it was actually written to be refilled monthly so I began using it nightly as a sleep aid.

It just really amazed me that I *could* fill it every month. Keep in mind this was the late 1990s and awareness of prescription drugs addictions didn't exist as it does today. At that time, trust in family physicians was at an all-time high and medications were to be taken as prescribed. They were almost considered deity among us laymen.

My aches and pains were eventually diagnosed and I had a reason for the prescriptions to roll on in; an opiate for pain, those Valium pills for flying tucked me in bed each night, with various anti-depressants and anti-inflammatory meds added to the mix.

When the medicinal hangover made it too hard for me to get up in the morning, I *developed* a case of ADD (Attention Deficit Disorder) to warrant a prescription for Adderall, which would wake me up. Adderall is nothing more than pharmaceutical speed. The generic title on the bottle actually says "Amphetamine/Salt".

Keep in mind that millions of American children are on this drug to help them pay attention in school. I had to get my insurance company to over-ride a denial of payment on the Aderrall. They said I was too old to take amphetamines. I found this ironic. Mom insists that I have always had classic ADD symptoms so I figured I might as well take advantage of a drug to remedy it, right?

This was merely the beginning of my prescription drug habit.

My motto in life has always been "Try anything once." Unfortunately, that has been the reason that I have no voice of reason when I am approached with possible dangerous situations for the first time, like drugs. The majority of people have that Angel/Devil Scenario playing on their shoulder when they are about to do something wrong. My motto "Try anything once" takes those reasoning little creatures out of the picture because "Hey, I'm only going to try it once, right?"

This was my excuse in the spring of 1998 when I tried cocaine for the first time.

Two young mothers, Lola and I, were visiting at her house. My husband was out of town working, which was the norm at this time in my life. Lola's was working out in a gym, an obsession with him. After tucking in our toddlers for the night, Lola and I had the house to ourselves. Lola had scored some cocaine from a friend who was a heavy user.

"Make sure the door's locked," I whispered to Lola. "The kids might wake up and come looking for us."

"In a minute," she whispered back, eyes aglow with adventure. "We'll be looking for *ourselves,* we're about to go on a *trip!"*

Our toddlers were four months apart. Lola and I had married within weeks of each other. We'd been friends since our early high school years, when, to hear Lola tell it, I had cheated with her boyfriend. When she caught wind of it, she called me on the phone.

"Is it true?" she asked.

I told her the truth. "I wasn't aware you two were dating. Honestly. If you are, I'm sorry, Lola." Lola forgave me and we'd been best friends ever since. We had, through the years, experienced many "firsts" together.

This being one of them.

~ ~

We crept into the bathroom with our little bag of white powder. Lola had tried it once before, at a party with her husband, but as far as I can remember, this was my first time trying an illegal narcotic other than marijuana. This was a serious street drug.

I was excited to experience something Lola so evidently enjoyed. She maneuvered the powder into little white lines while quietly giving me instructions on how to snort it. And though there was no one there but us girls and the sleeping toddlers, our voices never raised above a whisper.

On some moral level, we knew what we were about to do was wrong. That only intrigued us more.

Lola already knew she liked the powder. Instinctively, she knew her best friend would too.

Unfortunately, she was right. The rush of euphoria appealed to me. Immensely. I immediately wanted to take in my second little white line. Lola and I transferred our private party to the front porch, armed with a newfound force to marathon talk each other.

I'm still not sure who was listening because we were both doing all the talking.

The main joke was "Say Hello to my little friend." We did not tire of the Scarface saying that evening. After a couple more trips to the bathroom, Lola and I agreed this was something we would enjoy on "special occasions." We knew many friends who had let this drug take over their lives. We were adamant that we were *not* those people. "Special Occasions" only.

Over the next few months, Lola and I found innovative and creative ways to define a "special occasion." Basically, it just came down to the two of us being in the same room. But my first run with cocaine came to a dramatic halt on a couple's trip to Jamaica late that summer.

When I thought I was going to die.

~ ~

Lola and I, along with our husbands, Jack and Nick, planned an extended holiday in Jamaica, spending one week in Negril and one week in Ocho Rios. On our first day there, Lola and I took a "shopping trip" to the local flea market in search of cocaine.

Within minutes, I scouted out a local boy, whose demeanor smacked of *cool.* Moments later, Lola and I had scored. We hurried through the market, quickly buying things for the kids to legitimize our shopping excursion.

Back at the resort, we went straight to the bathroom of my suite (the men were already visiting the first of many golf courses).Why the bathroom? I'm not sure. Cocaine just automatically draws one to a bathroom.

We did our first line and then went about getting ready for dinner.

Our second line came just as we left to go to dinner. Now here we were at a five-star resort with exotic, tasty, once-in-a-lifetime cuisine spread before us. And Lola and I craved the one thing that kills your appetite.

I think I lost three pounds the first two days.

The third, and what I considered deadly line, came after dinner. Lola and I slipped back to the room and snorted. We left the bathroom. Within minutes, I knew something was wrong. My heart pounded like a bass drum and my head felt detached, like it floated.

"Lie down," Lola ordered.

But the racing heartbeat seemed to speed up. "Valium," I gasped, terrified.

Lola fetched the pill for me and I swallowed it with water, hoping it would calm me down.

Bad mistake. An innocent one.

I didn't realize that I was starting a speedball. Instead of Valium settling me down, it started me on an anxiety roller coaster. For the first time in my life, I was certain that it was the ride of death

Like a replaying video scene, the image of the local hospital rushed through my mind. On our drive in, our driver had pointed it out. A hospital it was *not*. It was a mere shack with dirt floors. One could stand in the open front entrance and see out the back door. Every time I thought of those local medical facilities, I would moan, *"Dear God, I am going to die!"*

Lola devoted the next hour to rubbing my back as I lay on the bed. As long as she caressed my back, the anxiety lessened. But she finally had to retreat to her room with her husband. My husband quietly snored on the bed next to me, unaware of what I was going through. Over the next two hours, the Valium overpowered the cocaine, finally, allowing me to drift of into a slumber. I awoke the next morning to an empty bed and an aching head. My husband had quietly slipped out of the room to venture to his next golf course.

Jack, an avid golfer, while not excelling at the game, did outclass others with expensive golf clubs, caddies, beer and anything else that would lend a luxurious hand to the sport.

"You what?" I peered at Jack later that evening as the four of us sat down to dinner at a nearby restaurant.

"We thought we were going to have to eat that golf cart," he said, laughing uproariously. Seems Jack and Nick had narrowly escaped being forced to buy a golf cart that they'd driven airborne. The golf cart flipped over four times during the flight. Mercifully, no one was killed or even seriously injured. The only reason they didn't have to purchase the cart was the all American threat of lawsuit. Nick and Jack somehow convinced the owners that the cart itself was faulty and had caused the accident.

As I lay in bed that morning, head aching and mind swirling eerily, one sentiment jumped to the forefront: gratitude. I was alive! *Thank you, God, for keeping me here*. I thought of my Mama and Daddy, who'd raised me right. And I thought of how they loved me and wanted the best for me and how, in doing this, I'd let them down.

The guilt popped up and disappeared like a startled raven.

Again, I cringed at the possibility of ending up in that primitive, horror chamber they called a hospital. I was certain Voodoo dolls and twirling witch doctors would dominate its décor.

I made a sober vow (the initial vow was the night before during my frightful speedball) — with all the strength and sincerity of a New Year's resolution — that I would never again touch that vile white stuff. Special occasion or not. I really was thankful just to be alive.

I scrambled to shower and remedy myself for a day at the pool. Standing under a battering hot faucet began to restore me.

I stopped by Lola's room after she didn't answer my call. I assumed I would have to drag her out of bed when to my surprise, she answered the door after the first knock.

"Hello!" she trilled. Tissues, stuffed in her nostrils, hung loose. Her saucer-sized, blinkless dark eyes seemed permanently surprised.

"Faith! I've been up all night. That was the best crap I've ever done."'

I rolled my eyes. "Come on, Lola. We're going to the pool."

At that point, she would have licked the proverbial frozen flagpole if I'd asked her.

To tell the truth, Lola looked plumb silly. That only fired my own determination to avoid drugs in the future.

I stayed off of cocaine for a few years after that and solely concentrated on my prescription drug habit. Cocaine, however was my introduction and my "gateway" drug." It introduced me to the drug culture.

~ ~

I don't know why I'm writing this. Today, I feel like my brain is fried from too much introspection. I've got to take a sabbatical from all this remembering.

More later.

Chapter Ten

"God never consults our past when planning our future."

– Ron Heiber

Deede

I dropped Faith's journal onto her cluttered bedside table, where she'd left it for me to read. I wordlessly turned to go. "I don't really know what you want, Mom," she said lackadaisically then shrugged. She lolled on her bed, still in pajamas at noon, watching a movie.

I turned back. "Honey, I don't want anything except for you to be enlightened. You know, learn something from the journey that may help you in future choices." *And give me a clue as to who you are. I haven't a clue. There was not, as yet, one shred of the whys and their repercussions on her psyche.*

And I don't know where this is going.

"I'll try to write more later," she said as I closed her door. Oh, well, some progress at least. She now saw merit in writing down her memoirs.

It was a start. But echoing in my head was *will she follow through?*

"By the way, Noni had her heart procedure last week."

"No." Her eyes widened with concern. "Is she okay?"

"She is." I shrugged, still feeling a bit hurt that Mom hadn't informed anyone in the family of her hospital stint until after it was over.

"Seems she only called Jensen to pick her up when all was over and they released her."

"He didn't say a word." I could see umbrage building in Faith and didn't want that to happen.

"Noni made Jensen promise not to tell. She wanted to tell us herself. So don't be mad at Jensen."

"Huh."

"Promise you'll drop it, honey. Okay?"

She nodded, her eyes bright with tears. "Is Noni truly okay?"

"She says she's good as new." I smiled, relieved that Mom's report had been so upbeat.

A couple of days later, Faith dropped more journal entries on my bedside table.

~ ~

Faith

Fast-forward three years and my prescription habit alone has caused me to leave my husband. I was now a single mom with a $500 a week Lortab habit. But I was working to make it work. It was only a matter of time before everything crumbled, but I couldn't see it at the time. I lived in my nice gated co-op, drove my Jaguar, carried

Gucci bags and thought I really had it all together. I can remember counting how long I had been taking Lortabs daily. A year was approaching. That was when I knew it was a problem. A whole year of abusing Lortabs. I ignored it and kept going.

Cocaine was about to rear its ugly head again. I would like to say that I could have kept it together on pills alone, but I wouldn't really know. I was about to juggle two addictions.

~ ~

Will? Now Will is definitely a chapter in my life. I have to introduce Will before I go any further. Somewhere during this time of being a single Mom and "having it all together," an old friend of mine decided to look me up. A friend I had not talked to in years. In those years, Will had gotten married, but from what I had heard through the grapevine, the marriage part never took. He was still running around acting single.

Will called under the premise that he wanted to have drinks and talk "business." I was leery, but we were in businesses that complemented each other so I went. I can remember Will trying to kiss me that night, and I made it very clear that we were on the "friend" track only. Unfortunately, this opened up my life to Will as a friend in his eyes.

He started popping by to use the pool at my co-op and eventually, just kept popping by. We actually became good friends. I enjoyed his eccentricities. Will was a very handsome, charismatic person, as a friend.

Will should have stayed "just a friend."

Will had a cocaine habit like I had my pill habit. On the weekends when my Maddie was with her father, I would let Will sit in my living room after I went to bed and enjoy his cocaine. Have you ever heard the saying that if you go the barber shop long enough, you're going to get your hair cut? Well, Will wore me down. He wanted me to use the cocaine with him so he wouldn't have to do it alone.

Later in our relationship, he seemed to be able to find scores of women to share his bed and his habit. Where were they all then? Nope, no other women to be seen. I fell head over heels in love with the idiot snorting cocaine on my couch.

As I stated before, I was about to juggle two addictions. Will was not going to be happy until I partied (using cocaine) as much as he did. Partying with Will took me to a whole different game level. I can recall seeing my first sunrise as a result of staying up all night snorting cocaine. Until this time, I had only partied to the wee hours of the morning. Never an all-nighter. The all nighters turned into two days and eventually three days. I one time stayed up for four days but didn't know my own name. This was when I realized my limit for staying up.

It also became a known fact with my partying friends. "If Faith has been up three days, put her to bed or everyone around will have hell to pay." In addition to not knowing my own name on the fourth day, I became ten feet tall and bullet proof. I would physically fight with a lamp post if it looked at me wrong. I also knew I had reached my limit with no sleep when I would drive home and I was waving at mailboxes like they were people. The real issue was that the mailboxes waved at me first! I was merely returning the gesture.

Due to the length of time we were partying, at days on end, we had to relocate the party. The most common location was hotels. We usually started the affair at the nicest hotels in our city. As the time and money disappeared, the hotel stars diminished as well. We found that if we partied at my co-op, someone would come looking for me and/or him and we did not want to be interrupted. We basically would disappear for days on end, inaccessible to our family and friends.

It didn't take long for my family to realize something was not quite right with me. It also didn't take long for me to abandon all responsibilities (my child, rent, etc.). Luckily, I had my parents to take care of my daughter when I went missing in action. Had I not, I feel certain Social Services would have intervened earlier and taken her.

Some people call my parents enablers here, but anyone who has children would agree that grandparents provide a better atmosphere for their children than DSS possibly could. At this point, Maddie was too young to realize her Mom was seriously screwing up. But that would change as she got older and her Mother continued to screw up.

Back to Will. I should have known it was not true love when I overdosed at the local Hilton and Will didn't bother to come upstairs and check on me because he was too busy having cocktails downstairs with a rival lady. I had let him know that I was not feeling well before he descended to happy hour. You would think that my power-dialing his phone would have tipped him off that something was wrong.

I'm not sure if I was aimed to go downstairs to get him when I headed for the door in our hotel room. I was dialing his cell when I passed out just shy of the door. I came to long enough to drag myself into the bath and turn the cold shower water on. Clothes and all, I drenched myself into a shock strong enough to wake myself and get into bed.

When Will did finally come around, he found the voicemail of me passing out amusing. I begged him not to leave me and to awaken me every 15-30 minutes to check on me. He promised he would and I awoke sometime later to an empty room. Comforted by the fact that I had awakened at all, I went back to sleep and awoke again a few hours later to Will back in the room with a male buddy of his. They were sitting at the table snorting the white powder as if I were in no way at death's door.

Fortunately for Will and unfortunately for me, Will redeemed himself when this happened a second time at a nearby La Quinta. I was trying to come down off of a two-day bender by taking Clonopin (a downer similar to that of Xanax) with Grey Goose. I was not a big drinker and sporadically took downers.

So, for me, the mix was deadly.

Lucky for me, Will enjoyed watching me sleep and realized when I stopped breathing. He administered CPR until the paramedics arrived. He did so with such force that my chest plate sustained bruises for weeks. The doctor informed me that had Will not done CPR, I would have died. I woke up in the ER with a tube up my nose, my mother and my godmother, Aunt Priss, by my bed praying for me. I will have to say that God answered their prayers that day.

I was not admitted. It was merely a stay in the ER for several hours. Will sent me two dozen roses to the hospital. I can honestly say that Will was worried about me. A good friend of his called me the next day.

"Will said he couldn't live without you, Faith. He couldn't quit crying!" Will's friend Otis told me.

"Really?" I drawled. "Funny. He didn't show up in the ER."

"Aaw, Faith. You know that boy loves you to death."

"Yeah?" I snorted dryly. "Well, Otis, I had two dozen roses to look at, but y'know, they didn't talk to me and they didn't comfort me. They didn't make up for Will's absence."

That was the beginning of the end for Will and me. It took me over eighteen months to admit that Will's only true love in life was cocaine, with himself running a close second. That boy truly was in love with himself. He got more manicures than two straight men should ever admit to.

Ending that relationship was difficult. I really loved Will. I took to my bed for two months with depression. Eventually, I turned to more drugs to get over him.

~ ~

Things began to look up when Joel came into the picture. Joel and I were past co-workers and friends so when we re-connected, he saw my angst and automatically reached out to help me. Joel's capacity for compassion was deeper than I'd ever seen in a friend. He just seemed to know when I was most vulnerable to using and would take me out for Italian food or a movie or simply invite me over to his place to chill out. He also understood about my grief over Will because he, too, had known romantic heartbreak.

Joel was battling alcoholism. "I have no choice but to quit," he told me in his laid-back way. "Abstinence is the only thing that will save my life. Alcohol has done a number on my liver."

Joel, a preacher's son, battled conscience, as well as temptations.

"I'm going to come over and nurse you through withdrawal," I insisted during one serious post-hospital episode. "You know what the doctor said. You drink, you die."

"Yeah," Joel agreed. I spent those four days keeping a journal of meds and treatment and keeping him from giving in to the horrible cravings. "No. You cannot have just one beer, Joel. No way."

In turn, Joel was vigilant over my behavior, turning me away from the hard stuff.

We were two lost sheep trying to help one another.

But I had moments when I simply let go and used. At such times, I did not answer my cell phone and locked myself away in my room. Mom and Dad never knew exactly what ailment I had that made me so "sick." It was so easy to fool them in their innocence. I wasn't proud of it. I simply walked through the darkness, seeing no further than the end of my red nose.

During one of those nights, my cell phone rang and rang. Irritated, I picked it up and gazed blearily at the caller ID.

It was Joel. I didn't answer but did later listen to his message.

"Faith, this is Joel," his words slurred. "Call me."

"Drinking," I muttered, angry and disgusted, never connecting the dots of "the pot calling the kettle black."

Three days later, Mom knocked on my bedroom door.

"Faith," she said and something in her voice, shock, disbelief made me uncover my head. "When have you seen Joel?"

I peered at her through a sleepy fog. "I don't know — why?" Then I saw she had an open newspaper in her hands.

"Isn't his name Joel Johnson? Lives on Mulholland Drive? If so, he's dead, Faith."

"No!" I sat up and snatched the paper from her hands. It was there, in bold type: Joel Johnson … died January 20 at his home …

It was the evening he'd called me. His body wasn't found for two days.

"Oh, Mama!" I wailed. "He can't be."

"I'm sorry, honey," she said, her voice breaking because she, too, loved Joel. She gathered me into her arms and we cried together, grieving the life gone too soon.

And secretly, I grieved that I had not answered his call that dark night.

Had I done so, he may still be alive.

~ ~

The next years were a typical "drug cliché." I lost everything bit by bit, the co-op, the cars, pretty much every material possession I owned.

Even my clothes and purses disappeared. I found out my cousin Chloe unashamedly took advantage of my altered state. Sometimes, during holiday gatherings, I would stay in my room. Other times, I would be gone partying, and Chloe would turn my closet into a shopping spree. The irony in that situation is that this same pilfering girl would guard her possessions like a prison guard when I visited their home.

But the worst of all was losing Maddie. Jack finally got wind of my "extracurricular activities" and demanded custody of our little girl. Mom and Dad were devastated because they'd tried so hard to pull me from the pit and had protected Maddie with their lives.

But, bottom line, I was not, at that time, a fit mother. I knew it, but facing that truth was the most painful moment of my life.

To escape the pain, I dove into drugs with a new passion. I spent three months after Maddie was taken from me so high I never touched the ground.

The next most difficult loss was the trust of my family. When your family finds out you are a drug addict, you don't have to steal anything from them to lose their trust. It just automatically goes.

Gotta stop for now. Head's spinning from all this.

~ ~

I'm back after a nearly sleepless night. Boy, did the crap hit the fan last night.

The one place I swore I would never go was back to my parent's house. Unfortunately, when I hit bottom, it was the only place left to go. The one place that there is nothing to do but lie around and watch TV. Talk about depression, that place is purgatory. My father sees me staying there as an act of grace, but it's basically jail with cable. His idea of keeping me away from drugs is keeping me away from life. My psychiatrist told him as much and that just offended my father. Nobody is going to tell him what to do.

We are alike in that respect.

It was during one of those times of being a nonperson, a thing, that I decided one day to hang myself on the ceiling fan. I waited for Mom to leave to visit Noni. I stared at the contraption for a long time. I had been thinking about it forever. Suddenly, I knew I could do it.

I had not, before, wanted to die. I'd simply not wanted to live, y'know?

Today, I wanted to die.

To check out.

The last thing I remember is stepping off the chair and dangling. Everything went black. Next thing I knew, I woke up in the ER with a king-sized headache, a raw neck and an extremely bruised ego.

God. What a fiasco. I don't even want to think back on it.

So I won't.

So now, two years later, things came to a head as Dad and I faced each other in the den and I asked for fifty dollars to pay the random court cost.

"It was just yesterday that I gave you forty dollars for a monthly drug test."

"Yes, but I'll lose my driver's license if I don't pay this."

"And, tomorrow, what'll it be? Huh, Faith? I'm a senior citizen, an old man who works and handles my responsibilities. I ask nobody for anything. Never have. And this is just not right." If he said this once, he has said it a million times.

"Dad, I appreciate you letting me stay here while I get back on my feet." I replied with all the respect I could muster up. It wasn't convincing enough.

"Faith, you're ruining our lives. Your mother and I are being punished for all your mistakes. We're constantly paying your attorney and court fees — all because of your mistakes, and I see no appreciation!"

"Dad! I'm always thanking you for everything you do for me. You just don't seem to hear it."

"It's not always what you say, Faith. It's what you do. Like helping around the house more without being asked. It's your attitude. Little things like being kind and considerate."

"Don't I try to do things for you, Dad? You won't let me."

"It's the way you go at things, Faith. It's chaotic ... I don't have any peace. No sanctuary. I'm getting old and I'm tired. It's time you get out on your own and make your own way. I've given and given and given."

And in that moment, like a starburst, I got it. I really *saw* the fatigue in Dad's lined face and the cry for help in his tortured eyes. I *heard* the desperation in his voice — the plea for mercy.

I nearly collapsed from the impact.

"Yeah." I sank into the nearest easy chair and stared at the floor, wanting to slide through the cracks. "You're right." I knew Mom was nearby in the kitchen. She didn't, as a rule, get into the middle unless necessary. Suddenly, I knew that she, too, felt violated. Used. And rightly so.

Dad handed me the money for the court cost, and I knew he did it only because it would ease some of his and Mom's financial strain. On another level, I knew he did it because he loved me.

But loving me shouldn't mean keeping me up all my adult life. Loving me shouldn't mean I was entitled to drain all their savings as I'd done, ruined their retirement years.

I realized another thing. Despite all my screaming and demands, all my bravado and arrogance, I'd been fearing this time — when being set "free" became a stark reality.

It was here. Now.

I have my space.

And it spooks me.

Chapter Eleven

"You must take the steps. There is no elevator."

– A Recovering Addict Proverb

Deede

Tonight, when Dan complained about Faith's deficits, I reminded him. "We've come so far, honey. If you'll just remember back to a little over two years ago when Faith went off the deep end ..."

Two years earlier:

I'd known something in Faith's behavior was off-kilter. Had felt it for weeks. It went beyond her sitting on the porch smoking herself to death and avoiding viable relationships. Her temper, never pleasant to deal with, grew increasingly caustic. Paranoia sprang up in every attempt at conversation, beyond her usual wariness. She kept to her room more with her door locked.

Unfamiliar cars appeared in the driveway and she would jump in and disappear with them for spells. Not overnight. She drew the fuzzy line there, just enough to keep from being tossed out. Dan fussed and I tried to calm him. "We can't expect her to vegetate here, Dan," I would say to placate him. "She needs a little time outside her four walls."

But I was uneasy.

Still, I didn't expect the axe to fall the way it did.

~ ~

"I'm so sorry," I said to the hospital medical staff at the nurse's station. They all looked at me with abject pity. Embarrassment overwhelmed me, and I turned away and went back to Faith's room in the ER.

"Get me some food!" she shrieked. *"Now!"* Purple stains blotched her hospital gown, medicinal remnants of the stomach purging. Her eyes remained glazed, slightly wild.

Her hateful, abrasive attitude and demands had, by now, driven the staff up the wall. She'd already insulted and ordered one poor nurse from her room. I'd overheard the staff discussing committing her to the psychiatric ward, but they had no available beds at that time.

I knew they saw me standing nearby, but by then, they didn't truly care that I heard them. After all, I was part and parcel of the package called Faith. It shamed me.

The crisis had erupted just hours before when Faith came stumbling down the stairs at home, nearly incoherent. "I want to die," she declared. "Just let me die."

I'd heard her dramatics before, but this time seemed different. And since her suicide attempt, I really heard her when she wished for death. She slumped into a kitchen chair, head on the table, and continued a black diatribe of pain and death wishes. Soon, the tone changed and she began twitching and screaming with pain.

Dan called 911 and the ambulance arrived within minutes. I followed the ambulance in my car and Dan followed minutes later in his. He never knew when he would get an emergency call from his asphalt crew.

Once at the hospital, Faith was able to sign herself in, taking responsibility for any arrears. This was critical because Dan and I could not assume any more liability for her. At the same time, she also forbade the staff to reveal any blood test results to her parents. *Déjà vu.* Again, there was nothing we could do about it because she was of age.

The day was a nightmare permeated with Faith's shrieks and demands. Both Dan and I felt shredded and helpless as she ran the show. Hours later, after pumping her stomach of whatever and running an IV, the doctor on call called us out into the hallway.

"Listen," he said quietly, "you two seem like good folks. You don't deserve this. I can't reveal anything about what we found in Faith's system because she's of age and insisted we not. But I will say this — if you don't put her out and force her to stand on her own two feet, she *will* end up dead."

We left the hospital in separate cars because Faith had focused in on me to browbeat and Dan refused to let her do that. By the time we all got home, the two of them were going at it like gangbusters. I knew the neighbors could hear them and no amount of my shushing them cut a dent.

The language was harsh and unrestrained. Faith's profanities went beyond her customary swearing.

"You're outta here," Dan yelled at one point and tried to bodily remove Faith. She went so limp he couldn't even push her. I was amazed at how strong she was following the health crisis she'd just experienced.

"I don't have anywhere to go!" she screamed at him.

"Call one of your friends who're always showing up at odd hours. Where are they now? Huh?"

"I hate you. I hope you drop dead!"

Dan laughed his angry laugh. "Tough. I'm not going to die any time soon so you just as well decide to leave peacefully because you ... are ... going."

I stood aside, shock splintering me as it all escalated, getting worse and worse. At one point, as Dan struggled with Faith to get her out of the bathroom with her holding onto the door with both hands, Dan fell against me and I nearly stumbled.

"Mama!" Faith screamed. "Are you all right?" I heard genuine concern in her voice as Dan turned to examine me. "Have you hurt her?" she cried, glaring at her father.

"I'm all right," I murmured through numb lips. "Look, all this fighting isn't solving anything. Dan, let's give Faith till morning to find someone to come get her."

So in the end, that's what we did. Dan didn't give an inch.

And somewhere deep, deep inside me, I knew that the end was here. That old familiar, sickening grip of betrayal held me captive, turning my insides and extremities numb and cold. It stole my hope.

Dan was right. We were, finally, on the same page.

I could no longer protect Faith from herself.

It was her turn.

The next day, Dan had relented but on the condition that Faith would submit to year-long drug rehab. Desperate to not be thrown out, Faith had agreed and faithfully completed the program.

Today, I reminded him. "So you see, Dan, she has come a long, long way toward at least a more normal life."

He sighed and rocked sedately in the chair next to me as we listened to April evening sounds. Soft mild breezes whispered through the Tulip Tree, whose huge buds now shriveled while vivid yellow and purple pansies still stood proudly along our sidewalk, unaware that in a few weeks, they, too, would succumb. Birds chirped and a squirrel frolicked along spruce limbs and sprang to a white-blossoming dogwood tree.

"Yeh," he said quietly. "You're right. One has to look back sometimes to gauge how much distance has been covered. I'm just so tired, honey. You know I love Faith. With all my heart, I love her. It's just hard for me to watch somebody waste their life away."

"I know." I sighed. "But she is looking for a job. Let's just chill out and trust God to set things right."

Dan winked at me and reached for my hand. "We can believe all we want for somebody. But that person must be willing to change."

~ ~

It happened out of the blue.

Priss called me. "Deede, can you come over here? I have something to show you."

"Sure," I replied, concerned. Priss never summoned me to her house. She usually came to mine on a whim. "Is anything wrong, Priss?"

"Just come on over."

By the time I got there, I was tied in knots. My gut told me something reprehensible had happened. But what?

Priss met me at the door of her beautiful log home. It was, like Priss, extraordinary. Its golden wooden exterior and interior were warm and embracing. Simple but elegant. The country décor completed the sense of welcome.

But Priss' face was ashen as she took me by the hand and led me into her bedroom with its Paul Bunyan furniture. "Sit on the bed," she said as she reached into the matching dresser drawer and pulled out a Greenville Newspaper and handed it to me.

"Wh—?" I looked over the page and then I saw her.

Faith. A photo of her lounging in an easy chair accompanying the half-page article. The heading read, "Woman searches for biological grandmother." The story told of my date and place of birth and expressed how nature itself compelled one to search out their natural roots.

My fingers lost their grip and the paper slid to the floor and landed with a quiet slide. So at odds with my churning insides. "Why?" I whispered.

Priss sat down on the quilted bedspread beside me and took my icy hand in hers. Hers, too, were cold.

"What are we gonna do," I murmured hoarsely. "What if Mom finds out?"

"Honey," Priss looked at me with stricken eyes, "she probably already knows. She takes the Greenville News."

"I can't believe Faith did this," I said as tears pushed behind my eyes. "Didn't she know that —" I couldn't say another word as tears spilled over.

For once, Priss couldn't console me.

She, too, wept.

~ ~

"Why, Faith?" I could hardly control my rage.

"Mom," Faith said gently and I knew she, too, fought emotions. "I wanted to do it for you."

"But Faith, why so public? Why didn't you do something more — subtle?"

"Because the block on adoption records is like an ancient castle fortified by not only moats and chains but crocodiles and every manner of fire-breathing dragon, Mom. It was the only way I could get your vital statistics out there, taking a chance that your birth mother might see it and recognize who you are."

"What if Noni sees it?"

"What if she doesn't?"

"But she subscribes to this paper."

A long silence. "Oh."

"Yeah."

Faith looked at me then, regret in her eyes. "I'm sorry, Mama." She shook her head slowly, her eyes misting. "I wouldn't hurt Noni for anything. I guess I just wasn't thinking." An elaborate, clumsy shrug. "Mark up another dumb thing for me. I just can't get things right, can I?" She got up and retreated upstairs, her steps slow and heavy.

I didn't know, in that moment, who was more deserving of my sympathy, Faith, Noni or myself.

~ ~

"Mom, I've gone through withdrawal from my last relapse," Faith insisted after the last ER episode. And I knew it to be so because I'd held her during the last of them. They were nightmarish muscle spasms and chills and all manner of physical and mental symptoms.

She'd done it cold turkey. For that, I admired her courage.

Not a pretty site.

But now, I wrestled with doubts in other areas of trust.

I dialed the number of the county probation department. My hands shook because somewhere deep inside me, I suspected what I would learn. Dan stood at the den window, looking out, hands shoved deeply in pockets.

I'd relayed my suspicions to him for once.

The clerk answered. I gave the information for her to check on. I waited, hoping against hope.

"Ma'am?" she said.

"Yes."

"No, ma'am. Faith Stowe Kenyan is not and has not been on probation here."

"Are you certain? I mean —"

"She's not listed here in our department. You can call the Federal Department. I'll give you their number."

Five minutes later, I knew. Faith had not been on probation in the two departments I'd contacted. Had not had fees, adding up to thousands of dollars over the past year. Nor drug tests for fifty-dollars a drop. Hundreds more dollars. She'd bilked her parents out of it for God only knew what.

Drugs? Probably. Most likely. My head was reeling with it all.

It all fell into distorted place; her insistence that I not accompany her into the probation office when she paid, nor circuit court. Always for the same reason. "It looks bad for me not to be handling this on my own, Mom."

And she insisted she was "clean."

"The tests always come out clean," she reminded me. "You talked to my probation officer."

Yes, I'd talked to James Bell. A nice sounding man

A thought hit me. A sliver of hope. I redialed both probation offices. "Do you have a probation officer named James Bell?"

Each replied "No one by that name."

And, I thought, *how naive* can one be?

Stupid? That, too.

I think it was just that I wanted to believe Faith.

Dan had been right all along.

Oh, Faith always produced a receipt but with her sharp intellect, she could have done that ahead. She could have had someone on parole to attach a copy of their receipt and edit it for her own purposes.

A memory popped up. One day, I took Faith to a district court to pay a fine. She pitched one of her most violent fits when I insisted on going inside with her. She ended up slipping through a door into a back section, leaving me in the reception area. She managed to get a receipt but claimed she'd dropped some money — other than the fine fee I'd given her, at least a hundred and fifty dollars — and insisted on turning around to go back and search the parking lot.

"It's gone by now, Faith." The characters that meandered about that parking lot would have snatched those greenbacks up in a flash.

The wailing escalated and Faith accused me of callousness. My nerves were near the breaking point.

I tried to calm her down, which only revved her up more. Something about it spoke of diversion. A smoke screen. She was hiding something. "Stop it!" I ordered. "You'll cause me to wreck."

True. I was on busy interstate I-85 with nowhere to turn around even if I'd chosen to. Her hissy fit pummeled her into exhaustion, and when we arrived at the house, she vanished up the stairs and into bed.

Now, today, I realized where all that emotion had come from. She'd dropped her coup of perhaps a couple of hundred dollars.

Our hard-earned money. Ill-gotten by her. And we were practically bankrupt, thinking we were keeping her out of jail.

Her betrayal hit me hard.

"I chose not to confront her at the time. It would not undo all the damage. The money was gone. Kaput. I chose not to tell you, Dan, either, because your health was suffering enough. I'm sorry."

He jiggled change in his pocket then sank into an easy chair opposite me.

Unfortunately, Faith walked in the front door just then. She'd been to visit a neighbor up the street. "Hi. What ya'll doing? What's wrong, Mama?" she plunged in with her forthright way and looking genuinely concerned, sank down in the seat opposite me.

"Nothing," I said quickly. I needed a rest from chaos and a confrontation would only let loose another vitriolic display of rage between father and daughter. Tonight, I needed a big dose of chill out.

But Dan had other ideas. Like Faith, his manner was never to retreat. It was up front and succinct. "Tomorrow, Faith, I want you to find somewhere else to live. Mom and I both feel it's time."

Faith looked at us, her mouth dropped open, disbelieving, like a bus had rammed into her. Tears slowly gathered in her eyes — then the blue turned to ice. Her mouth opened and a string of harsh expletives exploded from her. Hurt propelled her ... on and on, until she ran out of breath. "I hate you both," she concluded in a whisper. "I don't have a family."

Then she spun and dashed up the stairs.

Her door slammed loudly and I heard a wall picture crash to the floor.

It was definitely time for Faith to leave.

~ ~

The next morning, after a restless night, I decided to confront Faith with what I'd perceived to be her probation con game. I had to lay it all out and watch her reaction. I needed to know if I'd been right.

Or wrong.

She looked at me, her eyes red and weak as she lay in bed recovering from her previous day's breakdown. I tried to will my heart not to be too hard and just — love her. Dissonant echoes of yesterday's fracas bounced around in my head.

Dan hadn't addressed last night's edict that she leave today. Not yet. But I saw that behind those eagle green eyes a war raged. He now weighed things in his quiet way, going about his work as usual. Was this the time to toss Faith out? Ah, how well I knew that torn feeling he now experienced because underneath all that bluster and raging, Dan still loved that little girl inside Faith. And I was glad that he was not doing anything rash and furious.

Bottom line: Dan would come to a wise decision.

But was the evidence he now weighed correct?

I had to know.

Right now, Faith blinked and frowned at me, obviously confused. "Mom, I *have* been on probation. What department did you call for information?"

I told her. She shook her head. "That's not the right one. I'll go to the computer and pull it up for you."

Within ten minutes, Faith's probation sentence was verified.

I was glad I had been wrong. Very glad.

"Mama," Faith said hoarsely, "I wish you could trust me."

"I do, too."

"Don't you think you owe me an apology, Mama?" She said it so desperately that I heard her little girl's voice limning the woman's.

"I'm sorry, honey. I apologize." I gathered her into my arms and held her as she wept quietly. "So, so sorry."

"Apology accepted."

"Another thing," I said, figuring it was best to clear out all issues while I was at it. "What about all those court costs we paid? I was told that there are no court costs there."

Faith took a deep breath, blew it out and looked at me. "I'm sorry, Mom. That money was used to pay a traffic violation fine that ya'll didn't know about. I did it in increments. I didn't want to lie, but I knew that Dad wouldn't—" She shook her head and spread her hands. "I just didn't want to hear him fuss about yet another thing I'd done to screw up my life. I can only take so much of being told how bad I am." Her voice broke and she cleared her throat loudly. "How much I've stolen from you."

"I know. You don't need to be here. Like this. With us," I said, meaning it.

"I know, Mama. But I don't have anywhere to go. Believe me, if I did, I'd leave in a heartbeat."

Dan came in then. He dropped by the house during the day for short periods of time. "Faith," he got right down to business, "About the probation and--"

I stopped him. "Dan, I've checked out Faith's story. I was totally wrong about probation. I called the wrong department and got wrong information."

He looked at her. "What about all the money for court costs?"

"I had an old traffic violation charge against me and had a huge fine." She explained why she'd not told him. "I'm sorry I lied, Dad. I just —" She began to weep softly and sat down next to me on the sofa.

I put my arm around her. "Shh, it's okay, honey."

"No," Dan injected firmly. "It's not okay. She wasn't being truthful with us and that's not okay."

"I didn't mean that, Dan," I said, my stomach tightening. "I was just trying to comfort her."

Dan's features softened a bit. "Faith, I'll rescind my order for you to leave today. But I want more honor shown to your mother and me. I mean that. Another thing, I'll take you to get a drug test tomorrow. If you pass, we're in business."

Faith could hardly believe he was giving her a chance to redeem herself. I could see it in her eyes and feel it in her complete subjugation. Could hear it in the sincerity of her voice. "Thank you, Daddy. I won't disappoint you this time. I promise."

Chapter Twelve

"Keep Persevering and your heart will follow."

– Unknown

And Faith did not disappoint us. She did the drug test and came out clean. And her attitude began to mellow.

"Mama," she addressed me solemnly after the reprieve from her father, "I'm still struggling with guilt about that newspaper story, y'know, trying to find your mother." She shrugged tightly. "That was really dumb."

I sighed. "Well, don't worry. Noni apparently didn't see it because she's not said a word. Not to any of us. So, let's just be relieved. Okay?"

She smiled and wiped her eyes, obviously comforted.

I breathed a prayer of thanks.

~ ~

"I have this final court date and Otto said the record of my year-long rehab program should help my case," she reminded me a week later.

"What's Otto done to earn the last two thousand dollars we've given him?" Dan asked. I was wondering the same thing. But Faith's attorney had us because we didn't have the money to retain another defense lawyer.

Faith snorted. "Not a danged thing." Her language had smoothed out considerably lately.

"He's still committed to defend Faith in the upcoming court appearance," I reminded them both. "He's already been paid. My Social Security check will repay what I had to borrow for his fee." It would take months to pay off the latest loan.

Faith's attorney, Otto Winn, was a young, handsome, charismatic bachelor she'd met at a party of mutual friends after her divorce from Jack. When she began her criminal activities to support her drug use, she'd quickly migrated to him for help. From the very beginning, however, Otto was adamant that Faith involve her parents. "They must support you in this."

We soon learned what he meant by "support." He only included us in discussions when he wanted more money. That was the only time we mattered. Once he received the pay, we did not matter. He would proceed to usher us out of his office, smiling all the way. The thing lacking was, as Aretha Franklin belted out, *R-E-S-P-E-C-T.*

I understood that this was his profession and he deserved to be paid for his time. But in our financial bind, the fees were enormous to us and even though he gave us small, poorly itemized receipts, we were never sure of our status in face of his accountability. He was very skillful at tacking on "fees" and making it look like he was doing us great favors.

Otto was good at his game.

Now, after thousands of dollars in legal fees, Faith faced her final charge. Because Otto had flubbed one case by not getting it properly filed, it was filed in two different counties. Now, she faced two charges for the same shoplifting crime. Despite his promise that he would "take care of it" Otto never followed through. We were only just now savvy to that grave omission. Added to that was another misdemeanor charge. Totaled up, Faith had three charges stacked against her, which could, after President Clinton's "Three Strike" law was passed, reap her a prison sentence.

"I'm really nervous about this court appearance," she told me. "Really scared."

"It'll work out, honey. We need to rev up our prayers, huh?"

"Absolutely."

I wasn't as confident as I should have been. Faith didn't fret unless she faced something overly threatening. Her fear was contagious, but I wasn't about to let her see it.

Today, I simply wanted to enjoy the changes in our daughter. "What's playing at the movies?" I asked. "Dad's going to be working for a few more hours. We could catch a matinee."

"Sure we can afford it?" She cut her eyes at me, serious. Another change. Concern for our wallets.

"My treat," I said.

She looked up the movie agenda on the Internet and off we went to see Angelina Jolie and Johnny Depp's new flick *The Tourist*. As we sat in the darkened theatre and munched on buttery popcorn, I felt the difference in Faith. Little by little, she was allowing her affectionate side to emerge. Not in just word but in deed. Dishes regularly ended up clean and stacked in their proper cabinets and floors dusted. Laundry was completed, folded and put away.

We even read poetry to each other from my college textbooks collection. We had to wait until Dan fell into exhausted slumber before I ventured up to Faith's room to sprawl on her bed with her or join her on the softly lamp-lit front porch with background accompaniment of crickets. Dan remained vigilant, locked into his dark, rigid stance. I tried to encourage him to lighter ground while getting to know my daughter again.

Sometimes, Faith and I lounged in the den, plastered like boneless, curing hides to the naugahyde sofas, listening to Sirius XM music of every genre and time period. We would switch from Escape tunes like the Carpenters' *We've Only Just Begun* to Siriusly Sinatra's *Bewitched, Bothered and Bewildered* or Sammy Davis Jr.'s *I've Gotta Be Me* to Sirius XM Chill with Slusnik's *Luna's Sun*. From hip-hop to Broadway tunes to praise, Faith and I basked and reveled in our affinity for music, our genetically connected likeness. We sang together to the 50s and 60s tunes, as well as the 80s and 90s, sharing each other's musical repertoire.

We talked like old friends who hadn't seen each other in years. We discussed our family and friends, our likes and dislikes. She hated mayonnaise with a passion. I hated pickled beets. We both loved rich gooey cream cheese icing and Hershey's candy bars. With almonds. Faith wanted to know all about my younger years. My boyfriends. Why I liked them and why we broke up. I wanted to know about her crushes and date experiences because she'd not been one to share openly in those days.

I could now be her friend. Not her judge. What a glorious liberation.

We talked about our personality likenesses and differences.

"We're as different as Clint Eastwood from Jim Carrey," I declared, laughing.

It was true. My pragmatic approach and idealistic way of looking at life was totally at odds with Faith's in-your-face, impulsive shoot-from-the-hip near manic persona. When I entered a room, though not reticent, I observed and quietly mingled.

When Faith entered a room, it was hers.

When some of the family had remarked that Faith always seemed to be "on," she was hurt. "Mama, why can't they accept that this is just — *me*?"

I couldn't explain without deeply wounding her that her unique brand of sizzling energy was consuming and exhausted those who lingered long under its impact. Her presence sucked up all the space and radiance. I couldn't even put it into words. It was at its zenith during her slide into drugs. Now, with her having completed detox, her evening-out lent her a mellowing aura.

But few witnessed what I did. Few gained entrance into Faith's off-the-beaten-path world. Now, I just peeked through the cracked door. Dan had not sought access to her inner sanctum. I was now realizing that his domain was, in ways, just as extraordinary as hers. Just tuned a little differently.

At the same time, Faith saw me in a light that no one else saw me. It was evident that she looked at me through those 50s 3D glasses, whose *view* results in aspects of the *seen* leaping out and virtually attacking the viewer. It was also a classic case of projection, her analysis of me. Everything I even lightly criticized reaped a "well, you speak harshly to me, too," or "you think you have to have the last word, too." It was eerie, having my words bounce off her and return to me in their identical form. Faith never cut me any Mother-slack.

That set Faith apart from my family. Everyone in my family reverenced parents.

That was not to be in our household. Unless Faith herself decreed it so.

But our times together now forged new directions in our relationship. They could, with the help of the Almighty, be better than ever.

I was counting on that.

When ten-year-old Maddie came on weekends, Faith's room was meticulous. She now cared what her baby girl saw and felt when she was with her. Faith was also becoming more fastidious in her grooming, a ritual neglected during her downward addiction spiral. It was as though she'd come out of a long hibernation and was slowly acquiring new appetites.

My thoughts *poofed* when I felt her hand slide into mine in the darkened movie theater. I looked at her there in the silvery glow from the big movie screen and thought how beautiful she was. Now, the inner beauty was gradually emerging to join the outward.

"Love you, Mama," she whispered, gently squeezing my hand and smiling.

"Me, too," I whispered back, swallowed and turned my attention back to Angelina and Johnny on screen.

But, through tears, their images now blurred.

~ ~

We arrived at Lexie's house an hour early, Faith, Maddie and I. Dan was going to come on just a little later, when he finished mowing the grass on our lush lawn. April in South Carolina is heavenly. We have no extreme seasons here. They gently segue like a smooth-flowing creek with bends that magically unveil another time of year. Though rare, March may produce a light snow and then forty-eight hours later, the temperatures climb up into the eighties.

The past week had been mild. Today was short sleeve weather. The occasion was Mom's surprise birthday party. Thus the early gathering before her arrival. Priss would deliver Mom when she received the all clear call.

Mom had been doing well since her heart procedure. At least, she always insisted that she was.

Maddie dashed in ahead of us. I put my hand on Faith's arm, halting her. "What?" she asked, puzzled.

"I know I don't have to say this, honey. But just for the record ... please be careful not to touch anyone's belongings. Don't even give a hint of interest. Too many things have disappeared and should that happen with you here, you know that you'll get blamed."

Faith's ire visibly raised but she merely nodded. "I know, Mama. I'm not stupid."

"Definitely not."

Inside, Faith and I joined Lexie to hustle about setting things in order.

"Hi, Chloe." I stopped to give my niece a hug when she ambled down the stairs.

"Hey, Aunt Deede," she squeezed me back and gave me a big smile. She was in her final year of college now, close to earning her business degree. She would work in her Uncle Earl's bustling hardware business after graduation.

"How's it going, Chloe?" Faith asked as she passed, arms loaded with colorful streamers and balloons.

Chloe's smile dissolved as she mumbled something under her breath and spun in another direction. My heart plunged, but I managed to keep my expression neutral.

"Why is she so mean, Mama?" Faith murmured tightly as her cousin flounced away. "I've tried to be nice to her, but she's determined to be hateful."

I groped for something to say that might console Faith. It was true. She had gone out of her way to make amends for having offended Chloe in the past only to have them tossed back in her face.

"Just give her time, honey. Apparently, she still doesn't trust your motives."

"Huh." Faith scowled and attacked the decorating with a vengeance. I would have laughed at the vision she made — a so un-Normal Rockwell, furious artist at work — had I not felt so disturbed over Chloe's stubborn refusal to forgive.

Betty and Ginger had brought kabootles of lively decorations from their Simply Divine Gift Shop and worked together creating groupings of flowers and lacy napkin holders and all manner of pretty accents that reflected Noni's tastes.

A few minutes later, standing on a chair to stretch the streamers and balloons to corners, I heard Faith call out, "Chloe, come help me, will you, please?" I was in the kitchen and stepped to the doorway to gauge what Faith's needs were.

Chloe, standing only a few feet away, idly placing napkins on a table, cut Faith a cool glance and said, "Can't. I'm busy." Still reed thin, Chloe had morphed into a fairly attractive young woman, and I though how much prettier she would be if she would just lighten up and smile more.

Faith, struggling awkwardly with the paraphernalia, as well as her balance, snapped, "Can't you stop just a minute and help?"

"Sorry," Chloe intoned, a familiar retributive spark lighting her eyes. "Call Jensen."

"I'll get him," I said from the kitchen doorway, wiping away with a damp cloth remnants of homemade chicken salad and rushing to locate him. I hoped to maybe ward off a major clash. I would have helped Faith myself, but time was short and I needed to finish some of the food preparation.

I bumped into Maddie as I climbed the stairs to search for Jensen. "Maddie?" I caught her by her thin shoulders as she tried to turn aside, her face pale and somber. "Why the tears?"

Head lowered, gaze averted, she shook her head slowly as a tear trickled down her cheek.

"Tell me, sweetheart? Has somebody hurt your feelings?"

She sniffled and nodded, her face dissolving into grief as I pulled her to me. "Who?" The top of her auburn crown nearly reached my chin. It smelled of herbal shampoo. How she had grown lately.

Her tears continued for long moments, flowing from her tender heart. I hugged her to me, wishing I could protect her more. She was emotionally fragile, much like me at her age. Then she snuffled loudly, swiped her eyes and muttered. "Chloe."

My gaze narrowed. "What did she do?"

"S-she caught me in her room and told me to 'get out this instant.' I just wanted to look around because it's so pretty in there. She was so hateful, Mema. Why doesn't she l-like me?" The tears spilled over again.

"She does, honey," I improvised. "She's just having a hard day, apparently. Go help us in the kitchen. You can garnish the chicken and potato salads with olives and pickles. Tell Aunt Lexie I sent you to help."

That brightened her up and she rushed off to do my bidding as I continued my search for Jensen. "It's okay, Mama! Don't bother Jensen." Faith called from downstairs.

"Ginger's helping me."

Jensen was nowhere to be found so I returned to the kitchen. "I sent him to the store for more bagged ice," Lexie informed me as she put more seasoning in her delicious Sam's Club potato salad and mixed it thoroughly. "I didn't know you were looking for him." She'd been out of ear-shot of the snarking between our daughters.

As I started adding more chopped eggs to the chicken salad, I overheard Faith's voice, soft and entreating. I stopped and stepped to the doorway again. "Why do you insist on being this way, Chloe? You're grown now. Why don't you start acting more mature?"

"Hah! Look who's talking?" Chloe's bitterness smote me. It pierced my heart that she felt so bruised and battered that she couldn't let it go. I understood the why. I just couldn't understand the reason she clung to umbrage so desperately.

And now, her bitterness spilled over on little innocent Maddie.

Suddenly, I could hold my tongue no longer.

"Hey," I marched over to them. "Let's go sit down in the bedroom. We need to talk. Lexie?" I called out to my sister. "Come on, we need a conference here."

Lexie washed her hands and looking confused, trooped behind me and the girls up the stairs to her bedroom. "Close the door," I told her after we entered.

"Sit," I told Faith and Chloe. "This has got to stop. This fighting."

"I'm trying, Mom," Faith said.

"Yeh. Right." Chloe's eyes sparkled with the satisfaction of challenge.

"Okay." I held out both hands. "Lexie and I both want this to end right now. Isn't that right, Lexie?"

"Right." I knew Lexie and I were on the same page.

"Each of you will get your time to speak. In the meantime, do not interrupt the other. Okay?"

They eyed each other warily and nodded.

"You go first, Chloe," I said.

Chloe began to relate, one by one, the offenses she'd suffered at Faith's hands as calmly and matter-of-factly as I'd ever heard her. "When I have children, I don't want her to be around them because she's abusive," was her conclusion.

Faith rolled her eyes but held her tongue.

"Are you finished, Chloe?" I asked.

She nodded, watching Faith with an edgy wariness that could not be feigned.

"Okay, Faith." I gave her the go-ahead.

"Chloe, I was stoned many of those times you mentioned. I can't go back and undo a thing. I wish I could."

"Don't you think you owe Chloe an apology?" I asked.

Faith took a deep breath, slowly blew it out and looked Chloe squarely in the eye. "I'm sorry, Chloe. I really am. I'm doing my best to change the direction of my life."

Chloe watched her with great amused reservation. "This is about me."

Faith visibly reined in a smart-aleck-y reply. "I know. And I'm sorry for everything."

"Chloe," I urged gently, "do you accept Faith's apology?"

"Yes," Chloe said unconvincingly. And I wondered.

And hoped.

"She owes me an apology, too," Faith insisted. "She's been awfully snotty to me for a long time."

"I'm sorry," Chloe said automatically, staring into the distance.

Lexie got to her feet and suggested, "Why don't you two give each other a big hug?" I knew Lexie sought the same thing I did, family solidarity. She had lost some of her trust in Faith through the years, when she'd discovered things missing from her house following Faith's visits. But I knew that she struggled to love Faith anyway. I had to be thankful for that. Family meant too, too much to both my sister and me for us to give up on each other.

Only Priss, sweet Priss, still loved Faith unreservedly and trustingly welcomed her in her home. She merely put everything under lock and key.

Faith's horror now was in losing that space in the family, one reserved for her alone.

Her space.

Faith and Chloe hugged each other, but the gesture lacked conviction.

Lexie and I looked at each other, a question in our eyes.

Would our family ever find the peace it sought?

~ ~

Priss brought out the flaming birthday cake, whose white frothy center emblazoned in red letters, *Happy Birthday Noni!* Our sweet mother was overcome as we all, the entire clan, gathered around Lexie's long dining room table and sang an exuberant, if a bit dissonant, *Happy Birthday*.

"Make your wish, Mom," I said.

We all wondered, as the aging lids lowered over fading, once vibrant whiskey-gold irises, what would our mom, the family matriarch since Dad's death five years ago, wish for? Her salt and pepper, once richly sable hair, now sported a breezy, no nonsense style for minimum upkeep. Her face bore little makeup, only light powder and pale pink lipstick.

But to me, she was utterly beautiful with her diminutive, slightly plump silhouette neatly tucked into tailored navy slacks and a crisp white blouse. Her simple 14k jewelry represented gifts from Dad and each of her children and grandchildren over the years. Even the tacky *Grandma* brooches regularly found their niches on the pristine white collar or shoulder and her gold bracelet drooped from the weight of momentous charms denoting each family member.

Mom took a deep breath, leaned over and in one slow sweep blew out ninety candles.

"Good going, Mom!" we all cried out in unison.

"What did you wish," mischievous Lexie ventured, her eyes twinkling.

"Don't you wish you knew, Miss Nosey?" Mom shot back and hugged her. With that gesture, the entire flock, like love-starved, hungry puppies, converged upon *Nonie*, hugging and planting kisses on her blushing cheeks and wishing her many, many more birthdays.

Mom had chosen the Italian word for Grandmother, *Noni.* She was fond of saying, "If I had a second choice for who I could be, I would be an Italian. I love the language and the strong sense of family."

Buffet-style food filled our plates and we scattered all over the house for space in which to park, feast and chitchat. Jensen and Faith migrated to each other like magnets, to huddle and catch up.

Bachelor Jensen, due to family and friends' match-making efforts, never lacked for girlfriends. But today, he opted to simply be with family. His earlier chunkiness now had smoothed and lengthened to, if not thinness, a big, solid hunk of masculinity that seemed to thrill the opposite sex. His onyx, almond-shaped eyes, thick, near black wavy hair and strong olive features lent him a mystical beauty.

"You okay?" Priss took a seat beside me at the long table, which seated only part of the family. Others scattered about on sofas, easy chairs and even on the area rugs, plates parked on large, glass topped coffee and end tables and every available space, devouring a smorgasbord of delectable family favorites.

"Heck, yes," I reared back, stuck my chin in the air and demonstrated how okay I was. "Couldn't be better."

Lexie quickly joined us, pulling out a chair for Mom and courteously seating her. We all ate in warm camaraderie, our gazes sweeping the now grown brood whose lives were taking diverse turns and sweeps into this thing called life.

"Tell me, Mom," Lexie took Mom's surprisingly smooth, unspotted hand, "what does one like you, so strong and dependable, wish for?"

"Lexie!" Priss scolded, scowling comically, her own curiosity ablaze.

"Oh," Mom waved her free hand. "It's okay. I wished for all the Eagle clan to be happy and blessed. Do you think you can get their attention, Deede? I'd like to address my family."

I picked up a spoon and pinged it several times against a crystal glass. "Attention, everybody! Noni wishes to speak."

As one, the gathering fell to silence. Such was the respect for Noni. She slowly stood and swept her gentle smile over everyone. "Please continue to eat. You can listen at the same time. Don't want this wonderful food to grow cold."

Her voice, even at four score and ten, came out crisp and confident. "I don't know how long I'll be here to impart wisdom to you, my sweet ones." At her allusion to mortality, groans of protest arose. It struck terror in my heart. And when I gazed at Priss and Lexie, I saw reflected in their eyes the same stricken fear.

Did she know something we didn't?

Unruffled, Mom held up her hand, smiling. "That's not melodrama or a ploy for sympathy, it's a fact. But we have today, do we not?"

The nods were accompanied by misty-eyed adoration for Noni, this lovely retired school teacher who had a legion of students who still wrote her letters and called to thank her for making a difference in their lives. To have them drop by her house for visits and counsel was not out of the ordinary.

"I don't have anything profound to say, but I think these thoughts may have a place in your hearts to lodge if you will allow them to. The first thing I urge you to do is to live peaceably among all people. Don't give all of yourselves away, however. That's not good either. Always be honest. Don't think you always have to speak your opinion about everything. Silence can be golden. Listen to others, regardless of their station in life. Even the poor and ignorant have a story to tell." She smiled.

"Always be learning."

The reverential silence touched a spot deep inside me and I felt tears rush to my eyes. I'd already laid my fork aside. So, I noticed, had most of the others.

The wisdom of the words pierced my heart, from this woman who picked me up out of a cold, cruel world, whose warm arms embraced me as her own, who gave me a mother's love, and most of all, gave me a sanctuary in her heart to call my own.

I heard Priss sniffle, then Lexie. Then all over the living area, like leaves rustling, other sniffles and coughs.

Even Faith listened raptly. And I wished my own words would touch her in such a way.

Mom continued in her quiet dignity. "Be careful who you keep company with. The Bible says to avoid loud and aggressive people. That means they can steal your peace. Don't compare yourself to others because you will be disappointed. You were created to be you. Don't be too hard on yourselves."

She walked over to the younger generation and paused, her features grave. "Remember, you guys," she pointed a slightly crooked, arthritic finger at them, "God don't make no junk."

Everybody burst into laughter at Mom's brash, uncharacteristic departure from proper English usage. Then her gaze settled softly on Faith. "Don't think love has forgotten you. Love is as perennial as the grass. It finds you, somehow. You are a child of the universe. You have a right to be here." Mom's gaze now encompassed the others. "And whether or not you think so, life is unfolding as it should. And whatever your labors and aspirations in the noisy confusion of life, keep peace with your soul."

She now strolled back over to the older generation. "Grow old gracefully, willingly surrendering the things of youth. And know this, that with all its sham, drudgery and broken dreams, it is still a beautiful world."

She leaned to kiss each of us, Priss, Lexie and me. Then said softly, "Be cheerful and strive for happiness."

Mom stood erect and in her best teacher's voice said, "Now, I know some of you recognized those last words of counsel. Who can tell me what it is and who wrote it? A moment of silence, then Lexie's hand shot up. "I know! *Desiderata*."

"Written by Max Ehrlman," Priss chimed, grinning like road kill.

Mom beamed. "Correct. An A for both Lexie and Priss!"

I knew Mom's little aside was to break the solemnity of a joyful occasion. And it worked. Light banter and laughter coaxed back the levity. I shook my head in wonder. Mom was such a humble soul. Self-deprecation came easily to her and had brought much laughter during our growing up years.

So had Dad's. I blinked back the jolt of sadness at the void left by his absence.

"Hear this, hear this!" Priss startled me by banging on a serving tray with a huge spoon. When she got everyone's attention, she said, "Mom may have read that poem to us often before we left home, but the counsel she gave us today was hers. Exclusively hers. Because she's lived it by example. Take heed, you younger ones. You don't get this kind of wisdom many times in a lifetime. Take it to your heart. Live by it. You won't be sorry."

She sat down and one by one, we began to applaud, first Priss, Lexie, me and then Faith, Jensen, Maddie, Betty,

Ginger, Chloe, Dan and all the rest. Then we stood and I pulled Mom gently back to her feet to accept the homage.

Those huge soulful, generous eyes filled with tears as they scanned us, her family, one by one, lingering on each as love spilled from them and splashed over us. We were her life. And she was passionate in her love for each and every one of us. She *cared* and we felt it.

Moments later, Maddie sidled up to me as everyone settled down to conversations once more. “Mema,” she whispered. “I want to sit with you.”

“Sure.” I pulled up a chair and patted it. Now ten, Maddie was blossoming into a Faith look-alike. “I’ve missed you lately,” I said, feeling it from my soul.

“Me, too,” she said. “I wish Daddy would let me come over more on weekends.”

“Maybe soon that will happen,” I said, hoping it to be so. Despite the physical resemblance to her mother, Maddie was Faith’s emotional antithesis. She was gentle, polite and affectionate where Faith was impatient, forthright and often distanced. But their sharp intellect matched to a T. And with Maddie, Faith’s maternal leanings sprang forth.

They had been muted during her downward plunge into drugs. But I had been there to absorb some of the ugliness during Faith’s less than motherly times. I’d been like a she bear, protecting my granddaughter.

Now, Faith was loath to even discuss those black times. I don’t think she could come to grips with just how nasty things got. It was easier for her to block it out. But on some level, *she knew*. She was now trying to make it up to Maddie in every way possible.

And Maddie accepted every overture. She was a sweet, forgiving child, thank God.

From the corner of my eye, I saw Chloe plop down on a sofa nearby and begin to closely monitor Faith and Jensen. I tensed. Then I thought how much Faith had changed and that perhaps the dynamics of the Faith/Jensen/Chloe coalition would shift.

I thought of how they had each apologized to each other earlier today.

Had it taken, the forgiveness?

The younger women took charge of clean-up and kitchen duty. I breathed a little easier to see Faith and Chloe working together in what appeared to be a truce.

A little later, Chloe came up behind me as I aimed myself toward the bathroom. She whispered in my ear. "Faith has been going through purses when she thought no one was looking. I just thought you'd want to know." She left as quietly as she came.

Oh no. Shock gripped me. *Please, Faith.* I promptly found Faith and relayed what Chloe had told me.

She looked startled. "I did move some purses out of the way while cleaning, Mama. And I looked in your purse for some gum to kill that onion taste. But I didn't 'go through' purses. What's Drama Queen trying to do?" She was hurt. I could hear it in her voice and see it in her wilted attitude. The anger was just under the surface. But I was thankful that Faith kept it there rather than make a scene.

I also believed her.

In the meantime, I watched as Chloe furtively passed the word to others in the family. I chilled, thinking how much progress Faith had made and now to have this happen. To date, only Priss, Jensen and my Mom totally believed in Faith. They knew all her faults and all her ill deeds. But they loved her unconditionally. Still. They were rooting for her to overcome all the junk. To be restored.

I left Priss' feeling as sad as I'd ever felt in my life.

~ ~

The next morning, my phone rang as I drank my second cup of coffee.

It was Lexie.

"Hi, Sis," I said, "what's happening?"

Lexie took a deep breath. My antennae rose. "I can't think of an easy way to say this, Deede. But Adam is missing seventy dollars from his wallet. He left it in our bedroom last night on the night stand. He shouldn't have, but he did."

My heart was already pooled at my feet. "And you all think Faith took the money." It was a statement because I knew how fine that trust-line had been.

"Deede, who's to say whether she did or didn't take it? It can't be proven either way, can it? I'm sorry, honey. It has nothing to do with you or Dan. Faith was seen going through purses last night so her margin of innocence is very narrow to say the least."

I swallowed back the bitter gall of disappointment. "Faith says to wait and see if anyone reports anything missing from the purses before condemning her on Chloe's accusation."

"Chloe wasn't accusing her —"

"Okay, Lexie. Let's just drop it right here." I knew my voice was edgy, but I'd had it with Chloe's vindictiveness.

"Sure, sis. But I want you to know that, in the future, you and Dan are welcome at our house anytime, but Faith is not. Too many things have happened when she was around."

I hung up before I burst into tears.

Faith walked into the kitchen and quietly took the seat across from me, nursing her lukewarm coffee. "I heard," she said softly. "Most of it, anyway. I can read between the lines."

I wiped my tears away and tried to smile at her. "Oh, well. All families have disagreements."

I watched her battle the anger and the hurt. Her blue eyes began to shimmer, and I wondered which would win out, hurt or anger?

Anger won the first round. "I don't have any family except you, Jensen, Aunt Priss and Noni," she stated flatly. "I don't care beans about what any of the rest of them think."

"Now, honey," I said, "all of the family loves you. It's just that a lot has happened in your life. There have been incidents of things disappearing when you *were* culpable."

She cut her eyes at me and snapped. "You don't know that. Nobody could ever prove it was me who did all those things. Did it ever occur to you that Chloe was also around and she hated me so bad that she could have set me up just like she did yesterday?"

I shook my head. "I don't think Chloe —"

"Mama," her voice changed. Hurt was winning this round, "Chloe has bragged to Jensen and me how she takes hundred dollar bills from her dad's wallet all the time. She set me up, Mama. She can't stand for the family to love me. So she told everybody I was scrounging through purses so that when her dad's money came up missing, everybody would suspect me."

"And another thing," she added, "do you know what Chloe said to my little girl at the birthday party, when she caught her in her room?"

"No," I hedged. "Tell me."

"She said 'your Mama won't ever amount to anything. She's a druggie and she always will be.' She said that to my daughter, Mama. She made Maddie cry."

So I hadn't lied. I'd not heard this version and it made me sick inside.

She stood then, "I would have been a fool to steal anything there, Mama. We talked about it when we arrived, remember? And I may be many things but — now that I'm drug-free — I'm no fool. It's bad enough, my being the black sheep of the family. But when my child is penalized for my mistake, that's pure evil." Her words ended on a broken note as she left the room and slowly climbed the stairs to her inner sanctum.

For days, Faith stayed in her room for longer periods of time and came out with her eyes red and swollen. She began to feverishly look in the job want ads. She cleaned her room with a vengeance. I felt her desperation to salvage something of herself and to rebuild that which her addiction had destroyed.

Her spirit was crushed. I prayed that it would revive.

I suppose the most difficult aspect of that crisis was that, at first, Dan half believed that Faith had stolen Adam's money. "She *has* stolen before, Deede," he reminded me.

"You don't have to tell me that, Dan," I snapped at him. "I already know all of Faith's flaws and past deeds. But this time, I believe her when she says she's innocent. We had a talk just before entering Lexie's house that evening."

In the end, Dan did believe Faith. And it was a while before he would visit Lexie and Dan's home again. "If my daughter isn't welcome, I'm not welcome," he insisted.

I didn't want family dissension, but it was heaped upon me at that time. And one good thing came out of it. Dan was forced to take a stand. It didn't end his stand-off with his daughter, but for a brief span of time, I saw the fatherly side of him re-emerge.

~ ~

"Deede?" The female voice on the phone sounded familiar.

"Yes? I'm sorry, but I can't exactly place your voice.

"This is Shirley, from Temple Bible College in Charleston. How is Faith doing?"

I shared with my friend Shirley about Faith's recent turnaround and the difficulties she currently encountered. Shirley and I were childhood friends. She was now married with two adult children. She was an administrator at the coastal college. We kept in touch often and when Dan and I had gone down the past spring, we'd visited her and Jim.

"Faith needs to get away from here, Shirley. She can't pull herself up with so many significant others pulling her down."

"Hey!" Shirley's upbeatness caught my attention. "I just thought of a solution for Faith. Remember me talking to you about the Los Angeles Christian-based Drug Recovery center? Our son Scott was there for over two years and it totally saved his life and got him on the right path."

"Y'know," I said, "with Faith's spirit of adventure, she just might be interested in going to LA for this program. Do you think you can help her?"

"I'll see what I can do," she promised and we rang off.

Faith was excited. "I'll go! I'll go!" she replied before I'd finished my spiel. So she sat about readying for a transfer. Of course, we would have to have her probation transferred to Los Angeles. That would involve Otto, her attorney. But it seemed feasible.

The crushing weight of recent days began to lift. The light at tunnel's end blazed like a beacon. This way, we would, all three of us, finally have our own space.

~ ~

Just days later, it came out of the blue.

Like an atomic blast.

"My court date is Thursday," Faith said, her voice weak with fear. In the midst of everything else raging, we had all but forgotten this unfinished business hovering over our heads like radioactive nuclear fallout.

She got on the phone and called Otto, her attorney, who had been gouging us mercilessly all along. He could be charming, quite convincing that he was doing us the greatest of services getting Faith lighter fines and etc. Of course, we had our doubts, but with his hand out at every turn, he always owed us representation, and it was difficult to drop him after paying him ungodly sums.

It was a mutual, barely-civil relationship between Faith and Otto, whom she'd met through some mutual friends who lived on the fringes of addiction. "He makes his living off druggies, Mom," she would say disparagingly when especially ticked off at him. And then, when she needed him to get her out of trouble, she would backpedal and pay him half-hearted praise.

"Here," Faith held the phone out to me. "Otto wants to talk to you."

I sucked in a furious breath. I knew what that meant.

More money. I'd just paid him $1,700 a few weeks ago.

"I need at least another grand to cover this plea," Otto unapologetically told me.

"Otto, we are near destitution," I insisted, knowing I would be shown no mercy. I would have to borrow the money and pay it back with my Social Security monthly checks.

"Deede," he replied in his best lawyer voice, "I have to have this today. Can you come up to my office today and give me a check?"

"I don't know," I said, thoroughly agitated. I handed the phone back to Faith and marched from the room.

Dan dropped by the house about that time. "What?" he asked, seeing my face.

"Otto wants another thousand dollars for the court appearance day after tomorrow," I said. "What the heck did he do to earn that $1,700 we gave him recently?"

"Don't give him another penny."

"The court date is only one day away, Dan. He's got us over a barrel and he knows it."

"Deede, I wouldn't give him another penny until after the court thing. Let's let him earn it."

"That's not how Sir Otto does things, Dan. You know that. I'll have to go write him a check or Faith's up the creek without representation."

"I'm against it," Dan said, shaking his head disparagingly as he left to get in his work truck.

I was against it, too, but I had no recourse.

"He's a jerk," Faith said more times than I could count that afternoon.

Not for the first time, I whole-heartedly agreed.

An hour later, Dan called and wanted to pick me up and go for lunch in Greenville. On the drive to the Green Tomato Buffet, I answered my cell phone. It was Faith.

"Otto's furious," she said. "He said 'what does your mom mean going out to lunch when I told her to come immediately and pay me for the court plea?'" Faith snorted. "Can you believe his ego? Stop this world and cater to Otto."

"Yes. I'm acquainted with his ego. Mr. Otto will have to wait until I finish my meal, and if I have time, I'll go to his office and pay him." Then I laughed. "Why can't he wait until tomorrow? The court date is the next day. What's his hurry?"

"He says that if you don't pay him, *today*, he's not going to lift a finger to help me." She sighed heavily. "He'll squash me like a bug under his foot. I'm serious, Mom."

I feared that he would. I couldn't chance that.

So later in the afternoon, I arrived at Otto's nice office. He was the epitome of a gentleman when I sat down across his wide mahogany desk from him.

I described to him in detail the progress Faith had made in recent months. Told him of the year-long drug rehab she'd finished, the one that nearly bankrupted us.

"Otto, do you think you can get Faith's probation transferred to LA?" I clarified for him in detail the wonderful success stories coming out of church-based Daystar Center.

"No problem," he said. "I'll get her transferred and the first year she's there will be considered sentence served."

"Are you sure?" I asked pen poised over check.

"Absolutely. It's done all the time.

"Then write me a receipt showing what this check covers."

He did as I asked and I handed him the check. Immediately, he arose, "I'll walk you to your car."

I thought, it's not my imagination after all. The money is all that matters.

I am dismissed.

We chatted on the way down the stairs and when we reached the car, he waved goodbye without even pausing or looking back. I felt extremely *had.* But I reminded myself that I'm a fair person and know that lawyers are busy folks and they don't work for nothing. I brushed off the *used* feeling and, with no other choice available, entrusted Faith's future into Otto's hands.

~ ~

Two days later, Dan drove Faith to court. "I haven't heard a word from Otto so I don't even know if I'll go before the judge, Dad," she told her father. "There's no need for you to stay and wait. This could take hours so I'll just call you when we're finished."

Later in the day, when my phone rang, I expected to hear the good news of Faith's parole transference to LA.

Instead, Faith moaned, "Mom, Otto threw me under the bus. I'm so upset I don't know what to do."

"What?" Alarm buzzed all over me like a crazy swarm of bees.

"Otto only talked to me about three minutes before we went before the judge. I thought he was doing a plea deal — which he should have done — but he didn't. He told me to keep my mouth shut during the hearing. Not to say a word. Oh Mom —"

"What happened, honey?" I asked knowing she was torn to bits. Trying to hold together.

Seemed Otto had apparently decided to present her as a hopeless druggie, not allowing her to correct him at crucial misinformation points. Lies. Not a word about the drug rehab she'd completed the past year. At one point, when she tried to tell the judge that she'd not been on heroin, Otto told her to "shut up. I told you not to speak."

"It was so humiliating, Mom," she said.

Otto miscalculated. He thought erroneously that the judge would agree to transfer Faith to the Los Angeles recovery center as an extreme measure.

"The entire thing backfired, Mom. The judge decided that I needed a real lesson and placed me under house arrest for six months, and when Otto asked that it be transferred to LA, the judge almost laughed in his face. Then on top of that, I face *two years probation,* plus another round of drug rehab. It's horrible, Mama."

I was in total shock. "Oh God," I groaned, in tears, "Rehab? Why?"

"Because that jerk Otto convinced the judge that I was a hopeless druggie, that's why." Faith wept softly. She looked so exhausted my heart broke.

I groaned. "They'll put that awful chemical in you again. It did terrible things to you before."

"I know. I hated it." And she had. Methadone had nearly destroyed her health.

"This time, if it has to be, you will take suboxone. You did much better on that in the end."

"You're right," she agreed.

Dan was inconsolable. "I can't take this again, Deede. I can't. I've already put her through drug rehab at the cost of thousands of dollars, plus probation and other court related costs ... it's not fair. We're the ones getting the punishment."

We found out immediately that the extra costs for us would be over eight hundred dollars a month. The cost alone of wearing the house-arrest ankle bracelet was eight dollars per day. Then the weekly report-in to Sentinel cost forty-two dollars. Drug rehab was around $300 per month. Random drug tests were extra. And on and on. This — on top of our already overly-burdened finances — was more than we could bear at times.

This did not account for the extras of transportation to and from, with rising gas prices gouging us relentlessly. Dan rose early daily to transport Faith to the treatment center and later, the evening NA meetings.

We — Faith, Dan and I — could not even encourage each other, so we sequestered ourselves separately, as depressed as one can get. Desperation clawed. We'd been so close to the tunnel's end.

So close.

Now this.

And for the first time in a long, long time, I asked, *Why, God?*

~ ~

And then a miracle happened.

Not overnight. But slowly and steadily, our family began to come together in harmony. The house arrest made it impossible for Faith to abuse rules. She knew that any small violation would mean prison time for her. So she had to stick to the schedule, to the letter. She was accountable for her space and activities every minute of the day.

Dan began to relax and allow Faith some freedom from his policing. He now realized that he'd been obsessive at times. And he found that he could bend a little and allow Faith to drive our vehicles when absolutely necessary. After all, she was monitored every time she left the house and had to be back inside by a certain designated time. She didn't have time to gad about and get into trouble as she once had.

Bottom line: Faith knew that even one small violation could land her in prison.

Discipline was now the word. And Faith was the one who strictly adhered to it.

Me? With the terrible battle between father and daughter relaxing, my own stress began to wane. I tried to cut corners to help with the financial pressures. Faith did her part by revving up her coupon mania. She was a genius at it and ended up being paid to buy groceries at the best of times.

One weekend, when Dan and I took a trip to Charleston to visit our friends Shirley and Jim, Dan left Faith the key to his Land Rover.

"Thanks, Dad," Faith said. "I'll be really careful and return it as clean as it is now."

It was a great feeling, knowing that she was on a tightly monitored system, and we didn't have to worry. Not for a second.

We kept in touch regularly via cell phones. "Poopsie's really missing Dad," Faith said on our second day. "She watches the door constantly." We always got a big laugh over that one. Dan had at one time said, "I won't have a dog in this house." And then Faith brought Poopsie home one day. She immediately migrated to Dan, who, after a few days stand-off, melted into putty beneath her tiny paws.

Then on the third day, Faith said, "Aunt Priss came by today and stayed a couple of hours. She cooked spaghetti and homemade sauce. It was delicious. I love her, Mama."

"I'm glad she's there for you, honey."

We went out to supper that last night in Charleston. We had a wonderful seafood buffet and then Shirley spotted a friend and waved him over to our table.

"Dan and Deede, meet our friend Nathan Milton. He's a state house representative and he's also a criminal defense lawyer."

"I'm impressed," I said, shaking his hand.

"Call Kay over and join us," Shirley and Jim insisted. He collected his beautiful blonde wife to join us for coffee and dessert.

"Tell me what's happening with Faith now," Shirley said.

I began to fill her in on what had happened since she had put in an application for Faith's acceptance to the Los Angeles Daystar Center. "They agreed for Faith to come to Daystar Center, but the court thing really turned out badly," I finished up the account. "But all is not lost. We're learning to live together again without wanting to kill each other.'

Everyone laughed, except Nathan. He looked thoughtful. "Is Otto still on the case?" he asked.

"Well," I said, rolling my eyes, "as much as he's ever been."

"Get him to call me," Nathan said, handing me his card. "I might be able to help."

I put the card in my purse and forgot about it for a few days.

~ ~

Then one day, I got an e-mail. It was from my new friend Nathan, the criminal defense lawyer. "Is there anything I can do to help? There's not much I can do as long as another attorney has the case. I could only take charge if Otto is no longer on the case. I would do it without charge. But in the meantime, I do think he should file a motion for reconsideration."

I answered: "I'll suggest this to Otto."

I called Otto the next day. "Otto, I need to talk to you."

That apparently did not hit Otto right.

For the next twenty minutes, I listened to Otto. He was condescending and downright rude at times. But I let him talk and simply listened. "Faith told me that this politician wants me to file a motion for reconsideration. That's just not appropriate, Deede. You just don't do things like this. I don't trust politicians. You know why?"

Like I don't trust you. "No. Why, Otto?"

"Because all they're after are your votes. I don't trust 'em. Faith needs this time of house arrest. If she'd gone to LA, she would have been out on the streets within three hours, hunting drugs. She's a junkie, Deede."

I listened and absorbed the disrespect, my heart breaking a little that I'd allowed him to represent our daughter for this long. She deserved better.

Otto continued his discourse. "You went to these people whom you felt were influential and asked them to intervene for your little Faith. That's just not appropriate, Deede. I know you were ticked off when you called today. I could hear it in your voice, 'I need to talk to you,

Otto.'" He mimicked. Then, immediately, he switched to gentleman-icon. "Tell you what, Deede. I love you and Dan, and I'd like to sit down and talk with you. Without Faith. Could we meet somewhere today and have coffee?"

"Not today. I can't." *Not ever.*

"I'll meet you anywhere. We need to talk. Without Faith." And I realized anew just how much he disliked Faith. That was okay. But he had no business representing someone he could not even make himself like. I'd not paid him thousands of dollars for psychological counseling.

"No. Can't, Otto. Sorry. Let me get off the phone and absorb all you've said to me. I'll call you back."

I clicked off, stunned at the range of his manipulation and rudeness.

I waited five minutes, then called him back. He didn't answer, which didn't surprise me. So I left him a message I was certain he would get.

"Tell you what, Otto, I think it would be best for all concerned if you were off this case. Faith needs a fresh start and a lawyer with a fresh perspective on her. I appreciate all you've done to help Faith during our long acquaintance. But it's time for a change."

I rang off, feeling better than I'd felt in a long time.

Then I e-mailed Nathan. "I fired Otto today. Please feel free to file the motion for reconsideration."

And suddenly, I felt the impact of what had happened.

I had prayed recently for mercy. For a lawyer who would help us free of charge. And for peace.

God had heard me.

And He wasn't through yet.

~ ~

Dan's health steadily plunged downhill in those coming days. The added financial load of drug rehab and other monumental costs was the proverbial straw. On some level, I sensed it, but Dan had always kept on trucking no matter how tired or discouraged, regardless of what corner he found himself backed into. He'd always made a door where there wasn't an escape hatch or jumped out a window and landed on his feet.

That was his nature

At least, that's how I perceived him.

So when he woke me up at three a.m. a couple of days after Faith's sentencing, I thought it was a case of indigestion. "Here," I handed him a Zantac and he swallowed it with some water. "It was probably that spicy chicken you had for lunch."

But the antacid didn't help. "I — can't ... breathe ... good," he gasped moments later.

"I'll call 911." I jumped to get my cell phone

"No," he reached to stay my hand as I shakily dialed. "Don't. I'll ... be ... okay."

"Sit down, Dan, Relax, honey," I ordered and then gave our address to the 911 operator.

Faith appeared, no doubt having insomnia again. "What's wrong?" she asked, peering anxiously at her dad, who by now sat doubled over, elbows on knees, his face nearly ashen.

"Daddy?" she wailed and ran to him, dropping to her knees and taking his limp hands in hers. "Are you all right, Daddy?"

"I'm ... all ... right, honey," he murmured with difficulty.

"Is there anything I can do?" she asked him, tears gathering and pooling along her tired lids. Then she ran to the bathroom and grabbed the aspirin. She dumped two into her hand and grabbed the nearby glass of water for Dan to take them with. As he did that, she wet a wash cloth and gently applied it to his forehead.

"You're gonna be okay, Daddy," she crooned gently as she began to massage his cold hands.

I stood on the porch to signal the EMS as they arrived. Within minutes, they had checked Dan's vital signs and had him in the ambulance. Faith had tearfully hugged him as they started out with him on the stretcher. "Daddy, I love you," she sobbed. "You're gonna be fine."

Dan smiled weakly and patted her cheek. "I know, sweetie. Love you, too."

Faith stood in the doorway, frantic because she could not accompany him to the hospital. Her house arrest tethered her to the house during those hours.

"Oh, Mama," she moaned as tears coursed down her cheeks. "I love him so much. Why did all this have to happen now?"

I hugged her tightly, "I don't know, honey. But we can be sure that it's all going to work together. Remember Romans 8:28. So be praying."

"I will. And Mama?"

I turned from my car, I was going to follow the ambulance to Spartanburg Regional. "What, darlin'?"

"I love you so much."

I smiled. "I know."

~ ~

By the time Dan was wheeled into the ER, he was already hooked to oxygen. His vital signs were checked again. There, blood was drawn within minutes. And then an MRI was performed.

I sat beside Dan's bed, holding his hand. His eyes were closed, but when I moved, they would open and follow me. I could see confusion in them. Shock.

Dan had always been so indomitable.

I leaned to kiss him lightly on the lips. "You okay?"

He nodded.

"Scared?"

He shrugged then shook his head no.

"Good. You're gonna be fine, darlin'. And that's a promise." Inside, I was terrified and desperately sought to tether myself to the assurance of divine intervention.

This time, it was critical.

He smiled then, reassured, and closed his eyes to rest for a few minutes. His breathing was loud, laborious. I closed my eyes and prayed.

Two hours later, Dr. Chorness, the cardiac specialist, appeared. "He has a large blood clot behind his heart," he informed us gravely. "We're starting him on an anticoagulant to thin his blood and dissolve the clot."

The whammy of it took my breath. I sucked in a furious lung full of air.

"I'll have more to tell you in the morning after we get more blood work. In the meantime, we'll admit him."

"How long?" Dan murmured in true A-type style.

"At least eight days," replied Dr. Chorness.

Dan groaned in protest.

"Mr. Stowe," the physician said, not unkindly, "you are about to have a drastic lifestyle change."

~ ~

My cell phone vibrated against my side. I pulled my phone from my belt phone holder and clicked it on. It was Faith.

"We'll know more in the morning," I told her.

"Are you spending the night?"

"Yes. I'll catch naps in the waiting area. Not comfy but I won't leave him until he's on more solid ground."

"Mom?" her voice almost faded away and I heard, felt her panic. "Is he —"

"He's going to be fine, darlin'," I said more heartily than I felt. "I suspect he's passing over the most critical time tonight. So far, so good. Don't you worry now."

"I'm trying, Mama. I wish I could be there with you." The bleakness of her spirit bled through her words.

"I know. But you ask your Sentinel officer to allow you a time window to visit Daddy here. I'm sure they have provisions for family emergencies."

"I will. First thing in the morning. I love you, Mom."

"Love you, too, honey."

The next morning, Dr. Chorness came by mid-morning. "Mrs. Stowe, your husband has congestive heart failure."

I groaned and tears flooded my eyes.

"But you got him here in time for us to help him."

"But — I thought he would have had more warning than this. I mean, he was awfully *tired,* but then he works so hard — I thought that was why."

"What he had last night was a light heart attack. This always precedes congestive heart disease. We already started him on Coumadin last night. This anticoagulant causes the blood to flow smoother and begins dissolving the clot lodged behind his heart. Of course, we'll want to keep him here until we get his blood thinned down to a safe level, say around 2.5. We'll want to be vigilant in the event of a crisis, which we don't expect."

"Better safe than sorry," I murmured in a trembling voice.

I looked at Dan, wondering how he was taking in all this change in health status.

"Do you have any questions, Mr. Stowe," Dr. Chorness asked.

"How long before I can go home?" Dan rasped weakly.

Both the doctor and I burst into laughter. Dan was grinning, too. I was immensely relieved that he was taking it all in stride.

"About a week. In the meantime, rest. And leave all your problems behind. And that's an order."

"Yessir," Dan replied and stuck out his hand. Dr. Chorness gripped it warmly.

After he left, I leaned to hug Dan. He squeezed me firmly and murmured against my neck, "God, how I love you, Deede."

"And I, you," I whispered and kissed him soundly on the lips. "You are my rock."

He snorted. "Not so solid right now, huh?" And then he teared up, surprising me.

"Ah, honey," I hugged him again and sat down holding his hand. "You're gonna be as good as new. Just you wait and see."

"Naw. Not this time." He reined in his weepiness and looked at me soberly. "But that's okay. We'll get through this with the help of the good Lord, huh?"

"Got that right, Dan."

And suddenly, I knew that we would.

~ ~

Faith received permission from her Sentinel officer to visit her father at the hospital. Her Aunt Priss gave her rides to and from the hospital so I didn't have to leave Dan to chauffer. Faith was able to visit there for only short jaunts because of the limited legal time window. But while there, she held his hand and spoke life to him. I was awed by her sensitivity.

And so, I suspected, was Dan.

On her first visit, Faith had rushed to his side and embraced him for long moments, weeping openly. Dan returned her embrace, patting her lovingly and murmured, "I'm gonna be okay, baby. Don't worry, Daddy will bounce back."

Later, as we grabbed a bite at the hospital cafeteria, she told me, "I'd never seen Daddy look so — vulnerable, Mama." She puckered up again but fought back tears as we grabbed our trays and made food selections.

"I know." We took seats at an empty table. Priss, being sweet Priss, had volunteered to stay with Dan while Faith and I lunched. She knew instinctively that we needed exclusive mother-daughter time together. "I felt the same. He's always been so — so fiercely protective and giving …"

Faith opened her carton of milk and stuck a straw in it. "I've been really thinking about all the things I've said to him in anger." She looked at me then, and in her bright blue eyes glistened sorrow as I'd never seen it before. "Do you think he can ever forgive me?" Tears gathered in those blue depths as I sat and watched. A knot leaped to my throat. I gulped it back.

Then smiled. "I'm sure he can."

"I hope so." She didn't sound so sure. And I understood.

But I understood, too, that Dan's life had taken a sonic turnaround.

He would not be the same. About anything.

"Remember, Faith, love is the strongest emotion we can experience. And one thing I know — your Daddy loves you."

~ ~

The house sparkled for Dan's homecoming. Faith had outdone herself this time with cleaning. She even arranged vases of our in-season hydrangeas, placed strategically for splashes of blue and white.

Poopsie did an exuberant series of celebration dancing spins, yapping furiously until Dan picked her up and tucked her against his bosom.

Food, from Priss and Lexie's kitchens, filled the refrigerator and counters. A baked, glazed ham — for Faith and me — nestled beside an extra golden rotisserie chicken — for Dan. My sisters had gotten Dan's food instructions from me earlier that week. Now, he would be treated with his very own special dishes of low sodium/ low cholesterol entrees.

"*Dash* is a wonderful friend to heart patients who can't have salt," Priss now told me as she rushed to greet Dan. "Much tastier than the old version."

She and Lexie were setting out tasty veggie dishes on the counters and from the oven came marvelous, mouth-watering aromas of heating rotisserie chicken and ham.

Their spouses, Earl and Adam, dropped by on their lunch break to enjoy the meal with us, making it an even more festive occasion. But soon thereafter, when the kitchen reverted back to spic and span, they prepared to depart.

I plumped up the pillows on our bed, got Dan settled comfortably and handed him the remote. "Rest," I told him and gave him a big hug. His eyes drooped tiredly and he was already breathing deeply by the time I left the room.

"Dan needs his rest," Priss said as she kissed my cheek on her way out. "Call if you need me. Okay?"

"Okay. Thanks for everything." I hugged her, then reached out and pulled Lexie into the circle and we three inhaled each other's love, embracing and enjoying the intimate sister-moment.

I heard them praise Faith for her housecleaning efforts as they left, thankful for their sensitivity toward her. She'd had so little to validate her for so long.

I shook my head, letting that train of thought go.

Things were beginning to look up.

~ ~

"Mama, don't get up," Faith whispered as I struggled to wake. "I'll get Daddy his medicine. You need your sleep."

Thankful, I snuggled back down. It was time for Dan's morning meds and he was already getting up to trek to the bathroom. I'd had a late night, catching up on my newspaper column writing. My boss had understood when Dan was sick I couldn't meet the deadlines. He graciously had someone else to fill in. But I only missed about four days so I wasn't doing too badly. I'd always made it a habit to have at least four or five columns in reserve. This time, it had saved me much stress.

I heard Dan and Faith talking quietly in the kitchen. I smelled Dan's decaf coffee perking, Faith's morning gift to him. He preferred "high test" but was beginning to reconcile himself to the lifestyle changes Dr. Chorness had warned him of.

Decaf coffee was among Dan's most difficult adjustments.

With my mind in motion, I gave up on sleep and shuffled to the bathroom, then to the kitchen for my own cup of decaf.

Her father's med agenda lay spread out before Faith. "I've already measured out your two liters of water for the day, Dad. Dr. Chorness said that under no circumstances are you to exceed that." This, said gently and I watched Dan's slight struggle to submit to her nurse-y orders. In the end, he relaxed.

"Imagine that," he said, grin stretching wide. "And me wired with the *thirsty-gene.*" He shook his head. "I never dreamed I'd be limited to drinking liquids. Thanks, Florence Nightingale, for measuring it out for me."

Faith blushed prettily, knowing his teasing was affectionate. "I also measured your protein intake for the day. It's exactly one quarter of today's entire food allowance."

"You're really on the ball, honey," I said, sipping my coffee, sitting opposite Dan, who still made a face when he tried to drink his black decaf.

"Sweetheart," I said, smiling — I hoped — winsomely at him, "a little fat-free milk and sugar can do wonders for its taste."

His expression grew even fiercer. "No self-respecting Stowe drinks milk and sugar in their coffee."

Faith and I burst into laughter, having heard this often through the years. Faith and I both took cream and sweetener.

"Aren't we considered Stowes, Faith?" I asked, feigning umbrage.

"Last I heard," she agreed, nose in air.

"Present company excluded," Dan tacked on and joined in our laughter.

My, my, how times had changed.

Faith got back down to business. She took the responsibility of her dad's care very seriously.

"Here's your med holder. I've got all of them in their proper time slots. You've already taken your cholesterol med, the simvastatin and warfarin, the anticoagulant. Let's get some toast in you before you take the diuretic."

"Which one is that?" I asked, confused at the array of meds in the small compartments of the plastic pill holder.

"This one is the furosemide. This one is digoxin, which treats the irregular heart rhythms." She pointed to yet another pill. "This is dietiazem, which works along with lisinopril, to control blood pressure and angina in congestive heart failure."

"I feel like a daggum septic tank," Dan groused good-naturedly.

"Oh, and Daddy," Faith reached for some tiny pink tablets, "don't forget the baby aspirin. Dr. Chorness says it's very, very important for heart patients to take them every day."

Faith jumped up and in no time had a slice of whole wheat toast and an egg white and veggie omelet placed before Dan.

"Do you want one, Mom?" she asked.

"No, thanks," I replied. "I'll just do some cereal and fruit."

After eating, Dan washed down the remainder of his meds with his disgusting coffee, still making fierce faces.

Stubborn. But my, oh, my, did I love that man.

"Oh, and Daddy, I got a job today. Burger King is only two miles from here so they were interested in hiring me

— even though I'm under house arrest — because I'm so accessible. Mom won't have to spend much on gas chauffeuring me, with me working so close."

"That's great, honey," Dan said. A job took some of the pressure off Dan, who now was forced to hire another worker to do the things he had been doing. But with Faith's job, the stress would not be as heavy.

Suddenly, the load didn't seem as burdensome.

We were together.

And as the three of us sat there, laughing together, it occurred to me how peaceful it all was. How the love flowed.

And I thought how many times we pray for a miracle, not always knowing the crooked, shadowy path we may have to take to get to it.

~ ~

Jensen and Mom dropped by the next day. She still drove herself places, but today, Jensen had called her and offered to bring her along for the visit.

"Noni!" Faith met them at the door, squealed and enveloped her Noni in a bear hug while Jensen scooped me up, spun me into cheap intoxication and kissed the top of my head before lowering my feet to the floor.

"I'm so glad you're home for good." I held his face in my hands and kissed each cheek soundly.

"Me, too," he said. Was his voice deeper? "I was glad to serve my country, but I'm glad my time's up. That hot, dry desert air was so not fun. I love the smell of honeysuckle and magnolia blossoms too much to stay gone for long. And the good ol' southern food of the Eagle clan."

"Lordy mercy," I said, cutting him an impressed look. "Listen to you, you ol' poet you."

"I was just going to say the same thing," Noni chimed in, giving me a big hug.

Faith and I fixed tall glasses of iced tea for everyone and lounged in the comfort of the den. Noni got the most comfortable chair with the ottoman today. Drinks sat on the glass-topped coffee table beside our propped feet as we rested on soft, leather functional sofas and chairs. In the background, from Sirius Escape softly flowed Claire de Lune as we chatted.

Dan joined us when he awakened from his daily nap. He stooped to give Noni a kiss on her cheek and shake Jensen's hand. "Good to have you back, Jensen."

"Tell me what's been happening lately," Jensen flashed his dimples and white, white teeth. "Have I missed much in the past year?"

Faith burst into laughter, shaking her head helplessly at him.

Dan and I looked at each other and we, too, began laughing.

Noni sat there with this Buddha smile on her sweet face.

"What?" Jensen spread his hands. "I've missed that much?"

"You don't want to know," Faith gasped, wiping her eyes. "Lord help us, Jense. You really, really don't."

"Hey!" He thumped his chest like King Kong. "I've been to Afghanistan. I can take it. Put it on me."

Faith and I took turns relaying the worst of the last months' events.

When we wound down, I looked at Mom, seeing moisture in her faded eyes. I slowly shook my head. "Mom, there have been times when I wondered *why*. The road has been so — rocky. The mountains so high and the valleys deep as the Grand Canyon."

Mom smiled that sweet smile of hers. "Remember the story I told you when you were kids, about the American eagle?"

"What?" Faith and Jensen spoke at once.

"Well, the American eagle has a significant symbolism to our country." She smiled then. "And I like to think there is symbolism there to the Eagle family clan. You see, the eagle has the longest lifespan among birds. It can live up to seventy years. But to reach this age, the eagle must make a hard decision in its forties."

Nonie had her audience in her hand at that point.

"Its long and flexible talons can no longer grab prey, which serves as food. Its long and sharp beak becomes bent. Its aged and weighty wings, due to their thick feathers, become stuck to its chest and make it difficult to fly."

Jensen muttered, "And we think we got troubles."

Noni chuckled and continued. "Well, the eagle then is left with only two options: die or go through a painful process of change, which lasts 150 days. The process requires the eagle to fly to a mountain top and sit on its nest. There the eagle knocks its beak against a rock until it plucks it out."

"Oh, God, Noni," Faith groaned. "Are you sure?"

"Absolutely. Then after plucking it out, the eagle will wait for a new beak to grow back and then it will pluck out its talons."

"Sheesh," Jensen growled, echoed by Faith's moans.

"Then," Noni proceeded, "when its new talons grow back, the eagle starts plucking its old-age feathers."

"It goes bald?" Faith squealed, seriously concerned.

"Completely. Of course, within five months, the feathers all grow back. Now equipped with new parts, the eagle takes its famous flight of rebirth and lives for thirty more years."

Dan coughed and I saw tears in his eyes. He winked at me.

Noni, too, was misty eyed. "You see, many times, in order to survive, we have to start a change process. We sometimes have to get rid of old memories, habits and maybe even past traditions. Only freed from past burdens, can we take advantage of the present."

She looked at Faith, tears shimmering. "Isaiah 40:31 says '...they that wait upon the Lord shall renew their strength; they shall mount up with wings as eagles. They shall run and not be weary, they shall walk and not faint ...'"

"Faith and Jensen," Noni's head turned to include Dan and me, "when it rains, most birds head for shelter; the eagle is the only bird that, in order to avoid the rain, starts flying above the clouds." She threw back her white head and laughed deeply, joy bubbling from her. "No wonder God wants us to spread our wings and soar with the eagles."

"Wow." Faith's expression of awe was soft, almost wistful. "That illustrates why we —" she suddenly choked up. Threw up her hand, shook it as if to stymie her emotional lapse and smiled through her tears. "Thanks, Noni. I'd never heard that entire story. "

Jensen reached over and took her hand. "We knew that eagles always fly high. Now we know why." He winked at her and released her hand. "Thanks, Noni. You're the best."

Noni and Jensen soon departed.

But Noni's words left us equipped to battle whatever lay ahead.

~ ~

The very next day, Mom summoned me to her house. The familiar smell of home hit me as I entered its quiet, peaceful portals, a blend of potpourri, baked bread and indescribable nuances of sweet fragrances.

We embraced and then settled in the den, where she'd set aside her embroidery paraphernalia. She turned off the television.

"What?" I frowned suddenly, feeling the import of her summons sink in.

"Oh," she waved a dismissive hand. "It's not anything bad. So relax."

Then she reached over to the end table and picked up a folded newspaper. "I need to show you something." She handed it to me.

My insides curled into themselves. She'd found it. With shaking hands, I reached for it.

There it was. The story. Faith's picture ...

I licked my lips. "Mom," I began, wanting to throw myself at her feet. "I —"

"No," Mom said so gently tears rushed to my eyes. "I'm glad I saw it. I had no idea you would —"

"But I didn't," I insisted. "Faith did it without my knowledge or consent."

Mom smiled wider. "Then she was braver than you."

My tears stopped and my mouth dropped open. "You mean — you're not mad."

She gave me this mock glare. "Of course, I'm not mad." Then she chuckled. "Nor am I hurt. You see, Deede, I always knew the day would come that you would not be able to deny your curiosity or your deep need to know your roots."

She went on. "Your father worked for the county and his job, as a tax delinquency officer, gave him access to records and such. Somehow, he was able to get some information as to the identity of your birth parents. But he didn't tell me this until he was dying. He said to hold the information until such a time as either of your girls came forth requesting permission to try and locate your biological parents."

"You mean?" I asked, feeling as though lightening had just targeted and struck me.

Mom laughed. "Yes. I have some information that will help locate your parents. But of course, you will have to pursue the search." She sighed deeply, contentedly. "I also have information concerning Lexie and Priss' birth parents. I'm just waiting for them to show a desire to know. Perhaps your search will prompt them into action."

I looked at her sitting there, so loving, so generous of spirit and burst into tears. She moved across the room and gathered me into her arms, settling beside me on the same sofa, many times recovered in different fabrics and colors, that I'd sat and played on all throughout childhood. The same one on which she'd held me in just this way, throughout the years, more times than I could recall.

"Shh," she murmured as my head lolled against her bosom. "It's all in the Divine order of things." Her fingers brushed my hair from my wet face until I quieted. Only then did she give me one last squeeze and return to her easy chair.

She pulled out another brown clasp envelope. "This has some data that may help you."

"But, Mom," I licked my dry lips, "I don't even know if I want to know ..."

"You will, darling. I won't always be here, you know. You deserve to know from whence you came. It won't change the way things are with us. Not one iota."

"You'll always be my Mama," I declared hoarsely, tears gushing forth again.

Mom laughed then. It was contagious, her humor.

I began to laugh, with tears rolling down my face. "Always."

"I know, precious," she said, nodding. "I know."

Epilogue

Other things may change us but we start and end with the family.

– Anthony Brandt

Faith left today for Los Angeles.

Nathan's motion for reconsideration succeeded in getting Faith's house arrest lifted and her probation transferred to LA, shortening the sentence and saving us thousands of dollars. But Faith did, once she started, have to wean off the suboxone medication in her rehab program before she could transfer.

That went smoothly and uneventfully.

Dan and I drove Faith to the Spartanburg-Greenville International Airport and were joined there by Noni, Maddie, Priss, Lexie and their entire families. Yes, they were all there, every single one, including Chloe.

Something mystical had happened in the past months between Chloe and Faith. In the end, I felt that Chloe simply sensed the real change in Faith. The changes had, despite Chloe's distancing, impacted her. Little by little, Faith had regained her trust. Chloe also realized that Faith was not a real threat in Chloe's sister-brother relationship with Jensen. In essence, Chloe had begun to mature.

Today, she hugged Faith for long moments, whispering something in her ear as they stood there amid the bustle of passengers and the roar of engines. Faith smiled and nodded as they released each other and Chloe stepped aside for Jensen to bid his soul mate goodbye. My eyes misted as I thought of the lifelong battle fought over this big guy's affection and allegiance and how it had, in the end, worked itself out.

"Hey! I'm gonna fly out and visit as often as I can," Jensen promised. "Maybe Maddie can fly with me. Huh, Maddie?" Maddie nodded, her eyes huge with excitement.

Lexie hugged Faith fiercely, with tears in her eyes. It had hurt her as much as it had me to have the blots on family solidarity pop up. We both had to give up our own space at times to appease our mates and children. To accommodate them, as it were. This space thing, when family is involved, is complex.

Priss' farewell was, as usual, upbeat and funny. "Don't you get out there in that big city and forget your ol' Aunt Priss, now. Y'hear?"

Faith kissed her cheek and hugged her hugely, rocking back and forth. They would miss each other. Next, Maddie threw herself into her mother's arms, tears gushing forth. And it occurred to me that she had just now realized that her mother was actually leaving on that plane to a far away place.

"Now, now, sweetie pie," Faith crooned. "Remember, I promised to save up and buy you a ticket to visit me soon. Won't that be fun, getting to fly to California two or three times a year? And I'll be home for Christmas. So it's not gonna be so bad."

"B-but will you be gone long?" Huge, bottomless sky-blue eyes dripped tears as they peered trustingly up into Faith's face.

"Just a year. That's not long, honey. Didn't you hear Jensen promise to fly out with you all along? We'll be writing letters daily and visiting so often you'll get tired of seeing me."

That won a shaky giggle and another big hug and kiss before the cousins all swooped in for goodbyes.

I turned Maddie into my arms and said, "darlin', I know I won't take your Mama's place, but I'll worry your daddy to death asking for you to come over for weekends with Papa and me. You won't be away from us as much as before. I promise. " And I vowed to myself that it would happen.

Today was overcast and the clouds above gray. Everyone was solemn as Faith boarded the aircraft, then turned, smiled and waved at us. We all felt it, the change in her life, the change in her direction.

And as the plane lifted off and disappeared into the clouds, I imagined all the darkness the three of us, Dan, Faith and myself, had weathered. And I knew just as Faith's plane would momentarily burst free of the dark clouds into sunshine, so were Dan and I facing our own transfer from night to day.

We dropped Maddie off at her house then drove on home. Silent.

Contemplative.

"We've finally got our own space back," I told Dan, smiling. "You happy? I know Faith is."

"Yeh," he said but not as enthusiastically as I'd expected.

"You know, honey," he said, taking my hand in his. "Having your own space is necessary sometimes. But if there's no loved one waiting for you just outside that space, it loses its sparkle."

I laughed and for the first time in years, it was a full, belly laugh. Full of joy and celebration.

"Y'know, honey," I said, reaching over to kiss his cheek, "you are so right!"

~ ~

On the second anniversary of Faith's recovery, she moved back to Greenville. She'd decided, in the end, to stay an extra year in the discipling program in LA.

"I need more time here, Mama," she'd told me of her decision. "Maddie is okay with it because she sees how different her mom is now. Besides, I think she loves those round trip airplane rides all along."

Faith now already had a job lined up. "A good one," she reassured me over the phone the day she settled into her nice apartment. "With a real estate agent I knew before I got into drugs. He's excited to have me work with him"

"I'm so happy, Faith. You've come full circle back to where you once were."

"Oh no," she laughed. Then she sighed. "No. I'm in an even better place, Mama. The person I became was not the real me. Working in the disciple ministry at Daystar Center made me aware of who I really am. Who I was created to be. That came through helping others to find themselves."

"Faith, I'm overwhelmed at what's happened in the past two years."

"The next thing on my agenda is to regain custody of Maddie."

"Yes," I agreed. "Next year, she'll be a teenager. She needs her mother more than ever."

"I want it to be amiable between Jack and myself. Maddie needs her parents to work together to give her what she needs in life. I'll do all I can to be conciliatory with Jack. The rest is up to him."

"Well, we know that it will all work out to —" Faith took it up from there, "— the good of them who are the called according to His purpose."

Tears filled my eyes and I thought how wonderful is our Maker.

"I'm coming over to see my Mom and Dad," she said.

I heard the uncertainty in her voice and it touched my heart. "Of course. You're always welcome here, Faith." And I recalled how many times both Dan and I had let her know that she was a bother.

In the way.

Taking up our space.

So these words today meant much to her.

We all had sustained wounds, our family. And the past years had helped them all to heal.

Two hours later, Faith arrived in her very own car, looking wonderful. I met her at the door. She was stylishly thin again. Her thick auburn hair was cut in a fashionable bob. And she smelled marvelous. No nicotine. Had she —

We had flown out to LA twice, but the trip was so quick and she had so much to show and tell us that I hadn't even noticed. Of course, Maddie had flown with us, as she had numerous times with Jensen. She'd become quite the seasoned traveler.

In the meantime, Faith had come home for both Christmases.

"I quit smoking when I went to Daystar Center," Faith said as if reading my mind. Then she smiled, a radiant, open smile I'd not seen in years. And she reached to hug me tightly. "Just want you to know that it really *took*," she whispered in my ear.

"That's great, honey," I said, my voice breaking. "I'm so proud of you."

We both wiped tears from our eyes and grinning from ear to ear went to the kitchen to sit at the table and chat. This had been our thing for most of Faith's life. We sipped coffee and nibbled banana nut muffins I'd thrown together after she'd called to say she was coming to visit.

Banana nut muffins were among her favorites.

"Where's Dad?" she asked. "Is he doing okay? I mean, is he behaving and not working too hard?"

"He's doing great. He does love to go out to the work site and chat with his workers. Sometimes he doesn't come in until dark. But his guys take good care of him — they yell at him if he so much as touches anything."

Faith burst into laughter. "I'd love to see that."

"Oh," I clasped my hands, excited, "I got to meet my birth mother."

Faith's eyes rounded like Cheerios. "Mom! When? How did you —?"

I laughed, thrilled at her response. "Believe it or not, Noni actually found her and arranged for me to meet her. It was about two months ago."

"Was Noni with you when you met her?"

"No." I shook my head in wonder. "She wanted it to be just the two of us. What a heart my Mom has."

"I know. Well, what does she look like? What did you say? When can I meet her?"

"She looks like you and Maddie. Spitting image. We talked about everything under the sun, and you can meet her as soon as we can set up a time. Doris Sisk is her name. She lives only thirty miles from here. Can you imagine? That close all this time."

"I can't wait to meet her." Faith's eyes glowed. Then they clouded. "What about your birth father?"

I sighed. "He died in an auto accident. Before I was born, actually. Doris was only seventeen and her mother insisted she give the baby up for adoption. It was really difficult, according to Doris, to give up her baby. She's always wondered about her little girl and had even tried to find me in recent years but was blocked at every turn. It took Noni to —" My voice choked off as tears flooded my eyes. I slowly shook my head. "I'll never get over her generous gesture." I snuffled soundly, turning to snatch a couple of paper napkins from the counter and passing one to teary-eyed Faith. "I would never have done it, you know. Searched her out while Mom is still living."

"I know, Mom," Faith said, wiping her eyes and reaching across the table to grasp my hand in hers. "Noni is my heart, too. Her space in my heart is non-negotiable."

We wept a bit more then dried our eyes and lapsed into a comfortable, silent contemplation. "Oh. I almost forgot," I said, "Priss is now working on locating her biological parents. Lexie," I grinned and shook my head, "at this point in time, says no way, José. She doesn't want to know."

Faith smiled. "Time may change that."

"Yeah."

Then she gazed down into her coffee, swirling it slowly. "Mom, I'm sorry." The words were heartfelt. Mature.

Tears welled up anew in me. They felt like a tsunami. I swallowed them back, nearly gulping.

"Here," she said softly, handing me a spiral notebook with a marked section. "My testimony."

I looked at her through a mist. "You're beautiful, Faith."

She smiled, a glowing, no-holds-barred one. "Getting that weight off was not easy. But working full-time helped me un-focus on food. Do you like my highlights?"

"Love 'em. But then, you always were lovely to me."

"*Hah.* I know how I looked, Mama, at my very worst times. Only a mother could have thought I was still pretty." But she blushed with pleasure.

She only stayed a little while longer. "I've got plans for this evening," she said and smiled mystically.

"Male or female?" I blurted out.

"Wouldn't you like to know?" She leaned and kissed me on the cheek, then whispered, "Male."

I watched her drive away in that plain little second-hand car and realized that my heart had lifted to the sky, just seeing her. Just hearing her voice, seeing her in her newness.

Dan came in about at dusk. During dinner, I told him about Faith's visit. He was disappointed he'd missed her. "How did she look? And act?"

"She's beautiful, Dan. The old Faith, BD. And she acted — normal." Then I laughed and shrugged. "Whatever *that* is. Actually, she acted very nice. Y'know, I think I really and truly like her."

"I'm glad," he said, slowly nodding approval.

"And she's got a date," I added, wiggling my nose bunny-like.

He laughed then. "Now that's good to hear. Reckon it's serious?"

I shrugged. "Don't know. I'm just glad she's doing well."

"Me, too." Then Dan stood and came around the table, pulled me to my feet for a long bear hug and a sweet, lingering kiss. And I knew that he, too, felt what I did. Joy that our girl had finally returned.

Later that night, after Dan slept like the dead, I took out the notebook Faith had brought with her that day. Anticipation prickled over me as I opened it and began to read.

~ ~

Faith

My testimony

In the first phase of my testimony, you learned of my junkie days. I became an addict and didn't know how to get out. Fortunately for me, I had a family who loved me unconditionally. To the world, they seemed to be my enablers. But I knew the truth. They never willingly contributed to my demise.

Mom gave me gentle love, the kind that doesn't always approve of what I did, but it never marked me off as a lost cause. Dad was my solid wall of boundary. He refused to bless my sorry ways. That was his way of loving. The tough kind.

For that, in retrospect, I admire him.

I called him many names, among them, "my jailor."

I thank God he *did* put boundaries on me during that time in which I made horrendous choices, ones that, had he loosened the leash, would have been catastrophic for me. I shudder to think what might have happened had he turned me out into the streets.

I did enough damage without any help there.

I look back now and realize what a wonderful father he is. If he had a flaw, it was that he couldn't bear to see his daughter do herself in. He loved me too much.

Funny what hindsight is showing me.

My parents sacrificed their own peace of mind — their own space — to help me find my way out of the dark place into which I'd stumbled. And I turned around and hurt them over and over.

I didn't mean to. But I did. Oh, how I did.

I lied, stole and dishonored them in so many, many ways. I even tried to end my life. And failed. But you know, God has the last word. Always. Sooner or later, I had to meet myself — not through a glass darkly but face to face.

I met myself when my dad had a heart attack and nearly died. And suddenly, everything I'd done for the past ten years paraded before me in 3-D clarity. It wasn't a pleasant scenario. It was brutally vivid, portraying every single lie, theft, betrayal and dishonor in its pure evil.

Drugs are a selfish lifestyle. It makes the drug user focus on themselves constantly. They are like chains binding you to a dark place from which there is no escape. That stronghold is powerful.

It's funny how my perception of myself changed that day I looked at my Dad lying in the hospital bed, near death. And my mother sitting beside him, so pale and distraught. I'd worked so long and hard at being "cool" and denying my feelings for them that when that terrible stronghold was broken in that moment of truth, it all came gushing, like when the New Orleans levee burst. Oh, how I loved them, and the entire time I've been in the Daystar program, I would think of ways I wanted to honor them when I moved back.

First, I would stand on my own two feet and give them back their life. Their well-earned space. I would take responsibility for myself and my daughter and become all I was created to be. I learned many things about myself while in the LA program, what my gifts and strengths are. I intend to use them to the fullest.

I learned what true character is. And I knew instantly that both my parents possess it. So does Noni and my Aunt Priss. And Jensen and Aunt Lexie. And many others I didn't take time to notice.

I can't wait to begin my new life!

I remember something Noni told us once: With all its sham and drudgery and disappointments, it's still a beautiful world.

I thank God and my family for rescuing me from a literal hell.

I can say, because of them, that it *is* a beautiful world.

~ ~

Deede

I read Faith's words through tears, wiping them away as my heart soared up, up, above all the dark memories of the past to new ground. Faith's surrender, after all the desperation, attempted negotiation, failures and prayer was like a newborn kitten's *meow* in the midst of pit bulls. The change in her was, to me, a dose of heaven.

It was stunning.

The three of us, Dan, Faith and me ... were finally on the same page.

Consequently, we were each granted our own sacred space.

And the most amazing thing about it was, family was right there, just outside.

Waiting.

Greetings, reader,

Now that you have celebrated with me the amazing eagle-flight triumph of the Stowe family, I hope you will look forward to an equally inspiring journey in my next novel. Soon to be released, *Unto These Hills*, takes readers into the deep South's Tucapau Mill Hill as the textile industrial heyday perches on the cusp of decline. Abandoned by parents, Sunny Acklin's worst fears—disgrace and a bastard child—manifest after a sinister, faceless rapist destroys her dreams. Deserted by her life's love, Sunny desperately weds another to save her reputation and in the process, realizes the cost is too great.

Meanwhile, she wonders who fathered her child. When the shocking answer comes, it threatens to obliterate her.

Will her true love's return to Tucapau compel life to give Sunny another chance?

Unto These Hills is a life-affirming story that I hope you will embrace.

Enjoy!

Hugs,
Emily Sue Harvey